BLEEDING INTO WINTER

A C.T. FERGUSON CRIME NOVEL

THE C.T. FERGUSON MYSTERIES
BOOK 16

TOM FOWLER

Published by Greenfield Press

Edited by Chase Nottingham

Cover Design by 100Covers

For Lisa and Isabel

I STARED AT MY ENEMY, and he stared back.

Forty-four feet of pickleball court separated us. My wife Gloria and I were playing in a mixed doubles charity tournament. She'd been a competitive tennis player for years and segued into pickleball once she turned thirty. I went along because it seemed like something fun to do together. We won the first game of the match thanks mostly to Gloria, but now we were down nine to six in the second game. My wife signaled timeout, and we huddled outside the baseline.

"We need a good plan to come back," she said.

"Have I mentioned my collegiate championship pedigree?" I asked.

She grinned. "Not in the last five minutes."

"High time for a reminder, then."

"Winning a lacrosse title over a decade ago isn't helping us much today."

"Remember Leslie Rusinko?" When I got shot about two years ago, I spent a few months convalescing. As I'm a terrible patient, I needed something to do, so I found footage of Gloria's upcoming opponent in a major local tennis tourney. While racket sports have never been my thing, my lacrosse team went over film. I can spot when someone is moving well . . . and more importantly, when they're not. "You beat her."

"I know." Gloria nodded, and her chestnut ponytail bobbed with the motion. "You helped me with that one."

"The guy on the other side doesn't move as quickly as he thinks he does," I said. "He steals a lot of shots from his partner."

"Poaching," my wife said. "That's the pickleball term."

I frowned. "It sounds like he's hunting rhinos on some illicit safari. Either way, I think his partner is the better player, but he's not letting her get involved." The same was true on our side of the net—Gloria's skill easily outpaced mine—but I could admit it and had no problem letting her poach the occasional shot from me.

"I agree. What do you think we should do?"

"Start hitting the ball toward her more but not too close to the sideline. He seems willing to come halfway into her court. It might wear him out, and he'll be hitting more balls back at us than she will."

"All right," she said. "Let's do it."

We walked toward the baseline again. About two dozen people sat on metal bleachers to the side of the court. It was the other team's turn to serve, and I awaited their shot. The man hit a pretty deep one, but I got it back and even managed to place it where I wanted—about a third of the way across the center line. Sure enough, he darted sideways and took the ball from his more skilled partner. Doing so on the move caused him to hit the ball higher than he probably wanted, and Gloria was waiting to put it away.

The woman served next, and Gloria ripped a return up the line. The guy barely got his paddle on it. We got the ball now, and we had a chance to close the game out. It would be a slim chance with me up first to serve for us. I hit a decent one, and the man made the mistake of returning the ball to Gloria. Using her tennis experience, she blistered the ball in his direction. It was probably going long, but he stuck his paddle up, and the ball bounced harmlessly off it.

Seven to nine.

Now, I served to the woman, a short, compact lady with athletic glasses, a baseball cap, and a serious face. She hit a deep return, and my follow-up shot hit the net without going over. Gloria took service next and got us back to nine-all within about thirty seconds. Our foes now called timeout. My wife and I huddled beyond the baseline again and watched the opposition. Whenever the female player tried to talk, the guy shook his head and offered some rebuttal. He was about as tall as me at six-two, though he had at least thirty pounds on me and moved like he strapped weights to his ankles. "He doesn't get it," Gloria said. "She's way better, and he doesn't get it. Or can't."

"Some galaxy brain shit over there," I added. She chuckled. "Our strategy seems to be working. Considering these two might murder each other if we put this away, I think we should keep using it."

"Drawing on your priceless experience as a collegiate champion," Gloria said with a smile.

"You just wanted to mention it before I could."

"Maybe."

Play resumed when our opponents broke their testy *tête-à-tête*. The woman's serious face added a deep scowl and a light red color. Her partner seemed oblivious as he raised his paddle. A few volleys later, I hit a ball right between our opponents to make it ten to nine. Both looked disgusted, though I wondered if the man realized how much damage he alone had done. Gloria's serve was deep, and the return came to me. I didn't hit a good third shot, but the poach remained in effect, and Gloria ended the point, game, and match shortly thereafter. Following the perfunctory paddle taps at the net, the opposing woman stormed off the court.

"I hope they're not married," I said once Gloria and I were solidly back on our side.

"I think they work together."

"If she's his boss, he might be fired tomorrow morning."

"It'd be his own fault," Gloria said as she put her paddle into a large bag. I returned mine—really one of hers—as well. I've always lamented my wife's tendency to overpack, and this was no different. Her bag held at least eight paddles, two water bottles, two pairs of shoes, and maybe a kitchen sink. Wheeling it around fell to me, of course, allowing me to warm up and cool down without actually stretching.

The venue hosts presented us a mediocre trophy. Through her fundraising company, Gloria arranged the whole event. The twenty people in attendance heard we raised over fifteen grand for a local homeless children's charity. A larger audience for our win would have been nice, but considering recent snow bumped the event to a Thursday afternoon, I understood the light crowd. In the parking lot outside, I struggled to cram the bag into the trunk of my Audi S4 sedan. After taming the beast, I climbed in, and Gloria immediately leaned closer and kissed me. "I love winning."

"Me, too."

"We should celebrate," she said, giving my leg a squeeze as I started the car. "Drive fast."

So I did.

After showering and celebrating, Gloria and I ate dinner in her house.

She lived in the posh Brooklandville area of Baltimore County. Always a city boy, I maintained my own home in the Federal Hill neighborhood of Baltimore. We didn't need both places, but neither of us wanted to sell, so we settled on splitting time. Despite my location near the heart of Baltimore, I preferred everything else about Gloria's house. Three of mine could fit inside with room to spare, and the kitchen alone made every day and night spent here worth it.

As usual, I did the cooking. Despite the size of her kitchen and quality of the appliances, Gloria stopped well short of competency. She was smart enough to stock the fridge and pantry and turn me loose. "Good leaders delegate," she told me once, and I couldn't argue. Tonight, I put the finishing touches on lasagna. The sauce bubbled, and the cheese on top was the perfect golden brown. I let the large glass pan sit on the counter while I tossed a salad and poured us each a stemmed glass of Ruffino chianti.

"To victory," Gloria said as she raised her glass a few minutes later. "More importantly, to winning with the person you love."

"Hear, hear," I said, and we clinked glasses. As usual, I ate normal bites, and Gloria sliced off tiny portions she could have fed to a phalanx of pet squirrels. Before her tennis career ended, Gloria changed her eating and exercise habits, and she'd maintained them even in the absence of competitive play. She was stronger, a little leaner, and still beautiful enough to put an extra flutter in my chest every time I saw her.

After dinner, we adjourned to the living room, and Gloria put on the local Thursday evening news. As usual, the lead story tended toward the gruesome. "New details have emerged in the brutal stabbing of a woman in a Baltimore park," the news anchor said, his expression stern. "Twenty-five-year-old Kirsten Valle grew up in Carroll County but worked in the city." Her picture appeared over the anchor's shoulder. Kirsten had been a pretty redhead with bright green eyes and an easy smile. "Before the recent blizzard, Miss Valle visited Saint Mary's Park. Her body was found covered in snow the next evening. She'd been stabbed multiple times. Why she was at the park as inclement weather dawned remains unknown. Police are still investigating and have not found any suspects yet."

Gloria lowered the volume. "Has Rich talked to you about this one?"

"Nope," I said. My cousin worked as a homicide lieutenant with the Baltimore Police Department. When high-profile cases like this cropped up, he tended to remain tight-lipped about things.

"You could investigate," my wife said.

I shook my head. "Not how it works. I don't get to pick and choose what I work on."

"In a way, you do."

"Sure . . . but people have to try and hire me first. No one's reached out about this one. It's terrible, but the cops get killings like this pretty often."

"I wonder if the murderer knew it was going to snow." Gloria frowned. "If he did, he might have figured it would hide the body."

"Local forecasts were only calling for a few inches," I said. "We ended up getting about twice what was expected. I doubt he could have known in advance."

Gloria leaned into me, and I put my arm around her. "I still think you could help with this one."

"The cops won't ask me."

"They did about a year ago."

"Different kind of case," I said. Owing to my computer expertise, BPD Captain Leon Sharpe asked me to go undercover and bust up a band of hackers who targeted Baltimore with several malware and ransomware campaigns.

"It would be good for your agency," Gloria said.

"We're doing all right."

"Think of the good press you would get."

Her point was valid. Coverage would be copious and good on a case like this. My track record in similar matters—to Rich's chagrin and my clients' satisfaction—remained strong. However, the key word in "freelancing" was "free," and it didn't pay the bills. I needed to make rent, utilities, and the like, not to mention pay my assistant T.J.'s annually-increasing salary.

To avoid dumping all these thoughts on Gloria, I said, "I'd rather think about working off these lasagna calories later."

Gloria leaned her head back and kissed me. All thoughts of pretty redheads getting stabbed in Baltimore parks fled my brain.

CHAPTER 2

EASY ACCESS to I-83 South was one perk of Gloria's location. Taking it simplified my commute into Baltimore, where the highway ended and continued as President Street. The drive to Fells Point was usually quick and easy from there, though traffic lights did not always smile upon me.

Today, they did. I hit the lot a few minutes after nine. My office is the second-floor space above an auto repair shop. This means it gets occasionally loud, but Manny the owner has always been OK with some of the more interesting facets of my job. T.J.'s Mustang already occupied a space. I parked the S4 beside it, opened the building's outer door, and walked up the metal stairs.

Another door led to the office. It was a good-sized rectangular room with enough space for two desks, a table, a fridge, restroom, and the all-important coffee area with enough gaps in the layout for my assistant and me to move around. Speaking of T.J., she welcomed me with her favorite greeting: "You're late."

"The big perk of being the boss," I said, "is you're always right on time." I hung my coat on the rack and set my backpack down at my desk. The smell of coffee acted like a siren song, luring this weak sailor to the pot.

"I guess you're right. It's not like we have too much on the agenda today." T.J looked at me as I sat at my desk. My feisty secretary was 21 with the hardscrabble wisdom of an older lady. She was tall, blonde, and athletic, and despite several rough teenaged years, she was pretty but not to the point potential clients would gape at her. "The guy from the insurance company is coming over to settle up."

"With a check, no doubt. Did you tell him we don't accept his boomer currency?"

"No," she said, "I enjoy getting paid." T.J. crossed her arms. "You talk to Rich recently?"

"Was I supposed to?"

"I was hoping you did." My expression must have conveyed my confusion, because she added, "The park stabbing. I want to work it."

"Gloria was talking about it last night."

"I knew you married a smart woman."

"Me, too," I said. "I'll tell you the same thing I told her— as soon as someone hires us to get involved, we're in. Until then, we're sitting it out."

T.J. frowned but went back to something on her laptop. I logged into mine. My desk held a trio of twenty-four inch monitors. It was a call to my hacker days when unimportant matters like screen real estate were things we actually boasted about. Today, I imagined a large curved monitor or two conferred the greatest amount of street cred. I'd burned my major alias helping the BPD with their ransomware issue last year, so while I still kept my skills up, I'd basically exited the scene.

"I want to work interesting cases," T.J. said after a few minutes.

I sipped my coffee. "A woman is dead. We need a better adjective."

"You know what I mean. Something like this is a bigger deal than doing grunt work for an insurance company."

"Did you ever see *The Incredibles*?"

"Sure," T.J. said.

"Apply the lesson, then. If every case is interesting, none of them are."

"And here I thought you were going to quote an ancient Chinese curse to me."

"I felt more like pop culture this morning," I said.

"So we're still waiting on the dead girl?"

"Until someone brings us in, yes."

I knew she didn't like it, but at least for now, she stopped objecting.

Later in the morning, two men from the insurance company came in.

Doffing their coats revealed they were both dressed in cheap suits and in two different shades of gray. I directed them to T.J.'s desk. The firm was local, so they lacked the financial and personnel resources of the big ones who advertised on TV. "You did a good job with our case," the man on the left said. He looked a little older than his partner, but both of them got punched out of the generic middle management cookie cutter.

"We appreciate your discretion, too," the other one added.

"Absolutely," T.J. said. The case became fairly simple—locate a person the company couldn't find. She was the bene-ficiary of an eccentric woman who turned out to be her aunt.

The firm lacked the resources to maintain an in-house investigative arm, so they came to yours truly. A while ago, T.J. devised a higher rate structure for companies than for individuals. This marked the only time I considered deviating from it. It was rare to see a company try to do the right thing.

T.J. handed the pair a short stack of papers. It held the standard contract our corporate clients sign, a full report, and a summary of expenses. One of the perks of employing a secretary is delegating things I don't want to do—namely, reports and expense summaries. I contributed, but she did the bulk of the work and never complained about it. She flipped through the pages, going over the legal stuff quickly before moving on to the rest.

"Here's the breakdown of exactly how long it took us to find Wanda," she said. My assistant pointed at something on the page before skipping ahead. "This is where you'll find the expenses associated with the drive."

"You charge for mileage?" the older one asked.

"At the federal reimbursement rate, yes," T.J. said.

This continued for a few minutes. She was concise and patient but also willing to push back and defend our work if the tone of their questions indicated skepticism. I smiled. Hiring her remained the best decision I'd ever made for my business. A short while later, signatures went onto paper, one handed T.J. a check, we all shook hands, and the two men left. "Nice work," I said once their footsteps descended the metal steps.

"Whatever would you do without me?" T.J. asked.

"Do a lot more work I don't enjoy."

"Remember me when it's time for a Christmas bonus."

"You came to Thanksgiving dinner at my parents' house. I still need to give you extra money?"

T.J. grinned. "Well, the alternative is a bunch of work you don't enjoy."

"Fine." I was happy to give her a bonus, and she knew it. "I think Santa will find you on the nice list in a few weeks."

"Good. Let me know if he's hiring."

————

With our caseload light at the moment, T.J. left an hour early.

I stayed behind. When I first began working as a detective, I did it under the auspices of my parents' foundation. I'd been fully on my own for over two years now, and November and December were definitely slow months. I doubted we could do much to change this. The key would be making sure we worked enough cases in the first ten months of the year to carry a healthy war chest into the following January. We'd be all right this year—there was definitely enough to give T.J. a nice bonus—but I wanted to do better after the holidays. "Christ, I sound like such an entrepreneur," I said to my empty office. If I didn't get this under control, I would soon start writing clickbait posts on LinkedIn.

Footsteps thudded up the stairs. Definitely heavier than T.J.'s or Gloria's. The door opened, and my cousin Rich walked in. The circles under his eyes and the stubble on his face told me he'd had a long few days. "You have beer in your fridge?" he asked, and then walked to the appliance, opened it, and pulled out a couple bottles before I could answer.

"Help yourself."

"Dos Equis?"

"Why have one equis when you can have two?"

Rich shook his head, sat in one of my guest chairs, and handed me a bottle. He was about six and a half years older than me—meaning he would turn forty in the coming year—

but whatever troubled him also added some age to his appearance. Since becoming a lieutenant, Rich evolved into more of a supervisor than a crime-solving cop, and I knew he struggled with the balance even if he'd never admit it. With his eyes on the bottle's label, he asked me, "You still volunteering at the Esperanza Center?"

"When I can. I try to go once a week." I'd initially donated some time there after returning from Hong Kong about five years ago. More recently, a priest who worked at the Catholic-run center came to see me regarding a murdered colleague. "In the meantime, I figure buying Mexican beer is a way to keep my Spanish from getting dulled."

"Not sure it's a lot of practice."

"*Disfruta tu cerveza, gringo.*"

"You're as much a gringo as I am," Rich pointed out.

"Yeah? What was the rest of what I said?"

He frowned, and his face took on a serious look. This was how my cousin worked out even trivial problems. I sipped some of the beer while he puzzled out the phrase. "*Cerveza* is beer, so I guess you told me to enjoy my beer."

I raised the longneck in his direction. "*Muy bien.*"

"You hear about the dead girl from the park?" he said after a moment of silence.

"Hard to avoid it."

My cousin snorted. "Yeah. Constant coverage. A pretty girl dies, and the fucking news can't leave it alone."

"If you ever run for office," I said, "'Equal justice for unattractive people' isn't a very good slogan."

"It's just annoying." He took a long pull from the bottle. Rich's hair was a touch more gray than it had been even a few months before. Despite the longer hours his promotion demanded, he'd managed to stay in shape. Rich went an even six feet, and his weight hovered around two hundred pounds.

He'd always been strong and solid, and he didn't display any ill effects from months behind a desk and standing at a whiteboard.

"Hitting a wall?"

Rich pulled a face. "I don't think so. Not yet."

"So you came here to drink and commiserate because things are going well?"

He chuckled. "All right. Maybe there's a wall on the horizon, and we're headed toward it. I don't think we've hit it yet."

"You're concerned no one's going to turn the steering wheel, though." Rich frowned. "Hey, this is your metaphor, not mine."

"The investigation is ongoing," he said.

"I see you've been practicing for the press." We both drank some more beer. "Gloria and T.J. both want me to get involved in this case."

"What did you tell them?"

"We only get involved if someone hires us," I said. "Usually, it's a victim's family, but there's precedent for the BPD opening the checkbook."

"Not here."

"What if another woman gets killed?"

"This is Baltimore," Rich said. "There's a fifty-fifty chance a woman gets killed tomorrow."

"I mean like this one," I said. "If you think the coverage is bad now, what do you think a second body is going to do?"

Rich grunted. "I'd rather not think about it. Look, I know you're good for getting the bad guys, but we're not bringing anyone else in now." He looked at his watch. "I'm actually heading home at a decent hour. Too many late nights recently." He polished off the rest of his beer and left the bottle on my desk.

"All right. Let me know if you want the services of a brilliant and handsome private investigator."

"Will do." Rich stood and grinned. "Let me know when you find someone who checks both boxes."

"Fuck off," I said.

CHAPTER 3

A FEW HOURS after dawn on Sunday morning, I hit the mean streets of Federal Hill for a run. The last remnants of snow—turned black by car exhausts—clung to the gutters and the first few inches of asphalt in the streets. When I arrived at Federal Hill Park, some white stuff remained on the grass in the center. The paved trail and cannons were clear. After using the two-block walk to get there as a warmup, I fell into a nice rhythm. The cold morning meant not many people joined me.

Getting shot two years ago cost me my spleen, a lobe from one lung, and a little speed when it came to my runs. What used to take me thirty minutes now took thirty-five. I got my miles in, stretched my arms as I walked back up Riverside Avenue toward my house, and walked in to find Gloria downstairs. I could barely stand straight in many parts of my basement, but she could. Today, she toiled away on an exercise bike I bought about a year ago. "You could have joined me at the park," I said.

She glanced at the small screen, tapped a couple buttons, slowed her pedaling, and fixed me with a grin lascivious enough to weaken my knees. "How about I join you in the shower instead?"

"You can bike down here every morning." We hustled upstairs, ran the water heater empty, got dressed, and returned to the main floor. I fired up the coffee maker and surveyed the state of my refrigerator. I'd stocked up before the snow, and thanks to splitting time between the two houses, I still had plenty on hand to make breakfast. A short while later, we enjoyed plates of wheat toast, scrambled eggs, and turkey sausage.

"Rich and Jeanne are supposed to come by tonight," Gloria said after cutting a mouse-sized sliver from one of the patties. "At my place."

"Let's see if they cancel."

"Why would they?"

"The murder case," I said. "T.J. wanted me to insert myself into it, too. If it's as big a red ball as it seems, one or both of them might get stuck working it."

"She's on homicide detail?" Gloria wondered.

I shrugged. "I doubt it, actually. Probably breaks some fraternization rules."

After breakfast, I gave in to my natural curiosity about the case and the investigation. Kirsten Valle died at twenty-five in a manner no one should wish on their enemy. The victim of multiple stab wounds, she bled out in a Baltimore park, and her body remained undiscovered for close to a day. Since someone brushed the snow from her corpse, the BPD had made very little progress, and the press didn't let them forget it.

The *Baltimore Sun* started questioning how things were going this morning. The deceased hailed from Carroll County, and the *Herald* began hammering the cops almost from the jump. I read a column posted earlier this morning.

*FRUSTRATION MOUNTS AS BALTIMORE INVES-
TIGATION FALTERS*

by Adrian Brown, News Editor

A week after the discovery of Kirsten Valle's (25) body in a Baltimore park, frustration is simmering in Carroll County. The Westminster native, known for her fiery red hair and infectious smile, was found nearly a week ago. While the Baltimore PD continues their investigation, details remain scarce, leaving Valle's loved ones and the Carroll County community with more questions than answers.

Valle, an associate at a Baltimore public relations firm, moved to the big city after graduating from Towson University. The lack of a clear connection to the city has some speculating whether the Baltimore PD is prioritizing the case.

"They treat us like a bedroom community, not a place where people's lives matter," said a tearful Sarah Miller, a close friend of Valle's from Westminster. "Kirsten was vibrant, full of life. This isn't some statistic for them to bury in a report."

Carroll County officials are pushing for a more collaborative approach. Any progress would be welcome at this point. Murder investigations always take time, but the lack of a concrete lead or suspect leads this reporter to conclude the whole thing is an exercise in buffoonery.

The Carroll County community is holding a vigil for Kirsten Valle tonight at 6 PM at the Westminster Town Square.

"Wow," I said. "The Carroll County paper is pulling no punches."

"You think the coverage will keep Rich at work?" Gloria asked.

"It might," I said. "The BPD got a lot of bad press several years ago. They've been more sensitive to it since then." If

Rich and his girlfriend ended up not making it, I considered going to the vigil. Westminster was a manageable drive. Of course, going there would probably compel me to see if T.J. and I could get involved, and I wasn't interested in working off the books for free.

As Gloria looked across the table at me, I wondered how long I could hold out.

———

By late afternoon, we'd moved to Gloria's house.

Rich and Jeanne were coming by for a combination of Thanksgiving—a little more than a week behind us—and my birthday—tomorrow. Gloria and I went to my parents' house for Turkey Day this year, and T.J. joined us. Last year, we'd gone to her folks' house. Figuring out whose house we were going to on what time had become something of a holiday ritual already. Ah, the little joys of married life.

As she often does for any sort of event, Gloria got catering. She found a local place to deliver roasted chicken, gravy, mashed potatoes, fresh vegetables, dinner rolls, and a Dutch apple pie. The fellow from the catering company arrived about fifteen minutes before we were due to start. It took him three trips, but he got all the trays, warmers, and whatever else he needed inside and set up. Before leaving, he told Gloria someone would return to collect everything in the morning. I wondered if she paid more to have all this done on a Sunday.

Two minutes past the witching hour, a loud engine neared the house. Rich drove a Camaro with a V8, and it idled for a moment before cutting out. I only heard one set of footsteps approach the door, a fact Gloria confirmed when she opened up to find only Rich stood on the front porch. "Where's Jeanne?" my wife asked.

"Stuck at work," Rich said. He presented Gloria a bottle of white wine. She accepted it with a smile. The dark circles remained under Rich's eyes. I wondered how much sleep he'd been missing over the last week. Tonight, he wore dark jeans, loafers, and a tan sweater.

"Did she pick out your outfit?" I wanted to know.

"Why?"

"Because it goes together well."

"I know how to dress."

"You have a suit for every day of the week," I said. "Not the same thing."

"Fine," he said, relenting and showing a quick grin. "She might have . . . suggested a few things."

"I definitely have enough food for four people," Gloria said. "I guess you can take some to her for later."

"Sure." Rich nodded, but it didn't strike me as very convincing.

"Jeanne working homicides now?" I said.

"No, but we've pulled people from other details. The commissioner wants this solved. Jeanne's filling in somewhere."

We adjourned into the dining room. One end of Gloria's long table held all the trays arranged in two rows, plus plates, utensils, and cloth napkins. Four place settings adorned the opposite end. Each of us fixed ourselves a large dinner and sat. Gloria took two slices of chicken, a massive scoop of mashed potatoes, a bunch of vegetables, and a buttered dinner roll. I figured she would eat less than half of it, especially after performing surgery on the bird with her knife.

Rich and I inevitably talked shop during times like these, so we settled into our routine once everyone spent a few minutes eating. "Still no breakthroughs on the murdered girl?" I said.

He shook his head. "I wish we'd get one."

"What do you know so far?"

"She was in a park and got stabbed to death. No one seems to know why she was there, and we don't have any evidence putting another person at the scene."

"She must have been meeting someone," I said.

"Why?"

"Unless she was into painting winter landscapes, I can't imagine another reason for her to be there."

"It would take some dedication to meet someone in a blizzard," Gloria said.

"It would," Rich agreed. "She wasn't seeing anyone. Or if she was, none of her friends knew a thing about it."

"The first half-hour or so wasn't too bad," I said. "Then the snow really picked up. If she was waiting for someone there, I can't imagine she would've stayed very long."

Rich waved a hand. "We've considered all these things. The body being found covered in snow makes the ME's job pretty hard when it comes to time of death. We figure early on for the reasons you've already said. Hasn't gotten us any closer to solving it." He sighed. "With the press on the prowl, the pressure is on to get this one closed."

"I'm available to consult."

"We're handling it," Rich said. I bit down an uncharitable response. "Doesn't stop the reporters from buzzing around and saying all sorts of shit, of course. Some prick from Carroll County called us buffoons."

"I saw."

"You did?"

"Yes. I called to commend him for spelling *buffoonery* correctly. A lot of people forget the second F." Rich rolled his eyes. "If it's any consolation," I added, "I only expected the *Carroll County Herald* to cover large pumpkins and tractor pulls."

"They're not the only ones," Rich grumbled. He leaned to one side, removed a well-folded section of the *Sun* from his back pocket, and slapped it on the table.

"What is this relic?" I said, pointing to the paper.

Rich spoke as if I had asked nothing. "The local columnists are having a field day, too. The commissioner's pissed, and I get the impression the mayor is as well. Next year is an election year, and we can't have this get any worse."

"So long as the mayor gets another term, this young woman will not have died in vain," I said. Enough sarcasm dripped from my words to stain Gloria's white tablecloth.

"Jesus, you're cynical," Rich said.

"I'm also offering my services. Sharpe and the commissioner have reached out before."

"The commissioner doesn't like you."

"I'm an acquired taste," I pointed out.

"It seems like an all hands on deck approach would be best," Gloria said.

Rich's head bobbed a fraction. "Not up to me. I get barked at enough about overtime. I can't imagine how I'd justify paying your rates when we're already burning hours on this."

I spread my hands. "Because I'll solve it."

"Sure you will."

"It's what I do. Someone is pissed the police aren't making progress, they come to me, I figure things out, and you get to shake the commissioner's hand after I bring you in for the arrest. Kind of works out well for both of us."

Rich continued to disagree for all the good it did him. He was a smart and incisive cop, using what he learned in the army to help give his career a good early start. He made sergeant quickly and then lieutenant less than three years after. I couldn't take all the credit for his meteoric rise, of course, but I would carve out a little. After dinner, Rich left with two containers full of leftovers. "Happy birthday in advance," he said at the door. "You know Jesus died at thirty-three, right?"

"Good thing there are no more Roman soldiers around here," I said.

When he'd left, Gloria said, "I wonder what's up with Jeanne?"

"You didn't buy it, either?"

She shook her head. "Not fully. I don't doubt things are hectic, and maybe she needed to pick up a shift. I just think they both could have managed to get here. It's not like someone is chopping up people on the streets right now."

I looked at my watch. "It's early. Give it a few hours."

CHAPTER 4

T.J. DROVE to the office Monday morning.

She parked her Mustang in the usual spot. The car replaced an old battered Civic. Her new ride bolstered her self-image considerably. Having a steady job which paid a pretty good wage mattered more to her than she could have previously imagined. T.J. walked up the metal steps and unlocked the office door. She flipped the lights on and undertook the most vital task of the day—preparing coffee. C.T. told her he'd been a tea drinker during his years in Hong Kong, but he'd been a card-carrying member of team coffee since his return. They both drank more than their share during a typical day.

She took in the Spartan furniture and walls. Any seasonal spruce-up would improve the place, but it was soon time to decorate for Christmas. T.J. handled making the office look festive because her boss didn't care much about it. After spending a few years barely knowing what day it was much of the time, T.J. was happy to mark special occasions. The coffee finished, and she poured herself a cup before settling in at her desk.

Her time working for C.T. showed here there were ebbs

and flows to the business. Some weeks, they stacked cases back to back to back—C.T. disliked working more than one at a time. Other stretches, they went days with barely a nibble. Currently, the business found itself mired in one of the low points. The only emails since yesterday afternoon were the kind T.J. could delete without reading. No new appointments or even initial consultations awaited on the calendar.

T.J. understood not every case could be interesting. Right now, she'd settle for boring. She enjoyed learning the basics of the business from her boss. He relied on her more as the weeks and months piled up. With little work to do, she took a bright teal envelope from her purse and set it on his desk. A simple birthday streamer would have to suffice as the decoration.

C.T. would be in soon—a few minutes late as usual. Maybe he'd managed to drum up a new case since Friday.

———

As usual, C.T. arrived a few minutes after nine.

He spotted the card right away. Next, his green eyes took in the small banner. "You didn't need to do this," he said.

"It's your birthday," T.J. said. "I'm a little surprised you didn't take the day off, but if you're here, we might as well have a mini celebration."

"Thanks." C.T. opened the card, read the note, and chuckled. He held it up. T.J. saw her own words.

Happy birthday, boss! I'm gifting you another year of work in exchange for slightly more pay.

"You know gifts are supposed to be free, right?" he asked.

"Occasionally, they come with a string or two attached."

C.T. set the card down and poured a cup of coffee. "If we get a good case between now and the end of the year, you might even be able to affix three strings."

The office remained quiet for a while. T.J. didn't like having nothing to do. She felt like she was wasting her boss's time after he took a chance on hiring her two years ago. There were no more emails to check. No calendar appointments or requests for an initial consultation. Earlier in her tenure, T.J. used her downtime to organize old case files and notes, but her system had been in place for a while now.

She was about to unpack her lunch when footsteps came up the metal stairs, and a woman walked through the door. She looked to be in her late twenties, and red hair peeked out of the hood covering her head against the cold. "I hope you can help me. I've read good reviews."

"We'll do our best," T.J. said. "You want me to take your coat?" She stood, and the other woman doffed the jacket, handing it to the taller T.J. with a grateful smile. T.J. hung it on the rack near the door. The new arrival dropped onto a guest chair by the boss' desk, so T.J. grabbed her own chair and wheeled it to where they gathered.

"What can we do for you?" C.T. asked.

"You've probably seen much of the press coverage about the woman who got killed in the park." The woman paused and wiped her eyes. C.T. nudged a box of tissues closer to her. "Thanks. She was my sister. I'm Jessie . . . Jessica Valle."

"We're sorry for your loss."

Jessie nodded. "I'm sorrier about the official investigation." She sighed. "I know they can take time. I'm not expecting some *CSI* miracle. Maybe the coverage is influencing my decision, but I'm tired of waiting for the police to solve this. Whoever killed my sister is still out there, and he might do it again."

This was an angle most of the stories and columns ignored. They focused on justice for Kirsten and her family but fell into the trap of presuming her murderer must have been an acquaintance. It was more common, yes, but people fell victim to strangers every day, as well. Jessie dabbed at her eyes and cried. "You're right," C.T. said, the typical sarcastic edge gone from his voice and replaced with an uncommon sincerity. "Most investigations are hard. The police do a pretty good job overall, but sometimes, people need other resources."

"How would you tackle this?" Jessie wanted to know.

Most potential clients didn't pose the question. T.J. wanted to work the case, but she forced herself to sit still, not let her knee bounce with excitement, and take notes like a good executive assistant. "The case the police are building is stalled," C.T. said, "but it doesn't mean they've done bad work. The first thing I like to do is challenge their assumptions. I was never a cop, so I don't approach things the same way. From there, it depends on what we learn."

"All right," Jessie said. "I'd like to hire you, then."

"Here's a contract," T.J. said, taking one from the folder at the back of her notebook. "It goes over the rates on the first page." Before she came to work here. C.T. didn't even have a contract to present to clients. Despite his good work, it was something of a miracle he remained in operation for a single week once his parents pulled the plug on their foundation's support. T.J. needed a job, but her boss needed someone to come in and manage processes—after creating most of them— at least as much.

Jessie spent a couple minutes reading it over. "All right. Our parents are still alive, and we want to see this through. We don't have a ton of money, though, so if you haven't found out what happened after a week or so, we might need to pull the plug."

"I understand," C.T. said. "We'll start this afternoon."

After a few basic questions, Jessie left the office. T.J. stood and clapped her hands. "I'm not trying to sound ghoulish, but you know I wanted this case."

"Despite what the Rolling Stones told us, you can get what you want sometimes."

T.J.'s phone buzzed. Melinda was inviting her to lunch. "Can we start in an hour or so?"

"Hot lunch date?" C.T. said.

"Melinda wants to meet with me."

"Give her my best."

"I will," T.J. said. She shrugged into her dark blue coat and wondered what Melinda wanted.

———

Melinda Davenport already waited at the Fells Point iteration of The Abbey when T.J. entered the dining room.

Despite the chill in the air, The Abbey was close to the office, so T.J. walked. A burger and onion rings needed a little exercise anyway. Melinda was twenty-eight, vivacious, smart, and beautiful. She was also the mayor's daughter, and some people considered that her most important attribute. After falling out with her father and living for a few years as a prostitute, Melinda got her life together, reconciled with her dad, and started the Nightlight Foundation to help girls and young women who struggled like she did. T.J. was the first success story.

As T.J. approached the table, Melinda stood, and the two shared an embrace. Today, the older woman wore a smart cream-colored turtleneck over dark blue jeans. As always, she looked terrific. "Nice to see you," T.J. said.

"You, too." The restaurant attracted a good lunch crowd, and T.J. felt like she needed to talk louder to be heard over the buzz of background conversations. The smell of burgers and fries from the kitchen made her reach for the order form. She stuck to the basics. Melinda had already filled hers out, and they both handed the slips to the waiter when he came for their drink orders.

"How are things going?" Melinda wanted to know.

"Good. Been a little slow, but we just got a big case." Her voice lowered, and Melinda leaned in closer. "The poor woman who got stabbed in the park. Her sister came in today."

Melinda frowned. "Sounds dangerous."

"It could be." T.J. had gotten used to Melinda worrying about her. It was endearing in a way. "I wanted to work on it. I like interesting cases."

"They can't all be interesting," Melinda said.

"You sound like C.T. now. You going to start citing *The Incredibles*, too?"

"I still need to see it." Melinda chuckled, and a little pink came into her cheeks. "I know I'm years behind."

"It's fine." The waiter returned, dropping off two iced teas along with a pair of straws in paper wrappers before disappearing again. "It's not like you to want a lunch meeting out of the blue. Everything all right?"

"Things are great." Melinda ripped the end from the wrapper, extracted the straw, and plopped it into her tea. "I wanted to tell you a couple things." T.J. tensed for a bomb to drop, but Melinda's news turned out to be sedate. "First, I'm going on vacation soon. My first one in a few years."

"Congratulations!" T.J. said. "Where are you off to?"

"Australia." She smiled. "I've never been and always wanted to go. A couple girlfriends and I are flying out in a couple days."

"Bring me a souvenir . . . and not some toy kangaroo."

"I will." The server returned and dropped off their meals. T.J. went with the basic cheeseburger with a side of onion rings. Melinda chose one of the speciality options and a side of fries. It all smelled delicious, and T.J. took her first bite before the waiter even walked away. They ate in silence for a few minutes.

"There's another reason I asked you here today," Melinda said. "I'd like you to come home."

"What do you mean?"

"I want you to work at Nightlight. I need someone like you."

"I don't want you to think I'm unappreciative of all your help," T.J. said, "but I'm happy where I am."

"You've been there two years. I know C.T. values what you do, but at this point, couldn't he get another person to follow the processes?"

"It's not just about that," T.J. said. She paused for a breath. Melinda was the closest thing to a heroine she had, and the woman didn't deserve vitriol for an honest inquiry. "I like the work. We make a difference for people. I'm learning things, too, and C.T. trusts me with more now. I don't want to lose any of that."

"Just think about it," Melinda said.

"I will." T.J. offered the response to be polite. She only needed a split-second to consider and reject any offer from Melinda. Even if it came with a healthy raise attached, she would need more than money to seriously entertain the notion of leaving a place where she was happy. Where she belonged. T.J. hadn't experienced too many of those feelings over the years, and she wasn't about to cast them aside no matter who asked.

CHAPTER 5

AFTER T.J. RETURNED from a long lunch, we got to work.

"Kirsten Valle," I said. I found a recent photo of her on her Facebook page, and it now occupied the center of a digital whiteboard on one of my monitors. "Twenty-five. Came from Westminster, lived in Baltimore, and came here to work in PR. She also visited her folks frequently and would commute from their house when she did."

"Must be a nice gig," T.J. said.

"Would you drive from there to work here?"

My assistant blew out a deep breath. "I don't know. I love what I do and all, but we're talking an hour each way. Worse if traffic acts up. It'd be a tough call."

"You have a terrific boss, though."

"Tough call," she reiterated.

I moved on. "No doubt why she also had an apartment. She lived alone. We'll have to look into the company, but it seems like a pretty small operation. One sister, both parents still alive, and not dating anyone as far as I can tell from a quick look at her socials."

"What about before? A jilted lover?"

"Jilted lover? You been watching the Hallmark Channel?"

T.J. chuckled. "Fine. A spurned suitor."

"Now I think you've been reading too much of the Brontë sisters," I said. "Even going back a couple months, there's no one who jumps out as a romantic interest. Her status has been single for a while. I know the cops are trying to run down people she knows, but we need to consider the possibility a stranger killed her."

"You have the police report yet?" T.J. asked.

"I want to brainstorm first. Let's not have their work color our initial ideas."

"All right. You mentioned her firm is pretty small. Office rivalry?"

"Doesn't seem like it." I pulled up her Instagram on my other screen. "They had a party a couple weeks ago. Everyone looks happy." I scrolled through the pictures. The staff of Charm City PR comprised four women and one man. They all went out for drinks. The captions didn't list a reason. Everyone smiled in all the pictures, including the late Kirsten, and the lone guy on staff didn't appear to be a lech lusting after his pretty coworkers. "Let's look at where she died." I brought up a Google Maps view of Saint Mary's Park. T.J. stared over my monitor at nothing in particular. This went on for several seconds. "I think aliens beamed down and killed her." No response. "T.J.!"

"Oh." She shook her head as if roused from a daydream. "Sorry."

"You wanted this case. Try not to space out on me."

"I'm good, boss. What are we looking at?"

"This is where she died," I said. T.J.'s eyes narrowed as she took in the display. "Notice anything familiar?" When she didn't reply, I pointed to Franklin Street, which ran along the southern end of the park. Her eyes widened. "That's across the street from me!"

"Yes." My assistant lived in an apartment building called The 501. It was popular with people her age, many of whom went to the University of Baltimore. It also stood directly opposite a murder scene. "I'm surprised you didn't see the police and the medical examiners."

"We worked from home the next day." She shrugged. "My apartment doesn't look out onto that part of Franklin. I mostly see Paca. If I strain my neck, I can see the bookstore on the corner."

Based on her description, she wouldn't be able to spot anything in the park. The angle and the row of buildings across the way would make it impossible. "You've been there, I presume?"

"Sure," T.J. said. "It's a nice little place. I don't think you can really get into it from Franklin, though. I've always entered from Paca."

"There's a seminary right there, too. I don't see how it would be related to the murder of a young woman, but we can't rule it out." Ditto the Mother Seton House museum. Saint Mary's Park was roughly triangular with much of the area taken up by grass, trees, and walking trails whose color matched the low brick wall encircling the area.

"The seminary is closed for now."

"Even more reason," I said. "The point is there are multiple ways in and out on the east, west, and north sides. If someone were really determined to slip between a couple of buildings, they could even get away to the south. Whoever met and killed Kirsten could have come from anywhere."

"It was snowing. Is a walkup even likely?"

"There wasn't a lot of accumulation by then, but it was

falling pretty heavily. I wouldn't be out walking unless I really needed to."

"Which brings us to the question of why Kirsten was there," T.J. said. "The weather was sketchy and getting worse. Why sit and wait in a park?"

"A date?"

"I'd reschedule based on the snow."

"Me, too," I said. "And I certainly wouldn't ask anyone to meet me outside in such conditions."

"Did she live nearby?" T.J. said.

"She kept an apartment maybe a mile away. Decent walk but worse in the conditions."

"Can we get camera footage?"

"We'll try. Trees and other buildings are going to block a lot of what we'll be able to see, though."

T.J. blew out a deep breath. "I'm starting to see why the police investigation has stalled."

"I'm a little sympathetic to their cause," I said. "We're smarter than they are. Let's see what they have so far."

———

I'd always been able to pull police reports.

It wasn't supposed to work like this, of course. There were proper channels to go through, forms to fill out, rings to kiss, and the like. I've never been a fan of process for process' sake, so I tend to look for ways around silly procedural road-blocks. On my first case, my cousin Rich—then a uniformed sergeant—made the mistake of leaving me alone at his desk for a few minutes. I captured all the relevant addressing information, and ever since, I've been able to convince the BPD one of my virtual machines belonged on their network.

The ransomware kerfuffle of about a year ago caused

some issues, but otherwise, I've enjoyed uninterrupted access to any case file I wanted. Once the medical examiner started using the same network, things got even easier. I pulled down the reports for Kirsten Valle's murder while T.J. put a pot of afternoon coffee on to brew. It was basically never the wrong time of day for caffeine.

I sent a copy of the documents to T.J., and we each read at our own desks. She fixed two mugs of hot java, and then we looked at everything on my screen. "Turns out the cops don't have a whole lot more than our speculation," I pointed out.

"I still can't believe this was on the other side of the street from me." T.J. crossed her arms.

"I'll try to keep you out of the suspect pool."

She grinned. "Thanks, boss."

"The ME says Kirsten was stabbed six times." I displayed a photo of her body lying on the snowy ground. Someone brushed almost all the white powder off her. Much of what remained below her had turned red. All the wounds were to the torso area. "Any of them could have killed her."

"She probably didn't suffer at least," T.J. said.

"I like the ME's observation. The cold and exposure throw off the normal ways to calculate time of death, so he went by the amount of snow under her body. Clever. Puts it between nine and eleven on the night in question."

"You going to try for camera footage?"

"Might as well," I said. "The weather means we won't see the normal volume of people walking or driving, so anyone who enters or leaves the area goes on the list." I paused. "I wonder if the killer chose the time he did because of the weather?"

"Wouldn't it mean Kirsten would be likely to say no?" T.J. asked.

"I'm sure it was a possibility. If we presume our murderer is smart, he knew the snow would discourage people from walking by, cover the body afterward, and generally complicate the investigation."

"There's not an uptick in crime based on precipitation."

"I know," I said. "This was a specific crime. Nothing in the report suggests the police think this was random, so we shouldn't either."

"You suppose she knew her killer?"

"Maybe the date scenario is in play. Could have been their first or second time going out. They're still at the point where they're picking a public place. So maybe she didn't 'know' him, but she'd met him."

T.J. nodded, and her blonde ponytail bobbed along with her head. "Maybe." She frowned like she wondered if she'd left the oven on this morning. "There wasn't supposed to be a blizzard, was there?"

"No," I said. "I think all the local forecasters were calling for three or four inches right until the first flurries fell."

"I'm not trying to burst your bubble here, but if our killer counted on the weather to be a factor, he knew something no one else did."

I spread my hands. "We're spitballing here. Shoot down whatever you want. It's fair to say the forecasted amount wouldn't have produced anywhere near the same effect."

"This is a tough one." T.J. frowned. "I'm glad we're working it, but this isn't going to be easy."

"It's also not officially winter yet," I said. "We could get a bunch more snow."

"You think our killer might find another victim?"

"I'd like to stop the son of a bitch before we find out."

"Me, too," T.J. said.

T.J. and I kept working until a text from Gloria interrupted us.

Don't forget we're meeting your parents tonight. I get the feeling you did. :)

"Shit," I muttered.

"What is it?" T.J. said.

"Gloria and I are supposed to meet my folks for dinner."

"Are they going to get you cake and ice cream for being a good boy?"

"I doubt I've met the requirements there since I was twelve."

"We're putting a pin in this for today, then?"

I looked at my phone. It was 6:07. We were due to gather with my folks in 23 minutes at their house. If traffic cooperated, I could make it with some aggressive driving, but I wouldn't have time to change clothes first. This would expose me to a few bouts of sniffing and tsking from my mother, but she would have to live with it. "Yeah. We'll come back to it tomorrow. Fresh day, fresh eyes, and all."

"Maybe we'll get to make our epiphany faces," T.J. said. "I've watched some *House* like you told me. Even been practicing." Her expression went blank for a second, then her eyes widened and flickered around while her mouth opened like she wanted to say something. It didn't hold up to vintage Hugh Laurie, but it was a good effort.

"Not bad," I said. I dashed off a text to my wife. *Been working on the new case. It's the one you were asking about. Can you meet me there?* Her reply indicated she would and was in fact already en route. "If you ever get married, make sure it's to someone who understands your fluctuating ability to be on time."

T.J. wrinkled her nose. "No worries there."

My assistant said she would lock up, so I shrugged my coat on, grabbed my bag, and dashed down the stairs. I left the lot at 6:09. With a normal volume of cars on the roads, I could make the trip in under twenty minutes. Ten after six wasn't peak rush hour, but traffic was heavier than normal. I passed more than my share of cars on I-83 North, hit the exit for Cold Spring Lane at 6:27, and made the left onto Wood-lawn Road at 6:29. Two minutes later, I stopped the S4 next to Gloria's red Mercedes rocket.

My mother answered when I rang the doorbell. She was sixty-three and looked younger thanks to the finest hair color she could buy. She remained just as blonde today as I remem-bered from my youth. Owing to her hair and the skincare routine she occasionally tried to talk to me about, my mother could pass for a woman of ten years younger. "Coningsby, dear," she said, continuing the tradition of being the only person on earth to refer to me by my first name rather than initials. "You're almost on time."

"What's a minute between family?" I said as we embraced.

"Happy birthday, son," my father said. We shook hands and then did a back-clapping half hug. Unlike my mother, my sixty-four-year-old dad did not fight the onset of age. He, too, looked younger than his years, but his hair had been a mix of black and gray—with increasing amounts of the latter—for a decade.

"Thanks." My father shut the door. Their living room remained unchanged for eons. Even the flowery wallpaper border still ringed the area just under the ceiling. Plush carpeting covered much of the first floor, yielding to tile only in the kitchen and powder room. Gloria sat on a barstool at the kitchen counter. She smiled as I walked in, and I leaned down and kissed her. "Thanks for reminding me," I whispered. She winked. The doorbell rang again.

"That'll be the pizzas and salad," my mother said. When we initially made these plans, I was surprised she didn't opt for a catered meal. I loved pizza, however, and my father did, too, so my mother went along with it. A minute later, my father entered the kitchen carrying three white cardboard boxes and a bag which threatened to slide off. I grabbed it and set it on the counter. It held two large garden salads, which I tossed into a massive bowl.

A few moments later, we all sat around the dining room table with full plates, bowls, and glasses. "To the birthday boy," my father said, raising his soda. "Here's to a great year and many happy returns."

"Hear, hear," went up around the table.

"Thanks," I said.

"Gloria mentioned you're working a big case," my mother said.

I nodded around a bite of pepperoni. The boxes didn't identify the restaurant, but they made a good pie. "The girl who got stabbed in the park."

"Big story," my father said.

"Happened right across the street from T.J.'s apartment, actually. She didn't even know."

"Making progress?"

"We just started today. I can see why the police don't have much to go on yet. We'll figure it out."

"Be careful, Coningsby," my mother said.

"I always am," I said even though no one at the table believed it. My relationship with my parents acquired a significant amount of frost once they withdrew the support of their foundation. We'd thawed things considerably over the last couple years, but a little chill remained. I tended not to tell them a lot about what I worked on, they didn't ask too many questions, and we still managed to get together for big occasions.

When I wasn't late thanks to a big case, at least. I wondered what would happen if the investigation dragged on. T.J. and I often made lemonade out of the BPD's lemons, but the cops barely had a handful of seeds at this point. Being late—or absent—for Christmas dinner would earn me a lot more than a gently snide comment at the door. I'd deal with the situation if it arose. For now, I tried to enjoy my birthday dinner.

CHAPTER 6

CHARM CITY PR operated out of the second floor in a converted rowhouse. Their office was on Park Avenue—nice but far less fancy than its New York namesake—a few blocks from St. Mary's Park and T.J.'s apartment. "I could have gone directly here," my assistant said from the passenger's seat as I hunted for parking.

"But who would have made me coffee?" I said as I circled the block.

"I guess I can't quibble with your priorities."

I found a spot around the corner on West Hamilton Street. "I also decided to come here on the drive in this morning. I'm sure you were already at your desk by then."

"With a pot of coffee going."

"See?" I said as we got out of the car. "Everything happens for a reason."

T.J. snorted. "You don't believe that shit."

"You're right. Keep it in your pocket, though. A lot of people do."

We walked to the building, took a flight of stairs to the second floor, and rang the bell. One of the women I saw in Kirsten's photos answered the door. The pictures didn't make it obvious, but she used a wheelchair. I explained who we were and the reason for our visit, and she invited us inside. "Just two of us here right now," she said. "Everyone else is out meeting with clients."

Our hostess identified herself as Juana Rodriguez, and she used the Spanish pronunciation of her surname. She looked to be about my age, petite, with a classic Latina complexion and coal black hair. The other employee was Albert Harris. I pegged him for mid-twenties. Unlike in the social media photos I saw, he wore his hair in an absurd man bun, and I immediately disliked him for it. Other than his dreadful coiffing choice, Albert looked like the kind of guy women liked to hang out with after work. "We're so sad about Kirsten," he said.

Their office covered the length and breadth of the second level, with the whole area being turned into an open floor plan some real estate agent probably sold as an "advanced collaborative space." Other than a closet and marked unisex bathroom at opposite ends, the floor remained free of interior walls and divisions. This no doubt helped Juana move around. I couldn't imagine having to look at and listen to my coworkers all day with no possibility of privacy, but it was a single item on the long list of my unsuitability for many jobs.

Juana invited us into what passed for her office. It was a desk and sofa. I got stuck in the middle of the couch with T.J. to my right and Captain Manbun to my left. Another knock against this absurd layout. I summoned what professionalism I could muster and said, "Did Kirsten work a normal day the evening she died?"

"Yes," Juana said. "I don't think she went anywhere during the day. Kirsten has . . . had a car, but it's an old beater. I think she only used it to visit her folks back in

Carroll County. She lived a block away and walked pretty much everywhere."

"The park is certainly walkable from here even in the snow. Did she say anything about going there or meeting anyone?"

"No." Albert agreed with a shake of his head, and his silly bun wagged a little, like the stubby tail of a dog who's not sure it likes someone.

"Our theory is she was meeting someone on a date," T.J. said. "Maybe a first or second, so they would go to a public place at first."

"Why do it in the snow, though?" Juana said.

"We've had the same question," I said. "Ditto the police. No one's found an answer yet. Is there a friend she might have met there?"

"I don't think so." Juana frowned. "Kirsten loved to work. She put in more hours than she needed to. The five of us here would hang out afterwards sometimes, but I don't think she had a lot of other friends."

"None she'd go to a park in a blizzard to see," Albert added. "There are plenty of restaurants and coffee shops around here. Why not go to one of those?"

"What did Kirsten do if she needed to visit a client she couldn't get to on foot?" I asked.

"Uber or Lyft," Juana said. "She would ask for hybrids or EVs. Kirsten didn't want to leave much of a carbon footprint, and I like to encourage employees to live as their authentic selves."

"Authenticity in public relations?" I said. "Don't let people know. You'll be out of business."

She smiled politely. "We want our clients to tell the truth."

"I'm sure you do."

"Any clients who might have been unhappy?" T.J. wanted to know.

"None. Kirsten got rave reviews."

"Posted from computers running on windmill power, I hope," I said.

"We're gutted," Juana said, ignoring my comment. "Kirsten was great." Her voice cracked. "I'll have to hire someone else, but whoever it is won't be her. I wish you luck in your investigation. Wish we could tell you more."

"Me, too."

T.J. and I left without really learning much more about the victim. "I think Albert did it," I said once we were back on the sidewalk.

"You just don't like his hair."

"I despise it."

"Why?"

"It looks absurd."

"He doesn't think so," T.J. said.

"He's not to be trusted. Impaired judgment."

"Your opinions of his hair aside, we're no closer to figuring things out." We climbed back into the car. T.J.'s phone dinged, and she pulled it out of her jeans pocket. "Jessie just did an interview and mentioned she hired us."

"She named us?"

"Yeah."

"Shit."

"What?"

I started the car, put it in gear, and pulled away from the curb. "There's a lot of press coverage of this case. No new developments recently, so the reporters can only rehash the same old stories and opinions. Now, they're going to latch onto us."

"Maybe you should hire Albert as our spokesman," T.J. suggested.

"You're fired," I said.

———

While we were already out making the rounds, I figured we should talk to Kirsten's parents next.

Because I'm not some asshole journalist, I don't believe in ambushing grieving people. We called ahead. It turned out to be a good thing. Since their daughter died, the Valles had been staying with a longtime friend in the Fullerton area of Baltimore County. Much closer than a drive to Westminster or beyond. I knew how to get there without navigation, so we headed out of the city.

Fullerton is a short distance across the city-county line, and the Baltimore Beltway exit for Belair Road basically dumps out right into it. The neighborhood borders of Over-lea, Fullerton, and Perry Hall have always been a little fuzzy for me, but we found the street easily enough. The house stood on the left near the end. Most of the surrounding houses were duplexes. This one was the same size and shape with only one exterior door in front. "What do you call a duplex converted to one big space?" I wondered aloud as the S4 kissed the curb and stopped.

"A house?" T.J. offered, showing exactly how helpful she can be sometimes.

"A monoplex? A simplex?"

"Doesn't Gloria watch a bunch of home improvement shows?"

"I guess I'll ask her." We got out and walked up to the entrance. Two people whose eyes suggested they'd been crying for about a week answered the door and invited us in.

Kirsten Valle's mother was a redhead, and her father was a blond. I guessed them to be in their late forties or so, and despite the recent trauma of losing a daughter, they looked good for their years. They both sat on a sofa, while T.J. and I dropped onto separate recliners. Everything in the living room except the TV mounted on the wall was white, beige, or cream. My sleuthing powers sensed a motif. I also inferred the Valles stayed with a woman because no man would care enough.

"We're glad Jessie hired someone," the father said. "She told us she was thinking about it. I beg your pardon . . . I'm David, and this is Ingrid."

"We're very sorry for your loss," I said. "I know this isn't an easy time, but—"

"Do you?" Ingrid snapped.

"Yes. My sister died when I was sixteen."

She sighed and waved a hand. "I apologize. I . . . I guess I've heard people telling me they know how I feel for a week now, and most of them have no idea."

"I get it," I said. "We don't want to intrude, but we'd like to know a few things." They both nodded and huddled closer on the couch so they could hold hands. "I presume you've spoken to the police."

David snorted. "For all the good it did, yes." He paused and frowned as if realizing his words might have offended someone. "Don't get me wrong . . . if you know someone in the Baltimore police, I'm sure they have a tough job."

"My cousin works there." They didn't need to know Rich's job title. Our chat needed to focus on their daughter rather than any failings of the BPD. "We're looking at what the police have done but also making sure we go over everything. Did you talk to Kirsten before the night she died?"

"A couple days prior," David said, and his wife agreed

with a teary bob of her head. "Either she called us or we called her a few times a week."

"Did she move to Baltimore after college?" T.J. asked while tapping out a note on her phone.

"Yes," Ingrid said. "She was with us a couple weeks while she looked for a job, but once she found one, off she went."

I sensed a little resentment in her words and tone, but now didn't seem like the time to push it. The loss of Kirsten would still be too raw. Instead, I opted for, "She's been with the same company since then?"

"Yes," David said. "We've met her boss and a couple other people over the years. Some faces changed, but everyone seemed nice. Kirsten got along well with all of them. We never heard about any infighting." He let out a dry chuckle. "I don't think I've ever heard a young person complain so little about a job. She'd grumble about a deadline or a client who didn't listen to her every now and then, but those were about all."

"Do you know if she was seeing someone?"

"When would she have time?" Ingrid said.

"I don't remember hearing about her dating anyone in a while," David added. "Even then, it didn't seem like it went very far." He sighed. "Kirsten was a good student. I'm sure she was excellent at her job. She was very focused on school and then on work. She would get . . . kind of tunnel vision about things. I doubt she took the idea of dating very seriously. She was twenty-five. Probably figured she had plenty of time." His voice cracked at the end, and Ingrid cried quietly.

I felt like we were intruding now. "We won't take up anymore of your time. If we think of something or have a break in the case, we'll let you know."

"Thank you," David said. Neither of them stood.

"We're sorry for your loss," T.J. said, and we showed ourselves out.

———

After lunch, my cell phone buzzed. It was Manny, the guy who owned the building and ran the body shop downstairs. "Someone's down here to see you."

"Did you tell him to come up?"

"I think you'll need to make your way down."

"Did he say who he was?"

Manny chuckled. "Do I look like your secretary?"

"No. She's prettier than you. I'll come down."

"What's going on?" T.J. wanted to know.

I shrugged. "Manny says someone is downstairs for me. Didn't come up."

"Want me to go with you?"

I shook my head. "I'll be all right." I headed out the door and down the stairs. Instead of turning left to go outside, I made a right to enter Manny's shop. I saw why the man couldn't come up to see me—like Juana, he sat in a wheelchair. His height was hard to guess, but he had an average build atop atrophied legs. I pegged him for late thirties. His hair was a lighter shade of brown than mine—most of them were—and slicked back. "Adrian Brown," he said, extending a hand as I approached.

I shook his hand. "Your name is familiar."

"I'm covering the story for the *Carroll County Herald*."

"My compliments on spelling *buffoonery* correctly, then."

He chuckled. "Do you have a moment?"

Early in my career, when my parents' foundation supported my cases and I didn't charge my clients, I made myself available to the press frequently. Since going to a more traditional business model, I'd avoided reporters. I wasn't keen to talk to Adrian Brown, but he was in the city to cover the story, and he'd sought me out. We didn't need a parade of journalists stopping by, however. "Sure. Once you leave, though, I'm locking the door and greasing the stairs."

"Latter wouldn't work on me."

"No plan is foolproof," I lamented. "I will say I'd prefer you not run a picture . . . as disappointing as it will be for your readers."

"You want to be able to go undercover in the future?"

"More or less, yeah."

Brown nodded. "Sure. Manny said we could use this little office here." His motorized chair hummed as he wheeled into a small room which was half office and half parts storage. With the door shut, it offered a temporary reprieve from the smells of metal and oil, and it kept some of the sound out.

"If your chair isn't powerful enough, I'm sure Manny and his crew could put a turbo on it." I moved around the old wooden desk. A large cabinet radio like my grandparents had stood nearby, a couple of its panels off and its old electronic guts on display.

"I'm all right," Brown said with a grin. "I'm a little surprised his building isn't ADA compliant."

"He used the space upstairs as extra storage for years before renting it out." I shrugged. "I also don't know the building's age."

"This works out well." Brown set his phone on the cluttered desk, which was covered in both old papers and spare parts. "Mind if I record?" I shook my head. "As you've noticed, I'm covering the story for the *Herald*. Kirsten Valle may have lived in Baltimore, but she was born and raised in Carroll County, and we want to see justice done." I didn't say anything. After a short pause, Brown continued. "It seems Jessie Valle feels the same way."

"Victims' families are usually the ones to hire me."

"Because they're unhappy with the police investigation?"

"Usually the pace of it," I said. "TV has convinced people the police can solve every crime in a few days."

"You sound like their spokesman."

"I'm right. Look at the effect shows like *CSI* had on juries and what they expected law enforcement to be capable of."

Brown considered my words and then nodded. "You've seen what the police have?"

"Yes."

"And?"

"They haven't made an arrest, right?"

"Fair enough," Brown said. "How's your investigation coming along?"

"We're less than twenty-four hours in. I'm still learning some things."

"You mentioned TV creating expectations of the police. I think it's done the same for private eyes."

"Maybe," I acknowledged. "I'm not Adrian Monk . . . thank goodness."

"You've got a pretty good track record of solving cases the police can't."

"I like to think I bring a different perspective."

"Do you think they're incompetent?"

"Different perspective."

"Do you think you'll find the killer here?" Brown asked.

"Of course," I said. "I can't operate from the presumption I'll fail, so I operate on the premise I'll succeed."

"All right." Brown picked up his phone. "I think I have enough for now. Thanks for your time. I might reach back out depending on how things go."

"I hope I don't end up in the buffoonery column."

He smiled. "No promises." Brown pushed what looked like a small joystick on his wheelchair, and it moved out of the office. Outside, a handicapped-accessible minivan taxi waited for him. It was dark gray with red lettering I couldn't read because the vehicle badly needed a washing. I went back upstairs. Reporters could be annoying, but regardless of how many camped outside the office, T.J. and I had a murder to solve.

CHAPTER 7

AFTER AN EARLY RISE at Gloria's house, I slipped out Wednesday morning for a run.

There were no mean streets in Brooklandville. The area featured too many long driveways, manicured lawns, and sculpted hedges. I imagined the homeowners' association could levy topiary-based fines in a fit of pique, but such an action would be as close to mean as the place ever got. I'd carved out a jaunt of about three miles on nice streets surrounded by a backdrop of trees and returned covered in a sheen of sweat despite the chilly morning air.

I showered and selected clothes for the day. Ever since Gloria and I started using our houses about half the time each, I've moved more things here. She hasn't given me any more room to put my stuff, of course. I'm stuck with a small part of the walk-in closet, though at least I get full use of the chest of drawers in the guest room. Clad in black jeans and a French blue sweater, I headed downstairs to make breakfast.

Gloria was already in the kitchen drinking coffee. She smiled and fixed me a cup as I surveyed the options in the fridge. A few minutes later, sausage sizzled, eggs soon followed, and toast popped up to be buttered. Before I could put hers together, Gloria grabbed the plate. "Sorry, I need to eat and run today." She made a breakfast sandwich out of everything, cut it in half, and wrapped it in foil. "I'll see you tonight." We shared a quick kiss, and she headed out the door.

My wife owned her own company, and while it had been successful, it was still small. Unless she ventured out to meet with a prospective client or scout a new venue, she usually worked from an extra bedroom we converted to a double desk office. The garage door opened, a Mercedes engine fired to life, and she was gone. I ate my breakfast and wondered where she went in such a hurry. Alas, it was not the mystery my current client paid me to solve.

———

Following a stop at the office to confirm we had a wealth of coffee and a dearth of reporters, T.J. and I headed out again.

This time, we went to St. Mary's Park across the street from her building. "Here we are once more at another spot I could have come to before work," T.J. said. Before I could answer, she added, "You could make your own coffee."

"I'd have to dock your pay ten percent," I said. "Some duties are too important to shirk."

I curbed the car as close as I could, and we walked past the brick fence into the park. "I should come here more often," T.J. said as she turned her head from side to side. "It's really lovely."

"And a few hundred feet from your front door."

"What prompted this visit?"

"I want to see where Kirsten died," I said.

"It's been too long to find anything now."

"I know." Since the fateful night, Baltimore experienced

a brief warm period which melted all the snow, soon followed by more seasonally cold weather. While the mercury made it above freezing today, the ground remained nearly as hard as the paved walkway. I brought up a copy of the police report on my phone. "Here's the closest bench." T.J. and I dropped onto it. "She might have been sitting here before she died."

"She was in the grass," T.J. said. "You think she tried to get away?"

"Probably." We'd entered from Paca Street and headed down the paved trail. It stayed straight for a spell, did a forty-five-degree left for about fifty feet, and straightened out again. The bench sat off on the right side. A mostly open field sprawled behind us. I wondered if Kirsten Valle could have run away from her attacker there. A knife didn't add much to a person's reach, and in the open space, she might have been able to dash to freedom. Across from us, trees obscured much of the view of both Saint Mary's Seminary and Mother Seton House. Even if they were open, a direct line of sight would have been tough. "I doubt anyone would have seen what happened from the windows." I pointed to the seminary, the closer of the two buildings. "Even if people were in there, the branches, time of day, and conditions would have made visibility very dicey."

"You wanted to see it for yourself?" T.J. asked.

I nodded. "Could have had a maintenance worker or two inside. Now, we know it's not a valid avenue." I looked to the left of the bench where Kirsten's body had lain accumulating snow. Nothing remained except dirt and grass.

"It's weird to think about someone getting killed so close to my place."

"We'd better hope it doesn't happen again. You'll give the agency a bad name if you don't notice the second one."

T.J. punched me in the shoulder. "I told you it's hard to see over here from my apartment."

"I know. Line of sight is a challenge everywhere."

"I hope she didn't suffer," T.J. said in a quiet voice as she stared at the area where Kirsten's corpse had been. "Poor girl. Not very many friends, alone in the city, maybe meeting some guy despite the weather . . ." She trailed off and shook her head. "We need to figure out who did this."

"We will. It's still early."

T.J. stood. "Let's go back to the office."

I had no objections, so we left the park, got into the S4, and drove back toward Fells Point.

———

After returning to the office, we set out again later to pick up lunch. T.J. heard about a new gyro place on the edge of Greektown and wanted to try it. We got carryout and ate at our desks. My gyro was quite good. Not the best I'd ever had, but I would go back to the *taverna* again. T.J. mumbled something around a mouthful of food, took a gulp of her soda, and tried again. "We have a potential new client."

"Another one?"

"It's okay to have more than one, you know," she said.

"I tend not to agree when we're investigating a murder."

"You're also pretty lazy."

"I'll cop to being lazy," I said. "Though I prefer to phrase it as being judicious about how I expend my significant intellectual energy." My assistant shot me a look. "What? Even vast resources need to be nurtured and protected. Look at national parks."

T.J. chuckled. "Whatever you call it, you don't like doing more than one case at a time."

"I like to give them the attention they deserve."

"We have a homicide already," T.J. said. "I get it." She paused for another bite of lunch. "Considering we've had a lean month or two, however, it can't hurt to consider a second case."

"When does this mysterious person want to come in?" I said.

"Tomorrow."

"Too soon." I frowned. "See if they can do next week. Do you know what they want us to look into?"

"Not yet. Maybe it's something that can't wait."

"There are other PIs in the city. None of them have me or you, but we're not alone in the phone book."

"You sure you're only thirty-three?" T.J. said. "Maybe you shouldn't wax fondly about old relics."

"It beats talking about sponsored search engine results," I said.

While T.J. finished her lunch, I brought up the police and ME reports again and compared the photos to what we saw of the park. Kirsten didn't get far from the bench . . . if she in fact sat there. Her proximity to it in death didn't mean she'd been on it in the moments prior. Part of what I did was challenging assumptions made by other investigators—most often the Baltimore police. She could have been standing. She might have been walking out of the park on her way back home. Whoever she met picked the right night to kill her because the snow filled in his footprints as if they were never there.

"All right," T.J. said, "I asked if we could push it back. We're big-timing someone."

"Seems appropriate."

"I guess it does." T.J. collected her trash and mine into the restaurant's plastic bag and carried it toward the garbage can.

At the same time, footsteps thumped up the metal stairs. Unless this potential client happened to be in the area and be pretty large, someone else was coming for a visit. T.J. stopped and frowned. The door opened a second later.

A large man with a malevolent expression stared at us. He spotted T.J. and advanced.

CHAPTER 8

WHEN THE GOON BURST IN, T.J. was closer to the door. While I shot to my feet, she still needed to deal with him. His face was a mix of rage and glee, with knitted brows and a menacing grin. He struck me as the kind of asshole who enjoyed hitting women, and he justified this impression by taking a swing at my assistant as I closed the distance. She ducked under his haymaker and scampered backward. When his fist went back again, I barred his arm, but he managed to slither out of the hold.

At least he faced me now.

T.J.'s footsteps behind me told me she moved away toward her own desk. "Who sent you here?" I asked the muscleman. He was about my height but outweighed me by a good forty pounds. Even through a light jacket, his physique clearly communicated the extra mass came from lifting weights. Most enforcers have a size and muscle advantage on me, but they rarely get to use them.

"Don't matter," he growled. Yellow teeth showed in his grin, and he wore his similarly colored hair short. "You need to leave it alone."

"Leave what alone?"

My answer came in the form of another wild hook. I thrust my left forearm up to block it, turned my fist inward, and hit my foe on the cheek. Without a lot of room to wind up, it wasn't a powerful blow, but it showed him I wasn't going to knuckle under just because he was big and ugly. He scowled and fired off a series of punches. I spent years both here and in Hong Kong studying martial arts. My adversary didn't do anything new, and I tended to favor defense, so I blunted each of his attacks.

He backed up a pace and loaded his weight for a front kick. I turned it wide, stepped closer, and shoved him hard in the chest. With one leg still off the floor, the goon waved his arms in a futile attempt to keep his balance before crashing to the carpeted wood. I moved forward, but he recovered enough to keep me at bay with his other foot and leg. It allowed him a chance to get back to vertical.

"I been takin' it easy on you," he grunted. "Want to give up?"

In response, I did my best Morpheus impression from *The Matrix* and bade him to come at me with a wave of my hand. He obliged, unloading a series of punches. My forearms stung from the repeated deflections, and they would probably start to bruise soon. Still, my defense held, and his strikes lost a little speed and power as his breathing became faster and louder. After a big hook left my foe a little unbalanced, I hit him hard in the exposed side under the ribs.

When he twisted to protect himself, I elbowed him in the face. It wasn't enough to drop him, but the second one was. This time, he couldn't keep me at bay, and I walloped him when he lay flat. The blow didn't turn his lights out, but they were flickering. "Hey, asshole." I used a kick to the ribs as a nudge. "Want to tell me who sent you?"

"Piss off," he growled.

I shrugged. "Have it your way." While he blinked and grunted, I grabbed my phone and snapped his picture. I tossed my cell to T.J., hauled the enforcer to his feet, and steered him toward the door. "Make sure you tell whoever's signing your checks to pay you by the step. Be sure to count them on the way down." A jab to his stomach bent him over, and I used his collar and belt as levers to toss the goon down the metal stairs. He rolled and bounced before landing in a heap and lying still at the bottom.

I headed back inside and shut the door. "You all right?" I asked T.J.

She nodded. "Yeah. What the hell?"

"Someone clearly sent him to discourage us."

"We must be getting close, then," T.J. said.

"Maybe." She frowned, but I continued. "Normally, I would agree. Two things, though. One, we haven't talked to many people yet. Two, Jessie got the word out about us being on the case. We should presume whoever killed Kirsten is keeping an eye on the media coverage. He'd know we're in the picture."

"I guess." T.J. sat in her chair again. "You sure he's gone?"

"Once he comes to, he will be."

"What if he broke his neck at the bottom?"

I shrugged. "Manny and the guys have a forklift."

"I like the way you think sometimes," T.J. said. "Fuck that guy."

———

About an hour after our goonish visitor left, someone else came up the stairs.

The new arrival's footfalls were much quieter. The door opened, and a woman I guessed to be an age peer of our victim walked in. She was tall and very thin even with a coat on. Black hair spilled over her collar. "You're investigating Kirsten's death, right?"

"We are," I confirmed. Considering she didn't lead off with a question about a man lying at the bottom of the steps, I presumed the alleged tough guy dusted himself off and moved along.

"I read it online." When I gestured toward a guest chair, she took a seat. "I'm Rose," she said while T.J. wheeled her chair over to join us. "Kirsten and I have been close since middle school." She let out a humorless chuckle. "I think I was one of her few non-work friends."

"Thanks for coming in," I said. "We've talked to a few people so far, but I think you could have some insights we've been missing."

"Do you have a theory so far?"

Before I could answer, T.J. said, "We're thinking she went to the park to meet someone. It's odd considering the weather, but we don't have a better guess why she was there. Yet."

"You're probably ahead of the police already."

"Pretty low bar to clear," I said.

"Still . . . any progress is welcome. Someone needs to pay for what they did to her." Rose was a slender woman, but her reedy voice doubled in strength over the last sentence.

"Maybe you can fill in some gaps her family and coworkers couldn't," I said. "Let's start with an easy one. Was Kirsten going out with anyone?"

"Like, seriously dating? No. She'd been out with a few guys, but I don't think any of them panned out. Kirsten knew the dating pool in Carroll County was pretty shallow, so she was looking here in the city. Your guess about meeting a man in the park might be good." She frowned. "I don't know why they wouldn't reschedule with the snow, though."

"Have you talked to the police?"

"No," she said with a sneer. "They haven't done much. Our local paper is calling them out for it, thank goodness. Someone needs to."

While we tended to get paid thanks to the BPD's inefficiency, I sympathized with their plight here. Rose didn't need to know this, however. Having a resource Rich and company lacked could help us wrap this up faster. "Apart from her uneventful love life, is there something else we should know about Kirsten?"

"She was a fighter. We took kickboxing in college."

"I'm taking it now," T.J. said.

Rose smiled. "Good. It's a hard world out there for women. Your job probably makes it tougher." Today certainly provided an example.

"The ME's report doesn't mention defensive wounds," I said.

"So she knew her attacker?" Rose asked.

"Maybe . . . or she was taken by surprise and couldn't fight back."

Rose dug a phone out of her purse. "Kirsten didn't have the best luck with guys. There was one she dated a few times, but it fizzled out. I always got the feeling he wanted to reconnect." She showed us a photo of a reasonably handsome guy with his arm around Kirsten in a restaurant booth. "I can send this to you if you think it'll help. His name's Rider . . . Something."

"Please send it. We'll figure out who he is." I gave her both my and T.J.'s mobile numbers, and she got the picture to us quickly. "I'm not sure there's much more I can tell you. Hopefully this helped."

"I think it did," I said. Once Rose left, T.J. and I focused on the photo. I moved it to my PC, isolated the man, and used the BPD's access to the state police facial recognition system to run a search on him. We got a hit pretty quickly. "Fucking hell," I said when I saw his name: Ryder Long.

"What?" T.J. said.

"Look at the spelling. He's the killer."

"Because of the Y?"

"Yes."

"What about Captain Manbun?"

"He moves down the list. 'Ryder' is a worse offense."

"What if this guy also has a manbun?" my assistant asked with a grin.

"Then we shoot him on sight."

She pointed at my screen. "It seems more relevant that he has a prior arrest for assault."

"See? Sometimes, cases which look challenging at first blush end up being pretty easy. We have multiple reasons for him to be our guy."

"Are we going to rustle him up now?"

"Who am I, Wyatt Earp?" She rolled her eyes but couldn't help the amused grin splitting her lips. "Grab your purse, cowpoke. We're going to find this guy."

"Yee-haw," T.J. said.

CHAPTER 9

T.J. SAT in the driver's seat of her Mustang.

C.T. filled the passenger seat beside her. He'd insisted on taking her car because it stood out less. "It's a sports car," she protested.

He tapped the automatic gear selector. "Not with this transmission, it's not."

"My car is just as easy to spot as yours," she said.

"You may be right," C.T. said. "I delegate the task of getting a better stakeout vehicle to you. By Monday, you need to have an SUV. Preferably gray or black."

"Why don't you get an SUV? Your wife drives a two-seater. You all could use one."

"As the boss, I can assign things I don't want to do to you."

"Any special requests for my new ride?" T.J. said.

"Sure. Winter's coming. Heated seats would be nice."

"Piss off." T.J. chuckled. "I'm keeping the Mustang. No heated seats and all." She picked up her soda from the cupholder and took a swig. They'd been sitting outside Ryder Long's house for a few hours. At six, C.T. walked to a nearby Royal Farms convenience store for dinner—including a box of their amazing potato wedges. Both tried to keep their drinking to a minimum to avoid having to leave the stakeout and pee. Hoofing it to the nearest bathroom would take five minutes.

While they ate, Ryder Long returned home. He hadn't left the house in the hour since, and based on the interior lights remaining constant, he wasn't up to much inside. "Should we talk to him?" T.J. said after a few minutes of silence.

C.T. shook his head. "Not yet. If he's not our guy, he might not even be aware Kirsten is dead."

"It's all over the news."

"There are plenty of good reasons not to read or watch the news."

T.J. shrugged. "That's fair." She shot a sideways glance at her boss. "You're softening on him being the killer?"

"My distaste for the Y in his name aside, we don't have anything on him yet. I did a little research while we waited for him. Works pretty close to home. Goes into the office a few days. Bowls in a league. Otherwise, he doesn't seem particularly interesting."

"No manbun?"

C.T. smiled. "If he wore one, we'd be storming his place by now."

"Doesn't seem like he's up to much."

"No, it doesn't." C.T. opened an app T.J. didn't recognize.

"What's that?"

"I'm going to sniff his traffic."

"Legally?" He snorted. "I didn't think so."

"Most traffic gets encrypted in transit, so even if he were writing a long confession email, we couldn't see it. It'd be nice to know what he's up to at least."

"No matter his hairstyle," T.J. said, "why not knock on his door?"

"Let's presume he's innocent. The system is going to. His one time getting popped for assault wasn't against a woman and isn't a pattern. I'd still like to talk to him, but we don't need to spook him. It's the difference between being a suspect and a person of interest."

"Why'd we come, then?"

"I needed to tell you to get an SUV," C.T. said. T.J. arched an eyebrow at him. "Royal Farms dinner?" Her expression remained. "It's good to see if he's home. The press coverage keeps ramping up. What if he packed a suitcase and dashed for his car?"

"We'd upgrade him to suspect," T.J. said.

"Exactly. Just because a case is interesting doesn't mean everything we do to solve it will be. I learned my lesson early on."

"You're all about sharing the wisdom in your old age?"

"You're fired," C.T. said.

———

T.J. turned off the TV. She hadn't been paying attention for a while anyway. When her focus lapsed, she pictured the brawny goon walking in, seeing her near the door, and apparently being happy at the idea of beating up a woman.

He showed his joy by taking a swing at her. Thankfully, he was a basic goon, and the big windup meant T.J. saw the punch coming in plenty of time to get out of the way. She was mad at herself for freezing, though. She avoided the blow, got out of striking distance, and basically stood around while her boss ran in to deal with the enforcer. There were times in her past life T.J. felt helpless in the presence of large, angry men. Her pimps and their hired muscle took care of the problems sometimes. Others, she needed to improvise. This usually involved running, but she had ended up on the wrong end of more than one beating.

When she got out of the life and started working for C.T., T.J. enrolled in kickboxing classes. It doubled as exercise and a way to learn self-defense. Presented with a chance to use it today, however, she didn't. Or couldn't. The group only sparred in very controlled situations, and none of them came close to what she saw earlier today. Still, the goon was big and mean but not highly skilled. She could have kicked him in the balls and then given him a hard boot right in the head.

Instead, she stood and watched as C.T. took care of things.

T.J. spiked the remote onto the couch and walked into her bedroom. She pulled a heavy bag out of her closet, slung its straps over an exposed beam, and secured it in place. After a few minutes of stretching, she slipped on a pair of MMA gloves and got to work. A series of jabs got her arms loose, and T.J. soon alternated them with crosses. She mixed in hooks, doing ten sets alternating between dominant hands. Finally, she added an uppercut as the fourth and did two more sets.

Her arms ached, and she was already sweating. Her mind put the goon's creepy face near the top of the punching bag, and she attacked the canvas with a series of snap kicks. The first sets would have caught him in the family jewels, the second in the chest, and the third full on to the face. From there, T.J. pivoted and worked on her side kicks. She didn't have the flexibility yet to kick above chest level with her right leg and around the navel with her left. Still, the bag thumped and rocked every time her foot made contact. Power mattered, too.

Maybe she needed something beyond kickboxing. C.T.

told her how he started taking martial arts in middle school—his father's suggestion after a bullying incident. It meant he'd been studying to one degree or another for over twenty years. He didn't freeze. He jumped up, ran in, and dealt with the problem. Perhaps T.J. could get there with her kickboxing. Perhaps not.

She thought about the beatdowns she got in the past. A skinny teenager in a vulnerable position—and dangerous job—is going to run into trouble. Thanks to Melinda, her boss, and herself, T.J. wasn't that girl anymore. She'd come a long way, and now she recognized she still had significantly farther to go. She paused for a water break, clapped her MMA gloves together, took a few deep breaths, and went back to working over the bag.

———

As T.J. left her building's fitness center the next morning, she realized it was a mile marker in how far she'd come.

A few years ago, she was living wherever she could, frequently strung out, and skinny to the point she struggled to keep weight on. Now, she never lacked for food and needed things like her heavy bag and the treadmill to ensure she didn't gain too much weight. She felt healthy, and it seemed like such a lofty goal back then. She never wanted to take her circumstances for granted.

After a shower and a quick breakfast, T.J. headed into the office. She unlocked the door and set the coffee maker to do its thing. She opened email to see what came in since they left yesterday. As usual, most of it was junk, but the potential second client didn't like the idea of being rescheduled until next week and maybe beyond. T.J. knew C.T. wanted to push another case out, but she thought they could do both and said as much in her reply.

Good morning,

We are currently investigating a murder, and this is obviously a high priority for everyone.

These things are fluid, however, and if you're right that your matter doesn't need a ton of care and attention, I think we could work it in. Please note my boss doesn't agree with this yet. I'll work on him.

That said, we will have to wait until next week. Let's circle back Monday or Tuesday and see where we stand.

Thanks,

T.J.

Executive Assistant

She put a reminder on the agency's Google calendar about the case. C.T. would see it while drinking coffee and probably complain. He would get over it. This wasn't a one-man show anymore, and while T.J. was far away from becoming a full-fledged—let alone licensed—private investigator, she knew she could help. Multitasking didn't need to be a dirty word anymore.

Now, it was only necessary to convince her boss.

A quick glance at her phone showed she still had a few minutes until C.T. arrived. T.J. conducted research on Ryder Long. As much as they both wanted him to be the killer, it seemed unlikely. His assault charge came from a bar fight, and he never got convicted. He'd lived a clean life according to the police blotter ever since. Still, he was their only person of interest in what had been a vexing case so far. T.J. understood why the police gathered so little.

She and C.T. needed to do more . . . . both for the good name of the agency but most importantly for Kirsten Valle and her family.

CHAPTER 10

WHEN I GOT up the next morning, Gloria rose with me.

I hoped she was about to push me down and climb on top of me, but no such luck. She wanted to run with me. I tried to hide my disappointment as I changed into my Under Armour gear. I must have done a poor job, because she said, "Easy, tiger. We'll need to shower after." A little over three miles and thirty minutes later, we ran my water heater empty having spent the minimum time actually washing our bodies.

Gloria took longer to get dressed, so I'd already brewed coffee and mostly finished preparing a breakfast of an omelet and toast when she came down. She poured her java into a travel mug. "This looks great. Sorry I need to get going." I wrapped two slices of sourdough toast and forty percent of the omelet in foil for her and wondered again what she needed to get to with such urgency. Eating three-fifths of the omelet and pounding a mug of coffee did not lead to an epiphany.

I drove into the office in search of both more caffeine and a little inspiration. T.J. had made a fresh pot, so I was already one-for-two. I looked at our shared calendar at my desk. "I know what you're going to say," she told me.

"You do?"

"Yeah. You're going to talk about preserving your precious intellectual resources and not doing a second case. I get it. You used to be a one-man operation, but you're not anymore. I know I can't do some 'official' things . . ." She added air quotes for emphasis. ". . . but I can help. The client says it shouldn't be too hard."

"A few things," I said. "First, I would never sound so pompous." She rolled her eyes, and I deserved it, but I continued. "Second, clients don't really know how easy or hard an investigation will be. They only see it from their angle. Third, I'm glad you want to help, and I'm willing to explore it, but I'd love a breakthrough in our main case. Finally . . . did you consider this might be a fishing expedition?"

"What do you mean?"

"A goon visited us yesterday. He was unsuccessful. What if someone is trying to get information out of us about the main case?"

"I didn't tell her anything," T.J. said.

"You apparently told her we'd be chatting next week," I said.

"Okay, I might have said that much."

"Let's see how things go. If you want to be an executive assistant, you need to earn the title."

"I'm ready, boss."

I smiled. "I guess we'll find out."

"We should talk to Ryder Long," I said.

"Are you going to ask him about the spelling of his name?" T.J. wanted to know.

"Yes. Set up the interrogation room. Crank up the heat and lights."

"You want a set of scalpels for intimidation?"

"I was thinking a power drill and a few pairs of pliers."

T.J. chuckled. "I looked into him this morning. You know . . . since I'm always the first to arrive."

"Not always," I pointed out.

"I put what I found in our shared drive," T.J. said. I opened the document she added, yet she decided to summarize it anyway. "He might be a person of interest, but I'm not sure he's very interesting for this case. The Y in his name aside, he's not much of a suspect."

"I know. Right now, he's pretty much all we have to go on. Even if he's not good for the murder, maybe he can tell us something about our victim no one else could." I cracked my knuckles, opened a suite of hacking tools, and got to work.

"What are you working on?" my assistant asked.

"A little extra payload for something," I said. "We should presume Ryder knows what's going on. He hasn't fled yet, so you're right . . . he's a bad suspect. I think we can use the fact he might land on the cops' radar to our favor, however." I'd used this sort of attack before and chose a package I'd deployed previously. A quick code review showed it should still do what I wanted.

T.J. wheeled her chair beside mine as I worked. I found an article about Kirsten's murder, saved it, made it a PDF, and embedded my special payload in it. "How are you going to make him open it?" T.J. wondered.

"We'll spoof an email." I looked at Ryder's social media accounts. Like most people, he didn't lock them down enough. The first guy who appeared on his Facebook, Instagram, and LinkedIn was the winner. "We're going to be

Jimmy Henry," I said. "Never trust a man with two first names." I went to a site for disposable emails, set one up for our use, and emailed everything to Ryder.

"What will this do if he opens the attachment?"

"Allow us to track his phone. Location and apps."

"No data?"

I shook my head. "It's all encrypted. I could do another payload to try and break it, but the overhead is a lot higher. If he sends regular texts, we'll get those."

It didn't take long for Ryder to open the file. He even sent a quick and terse reply to our message. *What the fuck, bro? Don't send me this shit.* "He's big mad," T.J. said.

This status didn't compel Ryder to do anything, however. He remained in the house, and only his email and a few social media apps remained open. Around lunchtime, he opened DoorDash. "Is there such a thing as a person of no interest?" I said. "A person of boring?"

"Maybe we should rattle his cage," T.J. suggested.

"Let's." Ryder's cell number was easy enough to get, so I called him and put it on speaker.

"You got Ryder," he said, and I continued to dislike him.

"Ryder, this is C.T. Ferguson. I'm—"

"Do I know you, bro?"

"Not yet. I'm a private investigator."

"Is this about my application?"

"No, Ryder, it's about a murder. Kirsten Valle."

"I didn't do it," he said.

"Good. I actually believe you, but I'd still like to talk to you about Kirsten. Can you come by the office? We're in Fells Point."

"Not sure I can be much use to you."

I bit down an uncharitable reply and said, "Let me be the judge of your usefulness."

"I don't know, bro."

"Ryder, I'm going to give you a choice. You can come and see me, or I can tell the cops who you are with respect to the victim in their very high-profile murder investigation. You don't seem like a dummy, so I'd like you to spend a second or two doing the math on this one."

He sighed. "All right. What's your address?" I told him. "I'll be in around the end of the day."

"We'll see you then," I said and ended the call.

"You think he'll show?" T.J. said.

I shrugged. "I think I'll tell Rich about him if he doesn't." I tapped my phone. "Besides, if he decides to run for it, we'll know where he is."

"Let's see what happens, then."

A little after four, a single set of footsteps came up the stairs.

I opened the top drawer of my desk and took out a pistol just in case. The door swung in, and Ryder Long entered the office. He brushed a few flurries off his shoulders and out of his sandy blond hair. He had pale blue eyes, and an athletic physique showed through his jacket. He struck me as the type of fellow who was attractive to women and knew it. I empathized. "Thanks for coming in," I said, shutting the gun back inside my desk.

"Didn't sound like I had too much choice, bro," he said.

"Coffee?"

Ryder shrugged. "Sure." T.J. set a half pot to brew while he sat in one of my guest chairs. "If you don't think I killed Kirsten, why do you want to talk to me?"

"Do you have an alibi for the night of her murder?"

"Do I need one?"

"The cops will learn about you eventually," I said. "I'm ahead of them as usual, but they're not going to invite you over for coffee if they think you're a person of interest."

"I do," he said after a pause which didn't help his credibility. "I was at a work retreat. We ended up staying an extra day because of the snow."

I glanced outside the window. Flakes were coming down hard and fast now. I didn't even remember hearing about any snow in the forecast. "When did you get wind of her murder?"

"The day after I got back, I think. I was trying to implement some things from the retreat, so I didn't check the news."

"What do you do?"

"Sales," he said.

His personality seemed a little lacking for sales, though he could do well making visits to lonely women. "How do you take your coffee?" T.J. asked him.

"Just cream is fine, thanks." She carried over his and mine, and then went back for her own.

"We've talked to people who knew Kirsten," I said. "Her sister, parents, coworkers, and a friend she didn't make at the office. None of them know her the way you might have."

He put up a hand. "We only dated a few times. I wasn't going ring shopping."

"How many times?"

"Three, I think."

"You think?"

"Depends if we're counting hookups."

"I guess I don't need to ask if you were sleeping with her," I said.

"I was," he confirmed anyway.

"Was it serious?" T.J. asked.

"No. I wasn't dating anyone else, but we weren't exclusive." He met our eyes the whole time.

"Who broke it off?"

"I did. There were times she just . . . wasn't there. Thinking about work, I'm sure." He let out a dry chuckle. "Her job was her priority. I knew I would always come after it. We had some fun, but the spark really wasn't there, and I didn't see a future, so I called it off."

I sipped my coffee and asked, "Was she upset?"

"Didn't seem like it," Ryder said. "She didn't cry or even tear up. She just said she understood."

"So it was amicable?"

"Yeah."

"Did you keep in touch?"

"Here and there . . . mostly on socials."

"She was killed in a park near her apartment and work," T.J. said. "Our guess is she went there to meet someone. Do you know if she was dating again?"

Ryder shrugged. "If she was, she didn't tell me. I know the park. We took a couple walks through there. Nice place to meet someone if you want to be in public, but I think I'd rather be indoors during a snowstorm."

"Me, too," I said.

We chatted a few more minutes, and then Ryder left. A dusting of snow already covered the cars, and it showed no signs of stopping or even slowing down. "I guess he's no longer a person of interest," T.J. said.

"Nope."

"Despite the spelling of his name."

"I know," I said. "The disappointments continue."

"We might want to get a jump on the snow, boss."

"You go ahead. I'll see you tomorrow." T.J. left, and I continued sitting at my desk thinking about Ryder, Kirsten, and this case. I'd hoped we were ahead of the police, but now, it didn't feel like it. I watched the flurries fall, and something in the back of my mind hoped there wouldn't be a pattern to the unexpected heavy snow and a redhead being found dead in the morning.

CHAPTER 11

THERE WERE ALREADY a couple inches of snow by the time I got to Gloria's house on Thursday evening.

Salt trucks patrolled the roads, but the volume of precipitation combined with plummeting temperatures would limit the effectiveness of their treatment. "Looks like we'll be working from here tomorrow," my wife said.

"You'll need to make me coffee in the morning, then," I said. The look she gave me suggested she would not be putting a pot on anytime soon. I texted T.J. and told her not to worry about going to the office tomorrow. When Gloria and I went to sleep, at least another inch had fallen. When we woke up on Friday morning, I guessed eight to ten covered the ground, and a few flurries still fell.

While I made coffee—with Gloria's mocking encouragement—my wife put the morning news on. The weatherman, who looked flustered at the developments in the last twelve hours, said most parts of the Baltimore metro area got between nine and twelve inches. He did everything but drop to his knees and apologize for whiffing so badly. I drank some coffee and searched Gloria's garage for a snow blower. "Why would I need one?" she asked. "The neighborhood association pays someone to plow the streets and driveways."

I preferred digging out myself, but I couldn't fault her reasoning. The Brooklandville neighborhood watch probably patrolled the streets with their citation books handy, looking for anyone who attempted to remove their own snow. I worked on breakfast while Gloria confirmed arrangements for the driveway. We enjoyed a pot of oatmeal a short while later, and I sliced fruit to go with it. A loud rumble approached when we finished, and a large pickup with a plow on the front worked on several houses in the vicinity.

"How's your case going?" Gloria asked when we each partook of our second cups.

"Slowly," I said. "We thought we'd found a lead, and the guy had a little information, but it didn't turn into much."

"I'm sorry." She squeezed my hand. "I know it's going slowly now, but you always get your man in the end."

My morbid thought of the previous evening—wondering if a fresh body would turn up today—danced at the back of my head. I hoped Kirsten Valle's murder had been a one-time tragedy. Hope was often in short supply around Baltimore, of course. The clock struck ten, and I allowed myself a moment of optimism as I continued trying to sort out exactly what happened to our victim and whom she had gone to the park to meet.

T.J. and I dove back into the life of Kirsten Valle.

"Let's scrape her socials," I suggested. I ran a tool to accomplish exactly this, dumping her posts—with attached images—into a document I could share with my assistant for easy perusal. I used earbuds for the call. Gloria worked on the opposite side of the room, and she sported headphones, probably to tamp down the noise from my conversation with T.J. "You should be able to access the file now."

"I see it," she confirmed. I gave her a few seconds to look it over. "Nothing here about dating, looking forward to meeting someone . . . bupkis."

"Where the hell did you learn 'bupkis'?"

"Probably some boomer TV show you recommended."

"I don't suggest anything older than Gen X," I protested.

"Anyway," she said, "there's not much here. Her photos don't show her with anyone except her coworkers. Her TikToks are all about books she read and movies she viewed."

"I saw."

"Seems she didn't care for *Killers of the Flower Moon*."

"We can't arrest Scorsese," I said. Rich's name and number popped up on my screen. "Hang on," I told T.J. "Rich is on the other line." I switched over to his call. "Happy Friday."

"It's not," he said.

"What's going on?"

"We got another dead woman."

I closed my eyes and blew out a long breath. "Same as the first?"

"Pretty redhead . . . young . . . found stabbed in a park. I'd say the pattern holds."

"Shit."

"Yeah. Fucking press is going to be all over this if they catch wind of it."

"I'm not going to tell them anything."

"I know. You might want to get down here. I know you're on the Valle case, and Sharpe said we can include you on this one."

"I knew I liked the captain for a reason," I said. "Where are you?"

"Patterson Park."

"Wow." Located in Highlandown, Patterson Park was one of the largest in the city and much bigger than the site of Kirsten Valle's murder.

"Yeah. See you soon." He ended the call, and T.J. came back on the line.

"What's up, boss?"

"A second body."

"What?" she said in a whisper.

"Yeah. Pretty much the same as the first. We've been invited to the crime scene. I have all-wheel drive, so I'll pick you up."

"All right."

"I'm not sure what the roads are like, so give me forty minutes." I hung up with T.J. Gloria turned in her chair and frowned.

"Did you say a second body?"

"Yeah."

"My gosh," she said. "Both times in the snow."

I'd thought about this factor but also questioned its significance. Maybe it mattered a lot. I tended not to believe in coincidences. "Just one of many things we'll get to look into over the next several days, I'm sure." I walked to my wife's chair, leaned down, and kissed her.

"Good luck," she said.

I grunted. "We'll definitely need it."

———

I got to T.J.'s a few minutes early. Despite the rarity of me arriving anywhere ahead of schedule, she was ready to go as I pulled up. She hopped in the S4, and I headed toward East Baltimore. The streets remained slushy with a bunch of snow piled up at the curbs. A few scattered cars got plowed in and wouldn't be going anywhere until a full melt happened. "What the hell?" my assistant said as we were underway.

"I have to admit something like this was at the back of my mind."

"Me, too. I didn't think it would actually happen, though."

"Get ready for a lot of media attention," I said. "If this newest victim is anything like the first, the press is going to roll with a serial killer narrative."

"I didn't think two victims made a serial killer," T.J. said.

"You're right . . . but why let the truth get in the way of a salacious story?" I picked up Orleans Street, and the higher traffic volume reduced the slush remaining on the asphalt.

"Where was the body found?" T.J. wanted to know.

"In the dog park. The pooch's owner called nine-one-one."

We made good time. Baltimore Street formed the northern border of Patterson Park's main area, with Patterson Park Avenue to the west, Eastern Avenue to the south, and Linwood Avenue on the east. An annex containing a few baseball fields continued eastward to Ellwood. The dog park butted up against Linwood, and I took Orleans Street all the way to it. The directional designation changed from north to south as we crossed Baltimore Street.

A phalanx of police cars blocked the road ahead, with red and blue lights bathing the area and reflecting off of nearby house windows. I curbed the S4 as close as I could. The sidewalk had not yet been plowed, though the road remained reasonably clear. T.J. and I got out and approached the yellow police tape. A uniformed officer stopped us. I told him

Lieutenant Ferguson was expecting us and showed him my ID. He talked into the radio clipped to his chest, got confirmation, and told us someone would escort us inside momentarily. Sergeant Paul King picked his way through the snow a short while later.

King took Rich's spot when my cousin got the bump to lieutenant. Despite his long hair, slender build, and lack of a shaving routine making him look like a failed rock singer, King was a good and intuitive cop. What passed for his goatee looked especially patchy today. I suffered from a similar inability to grow facial hair, but I possessed the good sense to use a razor at least every other day. "You should go to the vet for the mange," I said, rubbing my cheeks and chin.

"I feel like it's my trademark at this point," he said. "Don't mess with what works."

"It works?"

King smirked and shook his head as he led us the short distance to the snow-covered grassy dog playground. All of us wore boots—my Alpago pull-ons were the most stylish, of course—so we made our ways easily enough. A black metal fence separated the dog area from the rest of the park. Benches stood scattered throughout. Varying amounts of snow, probably blown by the sporadic wind, covered the grass, paved trail, and canine exercise features. We entered via the gate at the far end.

A gaggle of cops and medical examiner staff—the latter in their white Tyvek suits despite the chilly temperatures—stood and huddled near a body lying in the snow. Rich nodded at us as we approached and broke away from the group. "This is where we found her. All we did was get the snow off her." From my distance of about twenty feet, this victim bore a close resemblance to Kirsten Valle. "Guy with his mutt found her," Rich continued. "I can't imagine taking a dog for a walk on a morning like this."

"A lot of houses nearby don't have much grass," I said. "Or any in some cases." The rowhouses surrounding Patterson Park often featured small concrete back yards with nothing in the front save a porch and a couple steps leading from the sidewalk. Facilities like this were essential for dog owners. We rejoined the main group.

"Lieutenant, you were asking about time of death," one of the ME's men said. "Like with the first unfortunate soul, the snow covering her for hours messes with body temperature. There's another similarity, however." He pointed to the ground, and I craned my neck to see around the burly cop standing in front of me. "You'll notice the snow underneath her. It's disturbed where the body fell, naturally, but there's not very much of it. My guess is she was killed while there were only two or three inches on the ground."

"Still after dusk this time of year," Rich said.

"Yes."

"But early enough there might be witnesses," I said.

"We have people canvassing the area," Rich said.

"You all right?" I whispered to T.J.

She bobbed her head. "Yeah, why?"

"I'm sure you saw things like this . . . before. Let me know if it gets to be too much."

"I'm good. I want to see this through."

"At least this one was pretty far from your apartment," I said. "You probably don't need an alibi."

A ruckus went up at the perimeter. Two press vans parked behind me, and a third approached. I groaned at the inevitable crush of questions. "They don't waste any time."

"Goddammit," Rich grumbled. "How did these jackals find out already?"

"We're not exactly in a remote location."

Rich grunted. Uniforms converged on the approaching reporters, a mix of men and women with their phones held out shouting in a cacophony of voices. The cops and the barrier would keep them at bay, but we could still hear them. Occasionally, the collective quieted enough for distinct questions to come out.

"Is this another dead woman?"

"Do the police have any leads?"

"Have you talked to the mayor?"

"Will the commissioner be on scene?"

"Are we dealing with a serial killer?"

Rich and I exchanged glances, frowns, and sighs at the last one.

CHAPTER 12

A BALTIMORE POLICE SUV joined the throng of vehicles outside. Captain Leon Sharpe got out and strode toward the park. He glared at the collection of reporters, and I imagined he wanted to bench press a few of them as they peppered him with questions. Sharpe stood four inches taller than me and outweighed me by a good sixty pounds. He looked like he could have played defensive end in the NFL, and even now, I wouldn't want to be an offensive tackle lined up across from him. His bald black head gleamed in the sun.

"This is already a shitshow," he groused as he joined the group. "How'd those jackals find out what happened?"

"This is the biggest park around, Leon," I said when everyone working for the BPD swallowed their tongues at a simple query from the imposing captain. "Even with the weather, plenty of people walk and drive by. Any of them could have tipped someone off."

We still heard the members of the press shouting their questions, but the volume and frequency both went down once it became apparent no one was going to give an answer. "Where are we, Rich?" Sharpe asked.

"Similar to the first case," Rich said, and he reviewed the ways in which the two were closely related.

Sharpe frowned. "I've heard a few of our friends over there asking about a serial killer. I know we're short of the definition, but this story's only going to gain traction."

A cop I didn't know had the temerity to ask, "So?"

Sharpe glowered at him, and I got the impression the fellow wanted to turn tail and run. "So the commissioner doesn't want to get bombarded with speculation like this at any press conference. So the mayor doesn't, either. So instead of standing here and trying to be contrary, maybe you can find some fucking evidence of what happened here."

Once everyone in uniform decided they needed to be doing something anywhere else, Sharpe pulled Rich, King, T.J., and me aside. "All hands on deck," he said, and his brown eyes landed on me. "I know the first victim's family hired you. I could tell you these are separate cases, but I know you won't care. Fine. Look into both. We want to get the books closed on these, and I don't really care how it happens." Rich opened his mouth to say something, but Sharpe continued. "Whatever overtime you need. The commissioner and the mayor will sign off on it."

"How about my usurious rates?" I said.

"You're already being paid." Sharpe jabbed his finger at me. "Don't try to double dip."

"I'm not trying to pull a Costanza."

"This is a different case," T.J. added before I could.

"She do all your talking for you?" Sharpe asked.

"Plenty for herself, too," T.J. said.

I grinned and shrugged. "I could only ask her to file reports in silence for so long."

The captain grunted. "We'll see how things go. I'm not committing."

"Then, just *most* hands on deck," I said. "Got it. I'm sure the BPD's stance will play well in the press."

Sharpe ignored me—probably to my benefit—and focused on the scene at hand. He walked around the body, careful not to disrupt the forensic crew's activities despite his bulk and general lack of grace. Everyone gave him a wide berth owing to his rank and the sour expression on his face. No one wanted to eat a military press slam even if the snow would provide a padded landing.

King approached me with an amused look. "You really know how to endear yourself to people, don't you?"

"My charm is boundless," I said.

"You got anything on the first one?"

"Not really. I thought we found a person of interest, but he turned out not to be very interesting."

"And here I was hoping you'd ride in and save the day."

"Don't tell me you're concerned about the commissioners Q score."

"What the fuck is a Q score?"

"I knew I liked you for a reason," I said. "Aside from any grooming tips you might offer."

"I'm thinking of starting a Substack," King said. He jutted his ill-covered chin toward the scene. "Looks like she was stabbed, too. Poor girl. No effects on the vic. Killer took her purse, phone, and everything."

"Unless we're dealing with a major-league moron, he ditched the phone. Still, once you know who she is . . ."

"We think of the obvious things, too, genius. No usurious rates needed."

The BPD's occasional inability to pluck the investigative low-hanging fruit made sure I stayed employed. Still, in the spirit of being collegial, I didn't pick this nit with a cop I liked. Instead, I kicked at a loose bit of snow. "Pretty crazy when you think about. Two times now we've had unexpected snowfalls, and a woman gets killed each time."

"Some rag from Carroll County predicted this."

I frowned. "Really?"

"Yeah. They brag about the accuracy of their forecasts." As if on cue, a minivan arrived, and *Carroll County Herald* editor Adrian Brown wheeled himself near the yellow tape to join the throng of journalists.

"I guess our killer must read the paper," I said.

———

We lingered at the crime scene for a while, but not much else happened besides even more reporters showing up. T.J. and I used our hoods to cover our faces—she even brought a base-ball cap—as we walked past the gathered throng. I tried to avoid having my photo in the paper, so I held up a hand to block their phones. "Keep walking," I told her as we approached the S4. "If these jackals do get a good picture, it'd be nice if we weren't both in it. I'll pick you up farther along."

She nodded and headed up the road. I climbed into my car, got it turned around as a few reporters took my photo, and picked my secretary up about five hundred yards away. "I think this is my first media circus," T.J. said as she buckled her seat belt.

"Too bad there are no elephants and popcorn," I said. We headed back to the office, driving through a Popeye's along the way. Once we sat at our desks, I told her, "The BPD won't have anything online for a while yet. I want to know what's so special about this Carroll County newspaper. They're two-for-two on big snowfalls when no one else was close, and each time, some poor girl got killed."

"You think the killer checks the forecast?"

"I think ten inches of snow throws a wrench into police investigations."

"It does," she acknowledged. "How does this get us any closer to finding a killer? Are you going to check the *Herald's* subscriber list?"

"No point." I opened the paper's website in an anonymous browser, clicked the Weather link at the top, and got what looked like a comprehensive rundown of the recent precipitation. *About ten inches fell across much of the region, as our forecast predicted. With temperatures remaining low for the next two days, we will see little melting. There is a risk of freezing overnight.* "The forecast details are on their website, which is accessible from pretty much anywhere in the world." I turned my screen so T.J. could see.

Her eyes scanned the page, and her brows knitted. "I know we're trying to challenge assumptions, but I think we need to make a few."

"Go ahead." I liked to let T.J. run with her ideas. She wasn't always right, but she had good instincts, especially for someone only twenty-one.

"First, we're dealing with one killer."

"Probable but far from certain," I said. "Similar MOs support your idea. Let's roll with it for now."

"All right," she said. "Moving on to number two. The killer is a man."

"Overwhelmingly likely."

"One more. He's local. You might be able to read the paper's website from anywhere, but no one is flying into town because of one meteorologist's prediction, killing a girl, and leaving."

"Agreed," I said. "Especially because getting a flight after would be dicey. This storm hit the neighboring states, too." I looked at the *Herald's* home page. It was nothing special.

Most online papers looked more or less the same, mimicking the classic print layout in several ways. "Why is their forecast right? They can't have the budget of other organizations in the area."

"They hired the right people?" T.J. suggested.

"I doubt it. Innovation like this probably comes thanks in part to AI." I hadn't heard of artificial intelligence tools being used in meteorology, but it made sense. Someone who knew what they were doing could adapt machine learning to any problem or field. A quick search confirmed this—rival papers accused the *Herald* of nebulous things like "selling out" and "having no soul."

"Their competition seems bitter. Probably don't want to fall behind in accuracy and cost themselves readers."

"Second place is just the first loser," I said. "Besides, where readers go, data and ad revenue follow."

"We're going to keep an eye on what this paper forecasts, aren't we?"

"It would be irresponsible not to," I said.

T.J. returned to her own desk. "I'm going to sign you up for the tractor pull newsletter."

"They don't have one for monster trucks?"

"No."

"We all need to get used to disappointment during big cases," I said.

Later in the afternoon, the BPD updated their online case file.

We got to work. "Our victim is Bernadette Holmes," I said, lamenting the lack of a large TV on the wall to project my screen onto. Maybe I would buy one with the windfall from this case. "Apparently, she went by Bernie." The recently deceased bore a strong resemblance to Kirsten Valle. Both were pretty redheads with very similar facial structures and eye colors. "She was thirty-two, but I'd guess her for twenty-seven at most."

"Do you always guess women's ages younger?" T.J. asked.

"A holdover from my bachelor years. Guessing twenty-nine or under never got me slapped."

She grinned. "How many were thirty or up?"

"If we're going to talk about my conquests as a younger man, this will be a long conversation. I'd rather focus on the case."

"Sure," T.J. said, chuckling. She moved her chair to put herself on a better line to my monitor. "Go ahead, player."

"Bernadette lived in Baltimore, but her address isn't very close to Patterson Park. It would be a nice walk in good weather. It would be insane in a snowstorm."

"Any siblings?"

I scanned the file. Considering the police only discovered her body a few hours ago, they'd managed to compile an impressive dossier already. Part of me wondered if Rich and Sharpe made sure to get it onto the network so I could see it and work this most recent death in parallel. The usurious rates would remain in play. "None. Her parents are out of state, too. I'm not sure how much information we'll get from family. We're also not going to harass them today."

"I'll start scraping her socials," T.J. said, using the script I developed and shared with her. "Looks like there's an ex-boyfriend, and it didn't end well." She glanced to an empty spot on the wall. "A TV would look good there."

"You're in charge of buying one, then," I said. "Let's wait until we get paid. I'd rather give you a bonus."

"Good. I'd rather get one." T.J. unplugged her laptop and wheeled her chair to my desk.

"Think of all the exercise you get pushing yourself back and forth across the office."

"Squats and kickboxing are more effective." She pointed to her screen. "Here he is." A man with spiky black hair scowled back at us from a Facebook photo. From the data our script compiled, Michael "Mikey" Grant was thirty-five and spent about a year in a relationship with Bernadette. Neither had anything good to say about the other in the intervening time, though at least Bernadette wrote in complete sentences with capital letters in the right places and solid punctuation.

"Anyone still going by Mikey at his age is guilty," I said.

"What about Ryder and Captain Manbun?" T.J. pointed out. "You liked both of them for the first killing, and neither did it."

I ran a search for Michael Grant and got some immediate results. "While we're assembling quite a rogues' gallery, the manbun guy didn't have a temporary restraining order against him." Bernadette filed for the TRO after the breakup, citing a few incidents of physical abuse. A judge granted her request, and the order remained active. Abused women had few legal recourses against the men who battered them, and as much as I wanted him to be guilty, I now hoped Michael didn't kill Bernadette.

"Are we going to dive into this guy?" T.J. wanted to know.

"I doubt we need to," I said. "The cops will already know what we found out. I'm sure he's their first suspect."

"Let's keep an eye on him. He seems like an asshole."

Based on Michael Grant's photos, my assistant's assessment was sound. His many shirtless pics—always a red flag for anyone much past college age—showed a range of tattoos. While ink itself didn't make someone good or bad, one of them read *He-Man Woman Haters Club* in a stylized font. It only appeared in one image, but one was enough.

My cell phone rang. Jessie Valle asked if we'd heard about the latest victim. "We were at the crime scene earlier today," I said on speaker. "We're reviewing the BPD's information now."

"Do you think the same man killed my sister and this new victim?"

"It's a presumption, but it's a reasonable one."

"I was hoping things would be wrapped up by now, Mister Ferguson. Does this help or hurt my sister's case?"

"It gets more eyes on it. We're going to attack both, but now the police will be forced to add even more manpower."

"We'll get to the bottom of it all," T.J. said. In general, I avoided promising things to clients, but I kept quiet.

"I certainly hope so," Jessie Valle said. "Please keep me updated." She ended the call.

"Her question is valid," T.J. said. "I'm not sure this helps her sister's case."

I stared at the unfriendly face of Michael Grant and wondered if he was a killer. "I'm not sure it does, either."

CHAPTER 13

AS AFTERNOON TURNED TO EVENING, the sun dropped, and the temperature plummeted. We'd barely gotten above freezing today, and the night would be colder still. T.J. and I remained at work. She continued using the results of our social media scraper to reach out to friends of Bernadette. Most didn't know she'd died. My assistant managed to arrange a Zoom call with three of them for six-thirty. "I don't know what to expect," she admitted.

"Probably tears," I said. "Memories. It'll be as much a platform for these women to grieve as for us to learn anything."

"You think they'll have something for us?"

"I'm skeptical, but it would be nice. The first victim is mostly a black box."

The witching hour drew near. T.J. brewed a half pot of coffee, and we each enjoyed a cup as she fired up Zoom and waited for our guests to arrive. Within four minutes, they were all in attendance. Their small windows identified them as Peggy, a round-faced woman of about thirty with large glasses; Angie, a pretty blonde who wore earbuds and bounced her head to a beat only she could hear; and Carla, who did not turn her video on.

"Thanks for coming, ladies," T.J. said. She arranged this virtual *tête-à-têtes*, so I let her take the lead. "I'm T.J. I'm the executive assistant at the Ferguson Detective Agency. My boss, C.T., is here, too." I leaned into the camera and flashed my best warm smile. "The first victim's sister hired us once the police investigation stalled. We're sorry to hear about Bernadette . . . and even sorrier if you found out from me."

"We'll all miss her," the invisible Carla said.

"Do you all know each other?" I asked.

"We've all met a few times," Peggy said. For her part, Angie's head moved as if a song played in her earbuds rather than our meeting.

"We were at the crime scene earlier," T.J. said. "Do any of you know why Bernie would have been in Patterson Park?"

"I can't think of a reason," Carla said. "She didn't live especially close. She worked from home most days, and when she went to the office, I think it was more to the north than the east."

"Was she seeing anyone?" I said.

Carla shook her head. "She didn't mention anything to me."

"Me, either," Peggy said.

"I think she told me something about meeting a guy on an app," Angie chimed in.

T.J. and I glanced at each other. This was new information. With Bernadette's phone missing, the cops could get her computer, but it would take them a while to recover the myriad data held on it. "Do you know which app?" I said.

She frowned. "No. It wasn't one I'd heard of."

"Was this recent?"

"Last week, I guess."

"The first victim died in a park, too," I said. "Our theory is she went there to see someone . . . maybe like meeting in public for a first date. Why anyone would choose an outdoor venue in the snow is weird, but there's not a lot out there about her. It seems like it might be possible here, at least."

"Do you think the same man killed both women?" Peggy wanted to know.

"It's an assumption, but it's a reasonable one. We're running with it for now. Did any of you get to know her ex-boyfriend Mikey?"

All three women groaned. "Prick," Angie said. "I never liked him." Carla and Peggy indicated their agreement. "He's one of those guys who just gives you bad vibes and throws red flags right away. I'm not sure what she ever saw in him." She snorted. "I wasn't surprised to hear she needed a restraining order."

"Any chance they were trying to reconcile?" T.J. said.

"None," Peggy replied. "Bernie was always too good for that asshole." She wiped a tear from her cheek. "It took her a while to get to this point, but she'd finally had enough and didn't want anything to do with him anymore. I was thrilled. If I saw him around her again, I might have killed him."

"Might not want to admit that over Zoom," Carla said with a chuckle.

"We're not recording," I said, "and I wouldn't dime you out, anyway." I paused. "Based on what we've talked about, it sounds like Bernie recently met someone on a dating app and might have been in Patterson Park to meet him." I realized I reverted to calling Bernadette by her nickname. When in Rome . . .

"It's possible," Angie said. "Mikey really hurt her . . . and

I don't mean just physically. It took her a while to get over all that shit. I don't think she dated anyone for months."

"She hasn't," Peggy confirmed.

We spent a few more minutes with the trio but didn't glean any other useful nuggets. After we'd signed off, T.J. said, "Which app do you think it was?"

"I have no idea."

"Do you think it's a good lead?" She leaned forward as she talked.

"Maybe. Look, I can tell you're eager for this to work out. Angie said it wasn't an app she'd heard of, so the major ones are off the table. There are plenty of smaller ones out there. Way too many for us to run down."

"So what are we going to do?"

"I'm going home. I'm happy to drop you off. We'll come back to this angle later. Could be the police will learn more, and we'll be able to narrow our focus." T.J. crossed her arms. "Simply because we learn something doesn't mean wc need to act on it right away. Sometimes, it's more prudent to wait."

"I guess," she said with all the conviction of a kindergartner who's just learned the lines in a school play.

We packed our bags, locked up, and drove away. I dropped T.J. in front of her apartment, waited for her to walk in the front door, and then continued to Gloria's house. I understood T.J.'s interest in wanting to chase down this lead. It represented the first real piece of info we'd learned. I hoped it would pay off.

———

Gloria and I relaxed on the couch after dinner.

She sipped from a glass of wine. Mine sat on the end table still almost full. I leaned against the arm of the couch, and Gloria nestled into me. She watched some romcom on Netflix. I'd seen it before and tuned it out in lieu of looking up the mid-sized and smaller dating sites. At some point, Gloria must have seen my screen. "In the market for a new wife already?"

"I need an offsite backup spouse," I said, and she elbowed me in the ribs. "You heard about the second woman killed, right?" Gloria bobbed her head. "Today, we learned she might have been meeting a man she met on a dating app. The woman who mentioned it told us it wasn't one of the major ones."

"How many does that leave?" Gloria asked.

"About a hundred thousand."

"Really?"

"I'm exaggerating but not by much. For every general site out there, there are several more designed for a particular religion or interest."

"I'm sure you'll figure it out."

I appreciated her confidence and hoped it came to pass. Considering I wasn't going to stumble upon whatever service Bernadette used tonight, I put my phone away and watched the movie with Gloria. About twenty minutes later, an incoming call made my cell vibrate in my pocket. "Sorry," I muttered as Gloria sat up so I could dig the blasted thing out of my pocket. The screen showed Rich on the line.

"Call off the dogs," he said.

"I don't have a dog."

"We made an arrest."

"What?" Gloria frowned as I stood and walked out of the living room. "You didn't even have a suspect this morning. How are you arresting someone all of a sudden?"

"We got a lucky break. Cameras showed the same homeless guy near both parks the day of the murders. We managed to find him. He said he did it."

"Really?"

"Yes."

"A homeless man?"

"Yes."

"For fuck's sake," I said, "how can you believe him?"

"He's good for it," Rich insisted, an edge coming into his voice.

"Sharpe mentioned all hands on deck. He wanted me cut in on this one, so I'm taking advantage of it. I'm positive you have the wrong guy, and I'm going to prove it."

"How do you know? You haven't even talked to him yet."

"Which will only make it more impressive when I point out how wrong you are."

"You're welcome to try."

"Where is he?"

"We're at Central Booking," my cousin said.

"I'll be there soon. Get a notebook ready. You're about to get an education in basic logic."

Rich hung up. Undeterred, I shrugged into my coat, told Gloria where I was headed, and grabbed my keys.

———

As its name suggested, the Central Booking and Intake Facility was a dreary place. It served as the first stop for anyone arrested by the police. Holding cells were numerous and often crowded. I'd endured a few hours as a guest here about four years ago when I worked a case counter to the BPD's interests. I'd never enjoyed any of my return trips even though I spent them on the good side of the bars. Tonight would be no different.

Piles of snow limited parking, but I managed to grab one of the few available spots. Rich waited for me just inside the front door, his arms crossed and his expression suggesting he'd sucked a lemon since our conversation ended. "So glad you could come and bestow your wisdom to the uneducated masses," he said.

I felt like I needed to check the floor to avoid slipping in a puddle of sarcasm. Instead, I said, "you should be. I'm going to save you and the department a lot of embarrassment."

"Before you put your syllabus together, come with me." I followed my cousin to an unmarked office where Sergeant Paul King waited.

"Two students for the price of one," I said. "The department's getting a good deal tonight."

"Watch the tape, smart guy," King said. "We combined footage of the two events." He pressed play, and grainy footage showed a man lurking near St. Mary's Park. I couldn't read any signage on the video, but the red path and surrounding buildings gave it away. Even at low definition, the figure in the video looked disheveled, and his gait was unsteady. He wore a black coat, brown pants, and a toboggan which covered his head. Stringy hair dangled out the back. An inch of snow already covered the sidewalk. "This was the evening the first victim got killed."

"Kirsten Valle." When King shrugged, I added, "She has a name."

Undaunted, he continued the playback. "Here's the second." A capture of similar quality played. A man who resembled the one in the first video ambled up the sidewalk outside Patterson Park. This time, he wore a brown coat and no hat. His movements remained unsteady, as if he'd been drinking, was unsure of the footing, or both. King spread his hands like he just proved a theorem in math. "It's him."

"There's no way to tell from those clips," I pointed out. "It might be the same guy, but you'll never get a clear enough shot to say for sure."

"We're pretty confident," Rich said.

"Well, it's a good thing 'pretty confident' is a legal standard. Oh . . . it's not, is it?" Rich crossed his arms again, and King mirrored the gesture. "'Your honor, the police watched two shitty camera captures, and they're pretty confident this guy is a killer. Life in prison.' I'm sure the prosecutors will be lining up for this one. Better get ready to fight them off now."

"We played the footage for him, too," King said. "The guy confessed."

"It might not even be the same man."

"It is."

"So you've gone from pretty confident to certain in the span of thirty seconds?"

"Why would you think it's not?" Rich wanted to know.

"Different coats."

"What?"

"This video isn't close to high-def," I said, "but you can clearly see a black jacket in the first and some shade of brown in the second."

"So?"

"So how many homeless people have multiple coats?"

"I'm sure the public defender will be all over it. 'Your honor, no homeless man could possibly get a second jacket in a week. We move to acquit.' You know, it's fun to be a pretend lawyer."

"A lot less so to be a real one," I said, "and I think you're a long way from anyone in the state's attorney's office taking up this turd."

"The guy admitted it," King said.

"Of course he did."

"What do you mean?"

"Can I see him?" They both shrugged and led me out of the office. We made a couple turns in the labyrinthine interior, eventually entering an observation area adjacent to an interrogation room. The homeless man in question sat in a metal chair, and handcuffs held his left arm to a bar mounted into the table. His hair was shoulder length and stringy, a brown mop hanging over the collar of his black coat. "Clearly, he had time to go back to his closet and get the first jacket."

"Why are you so sure it's not him?" Rich said. "King told you he confessed."

"What's the temperature outside?" I demanded.

My cousin spread his hands. "I don't know. Twenty or so? Less with windchill."

"Right. Plus, in case you missed it, there are ten inches of snow on the ground. Maybe not on major roads, but basically everywhere else. Parks. Alleys. Shelters are probably turning people away."

"They always are when the weather gets like this," King said.

"You want to know why this guy confessed?" I pointed to the man on the other side of the one-way mirror. "Because he's cold and hungry. If he goes to jail, he gets a warm bed, three meals a day, and medical care . . . . none of which he currently enjoys."

Rich snorted, and King scoffed. "This is your theory?" the sergeant said.

"You don't think those are factors in recidivism? What do they teach you in criminal justice classes?"

"Prove it," Rich said.

"Fine. Let me talk to him, and I will."

"I don't think so."

"Should we call Captain Sharpe? All hands on deck."

"Doesn't mean you get to question a suspect."

"When it has the potential to remove an entire carton's worth of egg from the department's face, I think you should make an exception."

Rich rolled his eyes, but he extended his hand toward the door after a few seconds. "Fine. Have at it."

"Get your notebooks ready," I said.

CHAPTER 14

THE FIRST THING I noticed when walking into the room was the smell.

The homeless fellow needed a shower and a bottle of mouthwash. I cleared my throat, shut the door, and approached the table. A lone unoccupied chair was the only other piece of furniture. A small red light glowed on a camera mounted at the far left corner. "Who're you?" he asked in an unsteady voice.

"I'm the man who's going to prove you didn't kill two women," I said. When he offered no response, I added, "I'm C.T. Ferguson, a private investigator. The first victim's family hired me."

The man's rheumy eyes fell on me before looking around the room. There wasn't much else to capture anyone's attention. "Never heard of you."

"What's your name?"

"Al. Al Lupton."

Al looked to be in his forties, but this was a guess. If he'd spent a significant amount of time on the streets, the hard life would add years to his appearance. Combined with the alcohol on his breath and the medical and psychiatric care he almost certainly needed, I wondered how old this man was . . . and the circumstances which drove his life off the rails. Gray mixed with the brown in his hair. "Al, you've confessed to two terrible crimes."

"I did 'em."

"Why?"

"Why what?"

"Why did you kill two women you'd never met?"

"Dunno," he said.

"Did you take their stuff?"

"No."

"Not a purse?" I said. "A phone?"

"Got my own phone," he said a little defensively. "God-damn cops took it."

This directly contradicted the events of the second murder, and I glared at the one-way mirror. Rich and King must have needed an arrest to make the commissioner or mayor happy. I couldn't think of another explanation for such shoddy work. "Al, do you know what happens to people who go to jail for murder?"

"They go for life. No death penalty anymore."

"You're right. Maryland got rid of it years ago. You ever been to prison?"

He shook his head. "Just a couple nights in lockup. You?"

I'd spent nineteen days as a guest of the Chinese penal system at the end of my time in Hong Kong, but this didn't seem like the time to bring it up. "I've managed to avoid it, too."

"How do you know what it's like?"

"I've talked to people who spent time on the inside," I said. "It sounds very unpleasant."

"They gotta give me a bed. Shower. Food."

"You can get those things at a shelter."

"Not tonight," he said, looking at me for a couple seconds before resuming his study of whatever else in the spartan room caught his eye. "All filled up."

"You need a place to sleep?" I asked.

"Of course I do. Snow is everywhere."

"What if there was an alternative? No shelter, no jail. Something else."

"Yeah?"

"Would you be interested?"

"Whaddaya have?"

"We can figure something out," I said, "but I need you to be honest with me, Al. Did you kill either of those two women?"

"No," he said in a small voice.

"Louder for the dumb cops listening in the other room."

"No. I didn't kill nobody."

I spread my hands and stared at the glass again. The door swung in a few seconds later. "All right," Rich said. "Al, we'll process you out. You'll be free to go in a few minutes."

"Go where?" he said.

"Meet me in the parking lot," I said. "We'll see what we can do."

———

Despite the beastly hour, I called Gloria. She mumbled something which was probably meant to be "Hello?" in a sleepy voice.

"I know it's late," I said. "Or early depending on your perspective. I need your help with something."

"Are you all right?" My wife sounded more alert now, but an alluring husk remained in her voice.

"I'm fine."

"What happened? You kind of bolted out of here talking about Rich arresting the wrong guy."

"He did, but I managed to convince him of it," I said. "It's part of why I'm calling. The cops arrested a homeless guy. He confessed in order to get a warm bed and three meals a day. Shelters are overcrowded now."

"What can I do?" Gloria asked.

"I know you had a lot of Marriott points back in your tennis days."

"Still do. Most of them, at least. I converted my account once I started the company, and the points carried over."

"Can we use some?"

"You want to put the homeless man up for the night," she said. It wasn't a question.

"Probably a couple," I said. "It's supposed to be cold through Monday. Maybe I should check the Carroll County *Herald* to be sure."

"What?"

"Never mind. I'll see which Marriott places are close and try to use some of your points. I'll just need your account number."

She told me what it was. "This is a big problem," my wife said. "It's not like homelessness is going away, and if shelters are turning people away on nights like this, you might have people dying on the streets."

"It's possible. I get the impression this guy sleeps in an alley, and it's one which now has ten inches of snow in it. Maybe more if something nearby got plowed out."

"Maybe you just found me a new cause for some fundraisers."

"We can talk more about it when I get home." Through the window on the front door, I saw Al getting a large envelope back from the officer behind the main desk. "I need to make some arrangements."

"All right. Love you."

"Love you, too." While Al finished, I checked for the closest Marriott properties. The nearest one couldn't help me, but I got connected to a helpful person at the Fairfield Inn and Suites near the Inner Harbor. I explained what I wanted to do and why, and the lady agreed to waive any points for tonight as it was already past one A.M. I made Al a reservation covering tonight, Saturday, and Sunday, with a checkout Monday morning. He exited the building when I was wrapping things up, so I waved for him to join me.

"I got you a place to stay," I said when I slipped my phone back into my pocket.

"Don't need your charity."

"Technically, it's my wife's more than mine." He frowned. "You have a room for the next three nights at the Fairfield near the harbor. Know it?"

"Yeah," he muttered. "What am I gonna do for food?"

"We'll pick a few things up on the way. I'll get you a DoorDash tomorrow morning."

"All right." He nodded as he put his knit cap back on. "Thanks. Nobody's done nothing like this for me in a long time."

"I've never stayed at this particular hotel," I said, "but I'm going to guess it beats jail."

"Probably does," he said, and we got into the car.

———

We made a slight detour to a 7-Eleven. For the first time since the meteor killed the dinosaurs, I declined to get a cup of coffee. Al chose some water, snacks, a couple microwaveable meals, and two sandwiches. I also suggested he get some soap, shampoo, deodorant, toothpaste, and a toothbrush rather than rely on whatever the hotel offered. He did so. I paid the sixty-dollar tab, and we got back in the car.

The Fairfield Inn was a four-story brick building on President Street. While some water would be visible from front-facing rooms, guests would need binoculars to see the Inner Harbor proper. Once inside the hotel, I checked in with the helpful woman I'd talked to. She looked close to my mother's age, with a slender but warm face and the voice of a patient teacher. I offered my credit card for incidentals, told Al not to go crazy, and the clerk handed him his keycard. Al thanked me and headed for the elevators.

I left the hotel, made a second trip to the same convenience store, and bought a spray bottle of disinfectant. I felt like a bit of a jerk for doing it, but Al really needed a shower and about an hour of tooth brushing. My car would smell like synthetic lemons for a while, but it beat the alternative. My olfactory senses abated, I got onto I-83 North and returned to Brooklandville. Despite trying to be quiet, my arrival woke Gloria. "You're back," she said, stretching and sitting up. The sheet and blanket fell away from her neck and showed her red button-up pajama shirt.

"I got Al checked in with some supplies. He'll need a DoorDash tomorrow."

"It's nice you want to help him."

"The cops weren't listening," I said. "They were so interested in making the commissioner and the fucking mayor happy they didn't bother wondering why a homeless man might confess to something he didn't do." Gloria and I differed on our opinions of Baltimore Mayor Vincent Davenport, and I rarely brought him up because of this, but his name slipped out. When it did, some invective usually came attached.

"I'm glad you got it straightened out," Gloria said, ignoring my barb at her former client. "This kind of leaves things back where they were, right? No one's a suspect now?"

"Pretty much. I don't even think we have a person of interest." I sighed and sat on the edge of the bed. "The weather is really messing with things. Snow limits the number of cars and people in the area, so the witness pool is limited. It covers the body, throws forensics off, and fills in any tracks the killer might have left."

"You'll figure it out. You always get your man in the end." She ran a hand through her long chestnut hair. "I'd like to do something to solve the problem Al experienced. It might be time for a fundraiser."

"My parents' foundation has worked with some homeless charities," I said. "You can probably get some ideas from them."

She nodded. "I'll reach out to them tomorrow. You coming to bed?"

"Yeah, I'll join you in a few minutes." While Gloria burrowed under the covers again, I brushed my teeth and changed into my own pajamas. A few minutes later, I crawled onto the king mattress beside her. I felt tired, but my mind raced, and I couldn't fall asleep. We had a pair of dead women, a thousand reporters crowing about serial killers, maybe one person of interest, and no real suspects. T.J. and Gloria both wanted me to work this case, and I did, too. Now, I needed to make progress on it. Victims' families expected it, and Jessie Vale wouldn't keep paying me for the same non-results the BPD produced.

We needed to turn things around, and quickly.

CHAPTER 15

T.J. WOKE up Saturday morning knowing she would need to go to work.

She was OK with it. Many cases didn't require her presence at the office on weekends. A double murder with no significant leads or progress did. She checked her phone. No messages, and it was almost 8:30. During the week, C.T. almost never made it in before nine. Add an hour or so for the weekend. She had time. T.J. changed into yoga pants and an athletic top and headed to the building's fitness center.

Management doubled the size of it recently, and today, this was a good thing. Other residents used most of the cardio machines, and a few people lifted weights on racks or benches. T.J. found an available treadmill, wiped down the handles and buttons—most users skipped this when they finished—and hopped on. She slipped her earbuds in, set the belt for three miles per hour to warm up, and started walking as high-energy hip-hop filled her ears.

She didn't need the motivation today, but it was still nice to have. Now, two families sought justice. When she first started working for C.T., she'd been happy to get a real job.

The fact she met him on one of his earlier cases—and he enjoyed the cachet of being Melinda's friend—helped. Back then, T.J. didn't know what kind of cases she'd be helping with. Today, she couldn't imagine being a secretary anywhere else. The stakes would just seem small by comparison.

T.J. increased the belt speed to four miles per hour and walked briskly to finish getting loose. Then, she turned it up to six and ran for twenty minutes. Her heart rate stayed in the zone. When she'd run enough, she turned it back down to four miles per hour and then three to cool down. The treadmills faced a mirrored wall. In the reflection, T.J. spotted a guy in the free weights area checking her out. Like many residents of the 501, he looked to be around her age. He was cute, too, and his body suggested he lifted weights here often. T.J. felt color come to her cheeks as she smiled. He smiled, too.

Once she'd finished cooling down, T.J. headed to the heavy bag. She left her MMA gloves upstairs, so she only did a few sets of punches, instead focusing on elbows, knees, and kicks. Once she'd abused the bag enough, T.J. stopped and chugged water from her bottle. Her admirer was busy on the bench press, so she left the gym. She knew she'd see him again.

Back in her apartment, T.J. refilled her water bottle and drank more. She turned the TV on to the Saturday local news. While the anchor talked about the effects of the cold and snow on the city, the chyron at the bottom said *LIVE COVERAGE OF MAYOR'S SPEECH IN 2 MINUTES*. T.J. knew she risked sounding like her boss, but she wondered how the mayor would spin recent events to try and make people feel better while also keeping his pending re-election campaign in mind.

At the promised time, the station cut to a shot of city hall. While the shot focused on a podium set up outside the main doors, bits of snow remained visible at the edges. Two newscasters talked about the mayor's hastily-arranged press conference and speculated he'd be speaking about the recent homicides. "What the hell else would he be talking about?" T.J. said, shaking her head.

A couple minutes later, Mayor Vincent Davenport stepped onto the platform. He wore a long black wool coat, the knot of a red tie peeking out at his neck. He looked to be about sixty with a full head of mostly black hair, round glasses, and an impassive face. T.J. sat on her couch and watched as the spectacle began.

"Ladies and gentlemen, fellow citizens of Baltimore,

"Today, I stand before you, not just as your mayor, but as a fellow resident of our beloved city . . . a city recently shaken to its core. In the past two weeks, we've experienced the heart-wrenching loss of two of our own—Kirsten Valle and Bernadette Holmes. Despite whatever you may hear or read, their tragic departures are not mere statistics; they are a profound loss, a reminder of the work that lies ahead of us.

"I want to extend my deepest condolences to the families of Kirsten and Bernadette. I have a daughter, and while our relationship has never been perfect, I can't imagine losing her. Your pain is Baltimore's pain. Your loss is our loss.

"In these times of trial, it's easy to succumb to fear, to doubt the strength of our community. But let us remember: now more than ever, Baltimore is not just a place. It's a spirit. It's resilience in the face of adversity. It's the unwavering belief in a better tomorrow.

"As your mayor, I assure you, the safety and security of

every citizen is my utmost priority. Our police force, under the leadership of Commissioner Ngo, is working tirelessly to bring justice to Kirsten and Bernadette. I've directed the commissioner to spare no expense when it comes to personnel and hours. Once the BPD catches the person responsible, we'll take a renewed look at investing in state-of-the-art technology for public safety and strengthening community policing. These have always been hallmarks of my office, and they will continue to be.

"But law enforcement alone isn't the solution. True safety comes from a community of people who stand together, who watch out for one another. It's in the eyes of one neighbor helping another, in the hands of volunteers tackling our toughest challenges, in the hearts of our children who dream of a safer, brighter Baltimore.

"As we move forward, let's channel our grief into action. Let's be vigilant, but not afraid. Let's collaborate with our police, report suspicious activities, and foster a culture of togetherness and support.

"I see this not just as a crime or a challenge but as an opportunity—an opportunity to prove that our city can emerge stronger and more united from these trying times. My office asks for your support to keep moving toward our collective vision of a secure, thriving Baltimore. Together, we'll get there, even though some days will make us feel like we're not making progress.

"Together, we can transform this tide of sorrow into a wave of hope. Together, we can restore and rejuvenate our beloved city. Baltimore is strong, Baltimore is resilient, and Baltimore will prevail.

"Thank you, and may God bless the city of Baltimore."

Despite a clamoring for questions, Davenport showed a quick smile he probably intended to be sincere before disappearing back into city hall. An assistant informed the press the mayor needed to focus on urgent matters of the day rather than spend more time at the podium. "Typical," T.J. said. She'd taken long enough to cool down by watching thinly-veiled re-election bids. It was time to shower and get to work.

———

Before heading out the door, T.J. texted her boss to make sure he planned to go to the office. He told her he did. She ate a quick breakfast, cleared a layer of windblown snow from her car, and fired it up. Her old Civic had been slow but easy to drive in bad weather. The Mustang felt different. She knew it was rear-wheel-drive, but it still felt composed on the road. As long as T.J. was judicious with the gas pedal, the car chugged along without sliding. The roads looked a little better than the previous night, also, though the far right lanes were often impassable thanks to piles of plowed snow.

T.J. unlocked the office and performed her most important duty right away—making coffee. While the machine dripped, and the aroma of brewing java filled the space, T.J.'s phone rang. Melinda called. "I thought you were going on vacation," T.J. said after the initial round of pleasantries.

"I did. There was snow on the ground when I left and then even more when I got back."

"It's been a pretty wild two weeks."

"So I hear," Melinda said. "As much as C.T. tries to avoid the press these days, they've picked up on him working the first case. I know this means you are, too. I'm also going to guess you're involved with the second even if it's unofficial."

"We are . . . and it is. So far."

"At least it seems like C.T. is keeping you out of the papers."

"Yeah," T.J. said. "None of them have come to the office, and he made sure we didn't leave the second crime scene together."

"Are you sure you want to do this?" Melinda asked.

"Is this about wanting me to come work for you?"

"Of course it is. You'd be perfect. Who better to be my assistant and serve as an example than the first girl we got hired?"

T.J. sighed. "Melinda, you know I'll always be grateful for what you did. If you want me to come back and talk to some of your new girls, I'd be glad to do it. I'm happy here, though. You placed me here because you thought C.T. would be receptive. He knew both of us."

"Two women are dead," Melinda pointed out.

"I know. If I'd never met you, or if I'd blown you off, one of them could have been me. Women getting killed doesn't make me want to run and hide. It makes me want to help figure out what happened because I realize I was only a couple different decisions away from being one of them." When Melinda didn't reply, T.J. added, "You keep rescuing girls, Melinda. Make sure one of them learns what I learned. Hell, Amy could probably be an assistant."

"She'd be better running social media. I'm close to getting her a job, too, but she's going to moonlight and help me on the side."

"You'll find someone," T.J. said. The coffee maker beeped quietly to indicate its completion. "I need to go."

"Are you working today?"

"Like you said, two women are dead. I can't help them much from the treadmill in my building."

"Be careful, T.J.," Melinda implored.

"You know me."

"I do . . . and it's why I told you."

T.J. smiled. "I'll be fine, Melinda." She ended the call. It was nice having someone to worry about her, though Melinda took it a little far sometimes. T.J. unlocked her laptop and poured herself a cup of coffee. The current case couldn't wait.

CHAPTER 16

I WALKED in to the terrific scent of fresh coffee.

T.J. sat at her desk, her brows knitted and lips pursed. "You must need another cup," I said.

She held up her mug. "Already on my second."

"The only thing better than your second cup is your third." I set my bag down and hung my coat on the rack. "Roads better today?"

"Yeah. The lot was clearer, too." T.J. paused and looked up. "I haven't had an epiphany yet."

"Me, neither." I fixed myself a cup of coffee—my first here but number two overall. "I'm hoping the caffeine will let the inspiration flow."

The wonderful brown liquid flowed, but the inspiration remained still. After ramming my head into an immovable wall for thirty minutes, I stopped, stood, and poured another cup. "I appreciate you coming in today," I said while T.J.'s face suggested she was as flummoxed as me.

"All hands on deck, right? I knew you'd be here, so I figured I should be, too."

"Is this a play for a bigger Christmas bonus?"

She grinned. "If I make a key discovery, you have to add a

zero." She paused and then added, "To the end" before I could say something else.

"I think one of the other numbers changing is more likely," I said.

"Are you hitting a wall, too?" she asked.

"Hard enough to risk damage to the moneymaker." I rubbed my cheeks.

My assistant rolled her eyes. "It's frustrating. We live in such an online, connected society, and there's nothing here to tie these two women to each other, let alone someone who might have killed them."

"I wonder if we should consider the possibility of two different killers."

"Really? So many factors are the same."

"I know," I admitted. "Statistically, it's more likely to be one guy. We don't solve murders with spreadsheets, though. Maybe we need to consider the alternative. There's been enough press coverage of what happened to poor Kirsten to enable some other twisted asshole to do the same."

"I guess." T.J. frowned. "If we're throwing statistics overboard, you must be getting desperate."

"We've had two snowstorms and two bodies. This is supposed to be a rough winter, and we haven't hit the solstice yet. It's still technically late fall. We don't want this one-to-one ratio to hold."

"You see the mayor's speech this morning?"

"No, thank goodness," I said. "I don't enjoy feeling nauseated over breakfast. Let me guess . . . it was mostly about what's been going on, but he threw in a few veiled references to getting re-elected."

T.J. nodded. "Pretty much. I thought you said Davenport had been doing a good job."

"He has." I shrugged. "He's still an asshole."

A buzzing cell phone interrupted my pending diatribe on the mayor. Caller ID showed Rich's name and number. "You really in for this all hands on deck stuff?" he asked.

"After saving you from arresting the wrong man? Sure."

My cousin didn't take the bait. "The ME found something significant. Sharpe told me to include you, so I am."

"I'll be right there." Rich disconnected.

"Something going on?"

I filled T.J. in on the poor homeless guy wrangled by the cops and nearly charged with two brutal homicides. "The wheels of justice keep grinding. This time, the ME found something." I got up and put my coat on.

"You want me to go, too?"

"Not this time. I'll tell you about it when I'm back. For now, you keep working on the possibility we might be looking for two killers."

"You got it, boss." I could see a flash of disappointment cross T.J.'s face. I sympathized. She'd been an eager learner ever since she started working for me, and made a better student than I did a teacher. Still, she didn't always need to tag along. Being able to work in parallel was a big perk of having an assistant, and she'd helped a lot simply doing this on previous cases. I knew she would again.

———

I walked into the ME's office about fifteen minutes later.

Dr. Gary Hunt, recently promoted to chief medical examiner, stood with Rich, King, and Leon Sharpe. I met Hunt early in my career, and when I kept a serious snafu of his under wraps, he fed me information in exchange. While he didn't strike me as the most ethical sort back then, he was good at his job, and the city agreed. Hunt looked much the same as he always did—slender, brown-haired, and serious—though he now sported glasses as a concession to the onset of middle age.

Everyone gathered to the side of the examination area. Medical tables dominated the middle of the room. The wall opposite us held refrigerated drawers to shelve the deceased. The ventilation system hummed, keeping the scents of death and chemicals out. A long workbench stood behind the small crowd, and a nice TV hung on the wall above everyone's heads. "Glad you could join us," Captain Sharpe said, his arms crossed.

"All hands on deck, Leon," I said. "Even ones with manicured nails like mine."

Rich did a double take. "Really?"

"I go once a month. Gloria found a great little salon near her house." Sharpe cleared his throat. "I guess we'll have to table discussion of my moisturizing routine for now."

"What a pity," the captain said. "Doctor Hunt?"

"Thank you," he said. "This is something I noticed on the second victim, Miss Holmes." He tapped a key on his laptop, and its display mirrored on the large TV. Another key changed the picture to a close-up of her neck. "You can see two small puncture marks here." Two tiny holes pierced the skin of her throat, and the corner of a large knife wound showed at the edge of the image. "I think we all know what this means."

"A vampire killed her," I said.

"I was thinking of the other meaning for these puncture marks," Hunt said.

"Do we need to start carrying wooden stakes? I cook with garlic already, so I think I'll be all right."

"A Taser," Rich said with a sigh.

"Thank you, Lieutenant," Hunt said while glaring at me.

"Yes, someone tased this poor girl before stabbing her to death."

"It was cold the night she died," King said. "Would the barbs go through something like a scarf?"

Hunt smiled. "An excellent question . . . and the answer is yes. I removed a woolen fiber from each small hole and several from the slash wound an inch away. Miss Holmes indeed wore a scarf when she was murdered."

"What about the first victim?" Rich asked.

"I went back and checked," Hunt said. "I didn't do the autopsy on Miss Valle, and the examiner who conducted it didn't mention anything like this. I re-examined her." He hit one more key, and an even more grisly image slid into view. "It's hard to tell because the knife wound is in the right spot to hide almost everything." He zoomed in, and at the end of the jagged injury, I thought I could make out a small circle.

"Is it . . . a Taser mark?" my cousin said.

"Impossible to say for certain. In my opinion, however . . . yes."

This meant we were back to the single killer idea. The Taser angle never got any play in the papers or on TV. It thus wasn't a detail anyone could copy.

"Did they suffer?" King asked.

"Being stunned by electricity wouldn't dull the pain," Hunt said. "It would immobilize the poor women by contracting the muscles. I'm sure they wanted to fight back, but they couldn't have done anything. Considering the conditions keeping people inside, the killer could have taken his time and enjoyed their suffering." He shrugged. "The bodies being cold for hours before we collect them makes the job harder in many ways."

"Does this mean our killer was some distance from his victims?" I wondered.

"I doubt it," Hunt said. "My colleagues in blue can give you more precise figures, but the effective range of a civilian Taser is about fifteen feet. A few factors make me think our guy didn't actually shoot the barbs. Chief among them are conditions at the time. Snow and wind can lessen the range. It would also make the darts diverge. These two marks are close together. I think he used the Taser like a stun gun in both cases."

"Meaning he was at personal range with the women."

"If you're suggesting they might have been talking closely, hugging, or even kissing . . . yes." Hunt bobbed his head. "Those are all strong possibilities."

"Discharging the cartridge also causes coded confetti to fly everywhere," Rich added. "The snow might make it hard to spot and recover, but no officers or technicians reported any at either scene."

"Thank you, Doctor," Sharpe said, and we all filed out. Before we all adjourned, he added, "We're keeping this detail out of the press. Those bastards don't need to know everything." The rest of us concurred. I considered a barb about arresting another homeless man but decided against it. This owed to both the maturity my thirties brought and self-preservation—Sharpe might have stuffed me in one of the ME's coolers if I mouthed off. The BPD contingent went back to their adjoining building. I returned to my car and pondered what this meant for the case. I would not have categorized any of my thoughts as positive.

———

"Who the hell uses a Taser?" T.J. wondered. When I returned to the office, I told her what we'd learned downtown. Bernadette Holmes definitely got tased . . . and Kirsten Valle also most likely. The voltage rendered both women unable to fight back, but they would have remained awake and alert as their killer swung the knife. The only small mercy was the fact the stab wounds targeted vital areas. It was unlikely either woman survived long, though their final few moments would have been horrifying in almost every imaginable way.

Some small mercies end up being microscopic.

My assistant's question was now the one we needed to focus on. The BPD would, as well. "It's what we're going to have to find out," I agreed.

"Are we hopping back on the single killer train?"

"I think so,. The Taser is a recent discovery. It hasn't been in any of the stories—and it won't be—so a hypothetical copycat wouldn't know he needed to include it."

"Could be two guys working together," T.J. said.

"Maybe. I'm going to stick to statistics here and go with the lone killer. It's more likely."

"What kind of man are we looking for?" T.J. frowned and stared at her screen. "I've never used a stun gun or been hit with one, but I know what it does. What kind of a sick bastard uses one on someone he's about to kill?"

"You said it. A sick bastard."

"We're looking for a sadist, then?"

"Seems like it," I said.

"I'm not sure either of our initial persons of interest qualify."

"Probably not. Bonus points for pluralizing the right word there, by the way?"

She grinned. "Another zero on my Christmas bonus?"

"Props for paying attention to my rants about bad grammar. I'll get you a couple extra Whoppers Junior the next time I'm at a Burger King." I pulled up the results of our social media scraping. "Bernadette gave Michael Grant the boot because he was an abuser. We've both checked him out. I'd call him more of the garden variety prick than someone likely to be a sadist."

"True," T.J. agreed with a nod. "Like you mentioned, the police will be on him, anyway."

"We need a different suspect. The challenge now is it might not be someone with an obvious connection to either of our victims."

"Any theories, boss?"

"I suggested a vampire when the ME first showed us the double electrode wounds," I said. "Doesn't seem likely to pan out."

"Let's wait for a full moon, then. Wouldn't want to miss out on a good werewolf suspect."

"Unfortunately, I think our killer is going to turn out to be far more mundane."

"They usually are."

"They are," I said, "which is why we're going to find him."

CHAPTER 17

"DO YOU NEED TO REGISTER A TASER?"

T.J. posed the question. I didn't know the answer. "I've never really encountered them during a case before," I said. "Police and prison guards carry them, but they're obviously allowed to. It might be different for the public."

Several keystrokes later, we had an answer. "It is." T.J.'s eyes scanned her screen. "Sort of like owning a gun as far as I can tell. Generally legal for anyone over eighteen, but there's a background check, and certain crimes in your past can disqualify you." She kept reading. "Carrying one is murkier. Public officials can. It seems like a stun gun counts as a dangerous weapon in Maryland, so a regular person would have to demonstrate some need to carry one."

"Much like a firearm."

"Basically."

"And much like guns, I imagine not everyone who owns one of these things went through proper channels. The black market supply is probably a lot smaller, though." I ran a search of my own. As I suspected, illicit firearms comfortably outnumbered Tasers at both the state and national levels. However, illegal stun gun sales were far from zero. "Whoever shocked our two victims likely went the black market route to keep his name out of the record books," I said.

"Maybe," my assistant said.

"Let's check the state's Taser records."

"You going to break in?" T.J. wheeled her chair to my desk.

"We're legit. I have access to it as a licensed private investigator." I found the link for the firearms registry in my bookmarks. Going up one level showed a page for the Taser records. I clicked the link. Whoever designed the site made sure the search function was at the forefront. I didn't want to use it, so I found the option to export a copy of the database in Excel format. A moment later, I sent a copy of it to T.J.

"Who are we looking for?" she wanted to know as she returned to her own station.

"Let's see if any interesting names appear."

"Lot of rows here, boss. It'll take a while to look over all of them."

"You got a hot date tonight?" I said.

"No."

"Let's start looking, then. I'll go down from A, and you work up from Z."

T.J. didn't say anything and got to work. I focused on the cells for registered user names. A few minutes later, my secretary cleared her throat. "Need a cough drop?" I asked her.

"I went looking for someone you don't like," she said.

"The mayor's on the list? He's probably authorized."

"Not him."

"You'll need to be more specific, then. I don't really like a lot of people."

"Ryder Long," T.J. said.

I confirmed this by searching and locating his name on the list. "Holy shit."

"Maybe he's gone back to being a person of interest."

"I think he has."

"What about his alibi?"

"We'll need to look into it," I said. "Work retreats often emphasize the second word over the first."

T.J. snickered. "Because you've been on so many?"

"No." I chuckled. "I'm dreadfully ill-equipped to work for someone else. I've read a lot of accounts over the years and heard some from friends. Anecdotal, sure, but there's a pattern."

"What are we going to do about Ryder?"

"Take a note," I said. "Anyone with a Y standing in for an I in their name immediately goes onto the suspect list. Ditto someone with an awful spelling of a common name."

"I'll be sure to add it to our SOP as soon as I start one. What about more practical actions?"

"We need to get back on him. It's a Saturday, and most roads should be passable now. Let's see if our friend is as much a homebody as he was earlier."

Before we could go anywhere, the office phone rang.

I didn't keep a traditional landline. The Voice Over IP phone came with the high-speed internet package. My agency's online presence tended to list this number, and neither T.J. nor I answered it regularly. It rarely rang on weekends, however. As usual, we let it go. Maybe this would constitute another entry to our nascent SOP. As soon as I came up with some more standard operating procedures, we could keep going.

A woman's voice came on the line once our recording finished. "Hello. This is April Holmes. I think you're working a case involving our daughter Bernadette." T.J. and I exchanged a glance. "The police aren't saying much, so I was hoping I could speak to someone in your office." I pushed the button to answer the call.

"Missus Holmes?"

"Yes."

"Hello. This is C.T. Ferguson. I'm here with my assistant T.J."

"Lots of initials in your office."

"Yes, ma'am. You could say we're A-OK with them."

"Thank you for picking up," she said. "I'm here with my husband Jamie, but he's got laryngitis at the moment."

"We're very sorry for your loss," I said.

"Thank you," she said again, and her voice cracked. After a few seconds of silence, April Holmes continued. "Like I mentioned, the police aren't telling us much right now."

"I'm not trying to defend them, but it's still a new case. My agency is involved because the family of the first victim hired us."

"Is it true that both cases are still open?"

"Unfortunately, yes. We thought we had a person of interest, and so did the BPD, but neither panned out. It's been hard to make any connection between your daughter and the first victim."

T.J. made a throat-slashing motion, so I muted the line. "This poor woman. We don't have very much to tell her."

"I know. She's looking for *something*. It doesn't have to be major. They just want to know people are trying to solve their daughter's murder, and the goddamn cops can't even clear such an easy bar." April Holmes talked while we did, so I took the call off mute. "I'm sorry . . . can you repeat what you just said?"

"I mentioned that it's nice to know someone is working on it and willing to talk to us."

"I can't say much for the police department's communications," I told her. "They're definitely working it. The city's top homicide unit is on the job."

"I'm sure this is impossible to predict, but when do you think you'll know something significant?"

"You're right. It's impossible to say with any certainty."

"We're going to look into something today," T.J. added, and I wished she'd refrained. "We think it's an aspect the police haven't considered yet."

"I hope it pans out," April Holmes said, and her voice cracked again. "We just want the man who did this caught."

"We want the same thing."

"Thank you for talking to me. Do you think you could let me know if you make some appreciable progress? Jamie and I don't want to fly to Baltimore before we need to."

I rolled my eyes, but T.J. kept driving along Affirmative Avenue. "If we have something significant, sure."

"Bless you both." We got the parents' contact information, and April hung up.

"Don't be a grump," my secretary preemptively said. "I know you don't like updating people."

"I like it even less when they're not paying us." She frowned. "I get it. They're gutted, and I want to help them. My priority is figuring out what happened, though. It takes precedence over calling someone with a progress report."

T.J. nodded. "I know. That poor woman just needed someone to hear her."

"I'm sure we'll need to talk to Jessie Valle at some point, too. I think she's going to can us if we don't have something worthwhile before long."

"Really?"

"Think about it. She came to us because she was frustrated with the BPD not making any progress. How much have we made?"

"Not much," T.J. said through a sour expression.

"Exactly."

"We're going to keep working this, aren't we?"

"Of course. I'm too invested now . . . as I'm sure you are."

"Badly-named men of the city, beware."

I smiled. "Speaking of which, let's get back on our Ryder Long detail."

———

We ate lunch and then headed to Ryder Long's house.

He lived near Harford Road and Walther Avenue in Northeast Baltimore in an area I'd learned as Waverly. My parents sometimes took me for snowballs not far from there on hot summer evenings. Unlike many areas of the city, houses here were single-family models with a lot of Cape Cods and Victorians. I pointed out the stylings to T.J. "You only know them because Gloria watches home improvement and house-flipping shows."

"You don't think I've studied local architecture in an effort to be even more awesome at my job?" I asked.

"No."

"Fair. You're right. It's how I know most of what I've learned about houses."

"Is he home?" T.J. asked.

My earlier malware to Ryder still worked as far as I could tell. The app showed the blue dot of his phone over his house, which was a white Cap Cod model. It sat on a small hill with a disjointed concrete staircase totaling nine steps in three stages leading from the sidewalk to the porch. "His phone is."

"Is he doing anything?"

"No traffic at the moment."

"Anything we can do while we wait?"

"Why not check his alibi?" I said. "We've acknowledged it might be sketchy."

"Yes . . . your expertise now includes Baltimore architecture and business retreats."

"I am neither stirred by praise of flatterers nor stung by the follies of unlearned mockers of learning."

T.J. blinked a few times. "What the hell was that?"

"Sir Thomas More. A light paraphrase." She said nothing. "*A Man for All Seasons?*" Still nothing. "Never mind."

"Are you putting yourself out there as a man for all seasons?"

"Here I am working in the very late fall with snow on the ground. It counts."

"With your executive assistant," she said.

"Yes, but *An Executive Assistant for All Seasons* isn't going to Broadway."

"Maybe a play on burning down the patriarchy, then?"

"I'm sure it would sell out for weeks," I said.

We tabled our conversation about long-dead saints and possible feminist plays. Minutes turned into hours, and we found a nearby convenience store to pee in shifts and get supplies. Ryder's phone stayed quiet. He opened WhatsApp, but as my exploit couldn't break the encryption, I didn't see his message. A few minutes later, he opened an app to catalog and recommend TV shows and movies. "Looks like he's in for the evening," I said as the clock struck five-thirty.

"How long are we sticking around?" T.J. wanted to know.

"Let's give it another half-hour." I sloshed liquid in my bottle of Gatorade. "Still have plenty left. Any luck running down his alibi?"

She checked her phone. "Maybe. I reached out to a couple people who are on both his LinkedIn and Facebook. Based on what I can see from our script, they seem more like acquaintances than friends. One of them is getting back to me now." She tapped out a few messages as I kept an eye on Ryder's house and location. "This is interesting," she said after a couple minutes. "Seems your cynical take on office retreats is accurate."

"As much as I'm used to being right," I said, "can you explain?"

"Seems like they had a fair bit of downtime, including most of the afternoon and all of the evening in question. Ryder's spot on that they stayed an extra day because of the weather, but it's not like they were in San Diego. The retreat was in Ellicott City."

"Certainly close enough to get to Baltimore and back even in deteriorating weather. Let me guess . . . no one checked attendance rigorously." She shook her head. "All right. Good work. Ryder is back to being a person of interest."

"We need to stick to our guns on these people with weirdly-spelled names," T.J. said.

"We do. 'It's always the quiet ones' is bullshit. It's always the people whose parents inflicted a bad name on them."

Fifteen minutes later, Ryder's front door opened. We spotted it easily, as I'd curbed the S4 in front of the next house. This also meant Ryder could see us if he peered down the hill in our direction. After locking his door and heading down the walkway, he did. His eyes took us both in as his boots hit the sidewalk, and then he did what I'd expected him to do.

He ran.

CHAPTER 18

T.J. and I both opened our doors and gave chase.

Like many neighborhoods in Baltimore, not everyone shoveled the sidewalks in front of their houses. My boots slipped on a patch of ice under the snow three houses down from Ryder's as he cut onto the grass. T.J. managed to stay on her feet while I avoided a faceplant thanks to a combination of solid balance and good fortune. While I got underway again, she caught up to the fleeing Ryder, dove forward, and tackled him by wrapping up his legs.

He made it back to vertical by the time I got there, and his focus shifted from my assistant to me. "We just want to talk to you, Ryder," I said.

"Already talked to you." He tried to shove me, but I swatted his arm away. He tried a punch next, and it met a similar result. "This is harassment."

"Actually, this is assault. I could press charges against you, and I have a witness." He went for another punch, and I deflected it with enough force to make him wobble on his feet. "I'm good at defending myself, Ryder. I'm not really pressing the issue because we only came here to have a conversation, but if you keep trying to hit me, I'm gonna knock you on your ass."

"Yeah?" He said. He threw a jab which I blocked, and I pushed his arm out wide enough on the follow-up cross to hit him hard in the solar plexus. Ryder sucked wind and bent over.

"You're okay," I said. "Keep breathing. You'll be fine. You want to keep pressing the issue, it's only going to get worse for you." I looked at T.J. "Nice tackle. They could use you on the Ravens."

She grinned. "They couldn't afford me."

"I'm pretty sure they can pay you more than I do."

"Not interested." She waved a hand. "Chasing down potential killers is way more rewarding than catching a running back."

"I didn't . . . kill anyone," Ryder said, still bent at the waist and breathing heavy.

"I hope you're telling the truth." I clapped him on the shoulder, and it almost made him pitch forward. "I also hope you're not going to tell us some bullshit story about your work retreat. I should've known as soon as you said it. When you're ready, we can talk in your house."

He stood up and exhaled loudly. "What if I don't want you coming in?"

"Then you're welcome to try and stop us." I shrugged. "Considering you're oh-for-two in the last few minutes, I'd suggest cutting your losses and pretending to be a good host." Someone in the house we stood in front of moved a curtain back to get a better look out their window. "Your neighbors are noticing, Ryder. Wouldn't want them to think badly of you."

"You think I care, bro?"

"Yes, I do."

He tried to glare at me, but considering the way the last several minutes unfolded for him, there was no power or intimidation behind it. After a few seconds, Ryder's shoulders slumped, and he sighed. "Fine." He brushed snow from the front of his coat. "You can come inside, and we'll talk."

"I thought you'd never ask," I said.

———

We filed into Ryder's house. The tan hardwood floors looked original—the neighborhood dated to the years following the second world war—and he either had a good eye for furniture or knew someone who did. The sofa, recliners, and TV console were the same shade of medium-dark brown and looked sturdy. The black glass-topped coffee table was an afterthought. I spotted two modern game systems tucked away in the entertainment console.

"Want tea?" our host asked, sounding as cheery as a funeral director.

"You have coffee?" I said.

"Don't drink it if I can help it."

Another mark against him. In Hong Kong, I got out of the habit of drinking coffee, and I quickly readjusted to the good stuff once back on American *terra firma*. "Tea's fine."

"Sure," T.J. added.

Ryder left the room. The first floor was mostly open, so we could see past the small dining room into the kitchen. Ryder added water to an electric kettle and flipped it on. He got three mugs down and dropped a teabag into each. A couple minutes later, with the water at a boil, he filled the cups, put them on a small tray, and carried them back into the living room. T.J. and I sat on the couch, so Ryder took one of the chairs. "You're probably wondering why I ran," he said, showing a little aware-ness of the situation.

"Innocent people rarely bolt," I said.

"I didn't kill Kirsten." He took a deep breath and cradled the mug in both hands. "Or the second girl."

"Why'd you take off, then?"

"You'd already talked to me once, and you threatened to put me on the cops' radar."

"I'm pretty sure they know about you."

"Really?"

"We make our bones cleaning up some of their messes," I said. "Along the way, they get a lot of it right. Don't quote me on any of this, by the way. I'll deny it to their faces."

"I figured something happened in the case," Ryder said.

"Another woman was murdered," T.J. said. "We looked at everyone and everything again . . . and we figured your work retreat alibi was dicey."

"Someone ratted me out?"

"Two people, actually."

Ryder snorted and shook his head. "All right, yeah. No one was really taking attendance at the fucking thing. It was pretty loose. I didn't go to everything I said I had. We were in Ellicott City when Kirsten got killed, though. I didn't drive into Baltimore, murder her, and then go back." He fell silent, and I let him stew in it. Many people in Ryder's situation will keep talking to fill what they see as a gap in the conversation. Sure enough, he continued a few seconds later. "The truth is I've been depressed since it happened."

"Really?" I asked.

"Yeah, really. I liked Kirsten. We split up, sure, but she was a nice girl. She deserved a good future, and I knew we weren't going to find it together. To hear someone murdered her . . ." He shook his head, drawing his knees up and holding the hot mug even tighter. "It really got to me. How could anyone want her dead? I just kind of spiraled. Before today, I don't think I've left my house since it happened."

"Where were you headed earlier?" T.J. wanted to know.

"I got tired of looking at the same walls." Ryder let out a dry chuckle which carried no humor. "I wanted to go for a walk. Breathe in the cold air. Then, I saw the two of you, thought you might try to pin what happened on me, and I panicked."

"And got laid out by a perfect tackle," I said.

"I think we covered this before," T.J. said, ignoring my props for her football skills, "but do you know why Kirsten went to the park that day?"

"I wish I did."

After a sip of tea and another brief period of silence, I got us back on track. "Do you own a Taser?"

"Yeah, why?"

"Do you have it?"

"It's upstairs." He paused and frowned. "Wait, did the killer tase the girls?"

"You ever use it?" I persisted, ignoring his question.

"No. I didn't want to get a gun, so I opted for something non-lethal. It's registered and all."

"I know. It's one of the reasons we came to see you today."

"It was still in my bedroom last night," Ryder said.

"You won't mind showing us, then?" T.J. said.

Ryder sighed and stood, setting his mug down. "If I have to." He walked out of the room, his footfalls went up and then down a set of steps, and he returned carrying a metal box. He opened it and showed the stun gun inside to T.J. and me. I was far from an expert on the things, but the device and its spare cartridges looked unused.

"All right. I don't think we need to take up anymore of your time." I swigged some more tea—it was an average black blend—and set the cup on a coaster. "If the cops ask me about you, I'll tell them to look somewhere else."

Ryder nodded but didn't say anything. T.J. and I let ourselves out. "No way he did it," she said once we were back in the car.

"You're right. Taser ownership made him a convenient person of interest again."

"The dreaded Y in his name didn't matter." My assistant chuckled. "What are you going to do if the killer is just a guy called Bob?"

"Not abandon my principles about spelling," I said as I started the S4 and pulled away from the curb.

———

"You want to go back to the office and get your car?" I asked T.J. as we headed toward the heart of the city.

"We working tomorrow?"

"I don't plan to unless something major happens."

"You're okay to pick me up Monday morning if we don't stop by the office?"

"Sure."

"You know this means you'd have to wait about ten minutes for coffee on a Monday, right?" she pointed out.

"Is there still time to revise my answer?"

"I don't think I'll need my car tomorrow." She shrugged. "Sure. If it's easier to drop me at my place, go ahead."

"All right." We headed farther into Baltimore, and I pondered where we were with the case. Being a professional sleuth and rather intelligent fellow, I quickly came to the conclusion we were nowhere. Every nugget of information we thought might be a lead ended up evaporating. Ryder Long rode the person of interest train twice for two different reasons, but he hopped off each time. The Taser development didn't lead us to anything of significance, and I'd heard nothing from the police since they dragged a homeless man into an interrogation room in the interests of closing the case quickly.

"Deep in thought?" my secretary said.

"While I might normally be deep, any thinking about this case is shallow. We're splashing in a puddle."

"We have two days until we're back at it. The cops might come up with something. Maybe the ME will find another new detail."

"Maybe," I agreed, though I was going along to get along.

T.J. called me out on it. "You don't think they're going to come up with anything."

"Nope."

"Why not?"

"Because these have been really smart crimes," I said. "I feel shitty giving credit to a murderer, but whoever he is, he's done these well. The snow has wreaked havoc with every aspect of the investigation. If he decided to kill these women in two months when it's cold and dry, he'd be behind bars already."

"Maybe the best thing we can do is hope for a warm winter going forward," T.J. said.

She had a point, though I let it pass. We approached her building, and I stopped at the curb. "See you Monday," she said as she got out.

"Enjoy your Sunday." T.J. smiled, shut the door, and walked up to the main entrance. Once she was inside, I drove away. The warm weather she wished for might stop things for now, but a killer would still be walking free. At some point, we or the police needed to catch a break. I'd worked challenging cases before and pulled a solution out of a mess of conflicting data, but this one seemed tougher. Normally, I wanted to keep slamming away and put something like this to bed as quickly as possible.

This time, I was glad to be taking Sunday off. I certainly needed it.

CHAPTER 19

I SPENT most of my waking hours Sunday going between trying not to think about the case, feeling bad I wasn't expending mental energy on it, and not coming up with anything when I did think about it. At least it got me a good night's sleep on Sunday night.

Monday morning, I felt glad to be back on the mean streets of Federal Hill. As I walked along Riverside Avenue and stretched my arms, smells of bread, coffee, and breakfast meats from nearby eateries nearly compelled me to take a detour. I stuck to the plan, however, pounding the pavement for about thirty minutes before heading back home. Once there, I did about twenty minutes of weight work in the basement. I couldn't stand completely straight up down there, so I limited my time.

After showering and sharing the room with Gloria while we both got dressed, I walked downstairs to find the coffee machine had prepared its morning magic. I made cups for my wife and myself and then set about breakfast. It was a brisk and windy morning, so I chopped an apple and added cinnamon to a pot where I heated milk for oatmeal. I used the quick kind, and it still took five times as long to steep and stir as the container claimed. Once it thickened enough, I spooned the oatmeal into two bowls and sprinkled a little more cinnamon on top.

Gloria came down a few minutes later, and she looked dynamite in a turtleneck sweater and a pair of corduroy pants, her hair styled into chestnut waves. "Someone has a meeting this morning," I said.

"I do." She picked up her coffee and took a sip.

"If I keep looking at you, I'm going to want to book an hour on your calendar. Maybe two."

Gloria blushed. "Easy, tiger." She looked at the bowls and frowned. "Oatmeal?"

"I hate to sound like I'm my parents' age," I said, "but it's a great morning for it."

"I really wanted to take something with me," Gloria said.

"You can eat this in the car. It'll be adventurous, but you can do it. I believe in you."

"Thanks." She chuckled. "I hope my leather interior shares your confidence."

"What's going on?" I asked as I sat at the kitchen table. "You've done a lot of eating and running this past week or so, especially for a woman who doesn't have a conventional office to go to."

"Maybe I'm having breakfast with my second husband."

I snorted. "Please. You're far too smart and discerning to go looking for hamburger when you have prime filet right here."

"Well," Gloria said with a smile, "I certainly didn't marry you for your modesty." She sat opposite me and grabbed the other bowl.

"It's hard to be humble when you have a lot going on," I said.

My wife's mirth faded. "It's work. My company is pretty

new, but the state is doing a compliance audit. I have to follow a bunch of regulations and all, and they want a ton of paperwork."

"You never hired an assistant."

"Not a full-time one, no, and I'm paying for it now. I need a T.J."

"Talk to the real one, then."

"I can't. She works for you, and you're busy."

"You'd have to pay her, of course," I said, "and she's already doing forty hours for me. When she went undercover in the Sterner Academy, the PTA president raved about her, and it was only for a few days. She'll help you out, and I'm sure she wants the money this time of year."

"I'm not going to mess up your investigation?"

"Not much to mess up at the moment."

Gloria took a bite of oatmeal, which is to say she filled the small spoon maybe halfway. On the other hand, I shoveled as much as the utensil could hold, daring surface tension to do me wrong. It did not disappoint me. "Sounds like it's not going well," she said.

"Definitely not." I set my spoon down and rubbed my temples. "Every time we think we have something, it turns out to be nothing. Another woman died, and we learned one new thing we can't do much with. The police seem to be banging their heads into the same wall. The first victim's sister is probably going to fire us because we've delivered exactly zero results."

"Sorry." Gloria squeezed my hand. "Sounds like you still need T.J. more than I do."

"She'll make it work," I said. "She's smart."

"Maybe you'll put your brains together and catch a break soon."

"Here's hoping." Even to my own ears, my voice sounded devoid of hope.

———

T.J. and I spent the morning trying to brainstorm plausible ideas.

"Maybe we shouldn't have dismissed the vampire angle so quickly," I said after an hour spent guzzling coffee and frustration. T.J. rolled her eyes. "The winter solstice is coming soon. There are more dark hours now than any other season."

"Let me check phone records for Dracula," my assistant deadpanned.

"Make sure you look for Vlad Drakul, too. He might not be so obvious." T.J. grunted. "You got anything?"

She shook her head. "I wish. The Taser angle was a good find, but we can't do anything with it. Too many registered, plus all the ones that aren't."

"Almost like knowing someone got shot."

"I think it does point to a sadist or someone along those lines," she said. "Maybe we could pull records for anyone arrested for torture or violence against women."

"Might as well," I said.

I helped her run the search. We started with state records. "Jesus," T.J. said as results filled the screen.

"I know. Unfortunately, beating a woman is some guys' favorite hobby. They spend a couple years in jail around people just as bad or worse, so they get out and go right back to what they know."

"This is a long list of abusers." A thumbnail image accompanied each record. None of the faces glaring back at us looked remotely friendly. "I used to see jerks like these a few nights a week."

"I can finish this if you'd rather not deal with it."

"I'm all right," T.J. said. "I can't run and hide every time something reminds me of what I did in the past. It might feel like a lifetime ago, but it was only a few years."

In the end, we got way too many results to sift through in a reasonable amount of time. "These guys are all assholes," I said after reviewing two fruitless records, "but we're going to have a hard time tying any of them to the two murders."

"You want me to run our script?" T.J. asked.

"No. Not yet. We still have way too many names here. I think it'll take too long."

"I think you're right. This will take a while. What should we do? "

"Let's get some lunch."

We put on our coats against the lingering chill and headed into Fells Point. At the Square, I got a hot dog, soft pretzel, and lemonade from two different vendors. T.J., carrying a roast beef sandwich and a lemonade of her own, sat beside me on the bench. I took in the smells of grilled burgers at The Abbey and fresh pizza from the brick oven place behind us. "That stuff will kill you," she said.

"I know. It's why I exercise. It's why anyone exercises . . . to keep our own demises at bay."

"What about feeling younger or building your endurance?"

"Welcome to America, where we work out so we can eat an extra slice of pizza and not have guilt be a topping."

T.J. chuckled. "You'll never break into the fitness industry with that attitude."

"Probably for the best," I said. "I'd be way too inclined to tell the truth."

The hot dog was large and juicy, and the man at the cart made sure to put plenty of mustard and onions on it. I told him ketchup was for Philistines, and he agreed. I learned he was from Chicago, and ordering a hotdog with ketchup was the mark of a tourist or an idiot. Or both, I concluded, but the fellow with the tongs didn't mention this reasonable conclusion. The pretzel was a little too salty, so I shook a few crystals off onto the sidewalk. A hopeful pigeon wandered closer, realized I didn't put any food on the pavement, and waddled away in a huff.

After sharing about a quarter of my pretzel with T.J., we headed back to the office. Another car had arrived in the lot while we were gone. It was pretty full, and opening the door let out the myriad noises from the busy body shop. It was only when we got to the top of the metal stairs when I realized I didn't see any customers in Manny's waiting area. T.J. unlocked and opened the door, and I realized why.

They were up here.

Two goons waited for us. One sat at my desk rifling through some papers. The other kept watch in the center of the room. I hadn't taken a pistol with me because we were only going a couple blocks and coming right back. Neither of these men looked armed judging by the lack of telltale bulges in their jackets. Both were taller and broader than me, though the one besmirching my chair looked a good fifty pounds heavier than his friend. "We were wondering when you'd be back," the one standing guard said.

"We encourage people to wait outside," I said.

"We ain't clients."

Despite their intentions being apparent, I asked the necessary question. "What the hell are you doing here?"

"You got two options," the mouthpiece said. "You can

drop what you're working on, or we can help you redecorate. The color scheme here could use a little more red in it."

"You been practicing your line while you waited?"

The other one stood and jabbed a meaty finger in my direction. "What's it gonna be, asshole? The easy way or the hard way?"

I stepped in front of T.J. and raised my fists. "Call me stubborn, but I tend to like making things difficult."

THE MOUTHY ONE MOVED FIRST.

It made sense. He had a clear path toward me, while his friend needed to maneuver his large frame around my desk. It wouldn't keep the second guy away for long, however. I heard T.J. step backwards behind me, so I edged forward to keep myself between these two and her. The chattier guy wore his blond hair short, and up close, I noticed he had a teardrop tattoo below his left eye. "You'll be crying for real soon," I said.

Rather than engage in trash talk, he kept silent, instead leading with a haymaker as his friend rumbled closer. I turned it aside, stepped back from a followup hook, and folded him in half with a hard kick to the midsection. The larger enforcer now waded in. I stepped to my right. T.J., potentially exposed by my move, walked around the perimeter and got behind the fracas. As I figured, the bigger visitor was slower but packed a wallop. If he hit me, he'd knock me down and potentially KO me. I blocked one punch with my left forearm and immediately turned it into a short jab. It was designed to stun or distract someone for a moment rather than inflict any real damage.

It didn't.

The large man surged forward and wrapped me in a bear hug as his friend straightened up and smiled like a wolf. I groaned as breath left my body, and my ribs felt like they were in a vise. My left arm remained pinned against my body and useless for the moment. The pressure felt intense, and I wondered how long I had before a rib succumbed. My foe's mistake was raising me off the floor, making me taller than him. Before the other guy could make things worse, I leaned my head back, drove it forward, and slammed my forehead down on the bridge of my adversary's nose. The crack sounded like a gunshot, and even the other goon paused and looked around.

The one holding me howled in pain, and I wriggled out of his slackened grip. He was too big to shove away, so with my left arm free again, I elbowed him in his ample paunch. This compelled him to step back. The other one was ready to fill his spot. His array of punches didn't find the mark. When he backed off a bit and tried a side kick, I turned it aside hard. It spun his body enough for me to punt him in the balls. His eyes bulged, and he whimpered before slumping over.

I stepped around him. "Want to tell me who sent you?" I said to the larger goon.

"Piss off," he said. When the big man tried to grab me again, I easily dodged the clumsy attempt. He threw several punches, going for a knockout each time. My arms stung from blocking the powerful strikes, and I would be sporting the bruises from it tomorrow. When my foe's breathing increased, and his punches slowed, I went on the offensive.

The guy's sizable midsection could absorb a lot of damage, so I avoided it. Instead, I hit his outer right thigh with a snap kick. I did the same to his left. He grimaced and dropped a hand to cover the affected area. I gave him a solid boot to the outside of his right knee, and he wobbled. A strong elbow to the side of the noggin turned his head and dropped him hard enough to shake the floor and rattle our monitors.

Another crack—this one quieter—sounded behind me. The trimmer enforcer held his head, and a line of blood ran between his fingers. T.J. held her big metal stapler, a scowl on her face, and she raised her arm to strike again. The guy didn't look to be in a position to defend himself. She delivered another whack. He winced and covered his head with both hands. I kicked him in the gut and knocked him flat with a short uppercut under the chin. The floor didn't shake as much when he collapsed. I briefly wondered if Manny and the crew downstairs heard our more tumultuous moments up here over the noise in the shop.

I pivoted to the larger one, who regained his feet. He pulled a switchblade from his pocket, pressed the button, and deployed the double edge. A scowl took over his face. I didn't like fighting people with knives. Even dealing with an unskilled opponent, one lucky swing could end the fight— and your life—in an instant. The enforcer waved the weapon around. I followed it with my eyes, also watching his body for the telltale signs of a weight shift or hip turn. Though she didn't sing about fights, Shakira got it right about feints and attacks—the hips do not lie.

The massive man's attacks didn't get any faster with him being winded and adding six inches of steel to his reach. He took a cut which suggested he wanted to decapitate me with the small knife. I ducked under it and moved behind him. Before he could bring the blade back around, I kicked him in the back of the leg. He fell to one knee. I grabbed his wrist with my right hand, elbowed him in the head with my left arm, and used his own hand to drive the knife into his right thigh. He yelped in pain again. "Leave it in," I said. "I don't want too much of your blood on the floor."

He slumped over, one hand closed around the knife as blood ran down his leg. The other guy got up, saw what was happening, and said, "Holy shit." He looked between me and his injured colleague.

"You might want to help your friend," I suggested.

"We ain't friends."

I shrugged. "Your water cooler buddy. The guy who beat you out for promotion to Goon Supervisor. Whatever. I don't want him bleeding out on my floor."

"You stabbed him."

"Technically, I guided his hand," I said. "Besides, he brought the switchblade."

"You could call nine-one-one," he said.

"You're right. I could. I won't, but I could. You want to get him help, you're going to need to provide the muscle. I doubt whoever sent you here hired you because you're a whiny wimp."

He sighed, moved past me, and assisted his larger accomplice to an unsteady standing position. Considering the trimmer man still bled from the scalp, I figured odds were fifty-fifty of a spill going down the stairs. "You're a prick," he said as they hobbled toward the door.

"And you're a sore loser," I said. "Emphasis on *loser*."

"Piss off."

"Why not tell me who sent you? Whoever did isn't helping you now."

He stopped, stared at me, and sighed again. "I got paid in crypto. I don't know who did it." The two of them squeezed through the door. I followed at a safe distance to see if they made it down the steps without taking a heels-over-head shortcut. They did, and the pair headed for the car I'd spotted when we returned.

"You going to need a new stapler?" I asked T.J. once I'd shut the door.

"I think it's still good," she said.

"Thanks for whacking him."

"You got it, boss." She looked at the blood on the floor and frowned. "I guess we need to clean this up."

"I'll have to ask Manny to build us a closet up here. We're going to need a steam cleaner."

"Or you could stop making goons bleed," my assistant said.

I waved a hand. "The steam cleaner is easier."

———

About ten minutes after the goon squad left, Manny called upstairs. "The reporter in the wheelchair is back again," he said.

"If he keeps coming by, you might need to add an elevator."

"Want me to double your rent?"

"Not especially, no."

"No elevator, then," he said and hung up. I would have to ask for a closet at some point when the landlord wasn't thinking about his potential exemption under the Americans with Disabilities Act.

"I'm headed downstairs to talk to the guy from Carroll County again," I told T.J. She grunted as she sprayed more cleaner onto the floor. As before, Manny situated Adrian Brown in a little-used office. A minivan taxi identical to the one Brown arrived in before idled outside, plumes of grayish smoke from its exhaust standing out against the bright morning backdrop. "Did you see two guys leaving here?" I asked Brown as I entered the office and nudged the door shut.

He shook his head. "Who were they?"

Considering the slower pace they would have been moving, it seemed surprising Brown didn't spot them. "Just a couple idiots who tried to deter me."

"And?"

"The wheels of justice continue to grind."

"You seem like a resilient man," Brown said as he took out his phone, a small flip notebook, and a pen.

I tended not to take bait offered by reporters—or editors, who were simply reporters with a few extra duties stapled on these days—so I simply said, "I guess I am."

"You mind if I record?"

"Nope."

Brown tapped his phone and set it between us. "I wanted to talk to you about the case so far," he said. "The first victim's family hired you, but a second woman has since turned up dead."

When he didn't elaborate or continue, I said, "Is a question in there somewhere?"

"Yes." Brown smiled quickly and without warmth. "The police and you now have two murders to solve, and if I'm being honest, there wasn't a wealth of progress when you just had the one. How are things going?"

"I can't speak for the police, but pretty slowly on our end."

"Why?"

"Not a lot of clues. We don't have much to go on, but we're trying. Two muscleheads aren't going to deter me."

"What about three?"

"I still like my odds."

Brown bobbed his head. "Are you presuming both murders are the work of a single killer?"

The BPD's spokesperson answered this question in the affirmative yesterday, so I followed suit. "Right now, yes."

"Would anything change your mind?"

"A significant break in the case, sure."

"Something you're still waiting on," Brown said.

"Yes."

"You've solved some high-profile murders. A kidnapping or two. For a few years there, you were in the paper pretty often. One might say you had a habit of making yourself available to the press."

"Those reporters were prettier than you."

Brown again showed the fast smile, which vanished from his lips almost as quickly as it appeared. "I guess I'm wondering why you've clammed up in recent years."

I shrugged as I looked around the small space. The old radio stood in a greater state of disrepair this time. "Maybe I realized publicity doesn't always help people in my business."

"You're talking to me, though."

"How many people read your paper? Like fifty?"

"Quite a few more, actually," Brown said, sounding a little perturbed.

"I'm sure the tractor pull section gets you good numbers."

"A large number of readers trust us for our weather. Most accurate in the state."

"I'm actually curious about how you manage it," I said. "There are plenty of bigger and wealthier news organizations in the state."

"It's proprietary . . . and not why I'm here today. Do you have anything else to say about the investigation?"

"We'll get whoever's responsible. One person, two, or

however many it is. Things are slow at the moment, but we'll figure it out."

"I'm not sure my readers will share your optimism."

"Just make sure you give us a good writeup at the end," I said.

Brown finished jotting a note. "Can I include your picture?"

"I'd rather you didn't. The whole not wanting a ton of publicity thing."

"All right. Thanks for your time." Brown tapped his phone again, turning off the recording, and packed up the rest of his things.

"Sure," I said. As I left the first-floor office, the minivan taxi remained idling outside. I headed back upstairs. This second major interruption of the day sapped whatever negligible momentum T.J. and I had built. We'd gotten photos of the goons on our cameras, but even after cropping them, those didn't turn into much. Each had the kinds of prior arrests one would expect of two enforcers, but neither existed in the orbit of anyone we'd encountered so far in the investigation.

"Someone had to send those two," T.J. said, crossing her arms and staring at the screen.

"Someone did," I agreed. "The same person who's managed to stay ahead of the police and us so far. We'll put it together at some point."

"All this difficulty because of two snow storms."

"Makes me wonder how police and PIs in places like Alaska get anything done."

"Maybe we should relocate operations to Florida."

I wrinkled my nose. "Pass. If I'm going to deal with humidity like we have here, I don't want the baseline temperature to be even higher."

Later in the afternoon, a Google alert I'd set went off. Adrian Brown penned a new piece regarding the investigation. As I read it, I realized he'd pulled no punches again, but this time, his pugilism targeted me.

Joining the police on what's turned into a fool's errand—with fools aplenty running around—is local private investigator C.T. Ferguson. In his nearly six years of operation, Ferguson has earned a reputation for closing difficult cases . . . several of which stymied the Baltimore police. Astute readers will know your columnist thinks this is a low bar to clear.

Despite joining the investigation well before the tragic murder of Bernadette Holmes, Ferguson has made no progress, contributed no leads, and mostly served to take money from the grieving Valle family. A handsome and affable fellow in his mid-thirties, one wonders whether Ferguson—who does not come from a law enforcement background—is out of his depth on the big stage. At least he seems to be trying.

The level of effort elsewhere in this sordid mess is questionable. Like its victims, the investigation is bleeding into winter.

"Son of a bitch," I grumbled.

"It's basically a hit piece," T.J. said.

"If he comes back, we need to figure out a way to get him up here."

"Why?"

"Because I kinda want to push him down the stairs."

"I think that might be illegal."

"Pity."

"Short of assaulting a disabled man," my assistant said, "what do you want to do about it?"

"Adrian Brown isn't the only one who can use the power of the press," I said.

"You're going to become a reporter?"

I scoffed. "As overqualified as I might be, no. His paper publishes letters to the editor. Most of them do. I'm going to drag him up and down, and the best thing is he's an editor. He'll read it even if he decides not to publish it."

"We're in the middle of a case."

"Let's not pretend we were about to make an arrest," I said. "Besides, this won't take me long."

I got to work.

CHAPTER 21

"AT LEAST HE mentioned I was handsome."

"And affable," T.J. added, "though you're not exactly living up to that description at the moment."

"It's only mostly a hit piece, then," I said. "It still deserves a response."

Her frown came with a shrug. "Maybe we need to look into taking another case?"

I'd started tapping out a few words but stopped and looked at my assistant. "I'm not a fan of working two at once."

"We're not making progress here," she said. "Brown might be an asshole, but he's right about the investigation being stalled." When I didn't say anything, she continued. "We're not getting paid for the second victim. I'm happy to look into it because I want this bastard found, but we're out of pocket there and can't justify billing much to the Valles."

"They might pull the plug anyway." I wouldn't blame Jessie and her family if they did. We'd delivered precisely zero above what the police had, which constituted a massive nothingburger.

"What do you want to get out of this?"

"Besides my literary revenge?" T.J. rolled her eyes. "I

don't know what kind of numbers the *Herald* is pulling, but I'll bet they've gone up a lot since Adrian Brown came to Baltimore. Their readers need to know people are working hard at this. We're stymied, and it sucks, but you and I are trying, and so are the cops."

She nodded. "All right. Go get 'em, boss."

I've always been a pretty fast typist, but the words—sprinkled with a dose of invective—poured out of me. It wouldn't count as my *magnum opus*, but it was still good.

Dear editors,

I feel Adrian Brown is doing your readers a disservice.

It's probably not his fault. He suggested I wasn't ready for the big stage. I think this was a projection. Mr. Brown shows his lack of crime writing chops with every byline attributed to him. He favors clickbait headlines and columns which are light on facts and heavy on poorly reasoned accusations.

The Baltimore police have yet to catch the man or men who murdered Kirsten Valle and Bernadette Holmes. This is unfortunately true. Yes, my agency has been on the case for a while, and it pains me to say we haven't brought much to the table yet.

We're giving it our best. Everyone involved is.

The BPD has authorized more overtime for this than any operation I can remember. Despite what Mr. Brown apparently thinks, detectives don't solve real murders in 43 minutes around commercials and quips infused with gallows humor. Some cases come together quickly. Others take a while. Several factors put the Baltimore double homicides in the latter category.

In spite of what Mr. Brown has written, no one on the case is a buffoon. No one is out of their depth. The stage isn't too big for any of us except the small-town editor who's desperate for everyone to believe he's a hard-hitting crime journalist.

The men and women toiling away on the case have contributed their work and ideas. Mr. Brown has contributed distractions, accusations, and vitriol. I will leave it up to your readers to decide which is more appropriate and useful for finding a killer.

Sincerely,

C.T. Ferguson

Private Investigator

Baltimore, MD

I sent it to the *Herald* once T.J. read it. "Sure you're not gunning for his job?" she asked.

"You should hope not. I doubt he has the budget for an assistant."

She grinned. "Let me earn my pay, then." We got back to work on the puzzling double homicide I'd just excoriated Adrian Brown for covering like a jackass.

We banged away at things for a while and came up with nothing. At about seven o'clock, we decided to adjourn for the night and come back with fresh eyes tomorrow. After a night of mediocre sleep, I arrived at the office in desperate need of fresh coffee. Thankfully, T.J. had a pot ready and waiting.

"It would be nice if we could establish a meaningful connection between the victims," my assistant said. "So far, we can't even tell if they knew each other."

"They probably didn't," I concurred. We'd uncovered nothing to put the two women in the same place at the same time, and they weren't acquainted on any social network besides having the occasional friend or contact in common.

"Why them, then?"

"Good question. So far, no one has been able to answer it. If they're really as unconnected as they appear, does it mean the killings were random?"

"I don't think so," T.J. said.

"Me, neither. There's no way an opportunistic predator happened upon two young women who share a resemblance sitting alone in the park during a snowstorm. These were coordinated somehow. Kirsten and Bernadette braved the elements to meet someone, and they died for it."

We weren't exactly on the road to an epiphany, but I still didn't welcome the distraction of the ringing phone. T.J. answered it, and after a grimace or two, informed the caller she would put the conversation on speaker. "Go ahead." Dread colored her voice.

"This is Jessie Valle," our client said.

"How are you, Miss Valle?" I said.

"I guess the best word to use is frustrated." She accentuated this point with a long sigh. "Have you come any closer to finding my sister's killer?"

"I won't sugarcoat it. No, we haven't. We stopped the police from arresting the wrong man, but someone we identified as a person of interest didn't do it and wasn't involved."

"So we're no closer than we were when the police worked it by themselves?" she wanted to know.

"Unfortunately, no."

"I'm trying here, Mister Ferguson. I'd like to keep you on this, but I also wanted to see results by now. Even if you found someone, and the police eventually cleared him, it would be movement, and it might be the first step down the road to finding who killed my sister." She paused for another sigh. "I think I want to cut the cord."

T.J. closed her eyes and shook her head. I sympathized. She'd wanted to work this case before it was actually a case.

Then, the Valle family hired us, and we found nothing of consequence. "I understand," I said.

"You're not going to try and talk me out of it? Tell me how difficult the whole thing has been?"

"Well, it really has been. The snow and conditions have thrown a wrench in our investigation and the police's. It's a reason and not an excuse, but I get why you might not want to hear it regardless."

"You're right . . . I don't. Thanks for what you've done. At least you identified someone who might have been involved. It's more than I've gotten from the goddamn cops. At this point, I feel like we're spending good money after bad, and I can't justify it."

"We're going to keep at it," T.J. said.

"You'll be out of pocket," our now former client said.

"We already are for the second victim," I said. "Unfortunately, we've never found a link between her and your sister. There's nothing to tie anything about those crimes together other than the methods and weather."

"If you end up solving it, I'll certainly be grateful, but I'm not going to pay for any more of your time. I'll settle up soon."

"That's fine," T.J. said. Jessie ended the call. "Shit."

"Inevitable," I said.

"It still sucks."

"It does."

"Maybe now is the time to take on the other client who might be interested . . . if she still is."

I waved a hand. "Pass."

"It would be nice to have someone paying us," my assistant said.

"Let's see how things go with our double murder."

T.J. fell silent and got back to work. Even though we no longer had a client, I did the same.

After lunch, footsteps rang on the metal stairs.

They were light, even more so than T.J.'s. I used my sleuthing prowess to deduct this could only be a goon if whoever walked through the door were the world's tiniest. Instead, a woman walked in. She was of average height and trim even in a coat. Worry lines were the only sign of age on her pretty face. I guessed her to be about forty, though if asked, I would go with twenty-nine to avoid getting slapped.

"I'm glad you could make it," T.J. said, standing to greet our new arrival.

"I'm grateful you and your boss could squeeze me in," she said, handing my assistant her coat. T.J. hung it on the rack.

"No problem," I said to be collegial. When the woman turned her back, I shot T.J. a look meant to be both confused and angry. She flashed a sweet smile in response and then got down to business.

"Coffee?" she asked. The lady declined. I didn't like her already. "Maybe you can tell us why you're here today."

The woman sat in front of my desk. T.J. joined her, notebook at the ready. "This is all a little embarrassing," the older woman said. "I'm Lucy . . . Lucy Russo, though I'll be going back to my maiden name soon enough."

"We don't do infidelity cases," I said.

"That's not why I'm here. My husband's philandering is well established. I was hoping he could change, but I'm done taking him back and wishing for the best. He hired some pretty new assistant recently, and sure enough, he started screwing her soon after." She snorted. "We're in the middle of a divorce. I need your help with a specific thing."

"What is it?"

"We're trying to determine assets. I know he has some

fancy sports car. A McLaren. He's hiding it, though, and trying not to declare it. I don't care about the car itself, but I want what it's worth. This was his major midlife crisis purchase. Frank is a decade older than me." Her lips twisted. "I also don't want him to be able to drive his latest side piece around in it."

"There can't be too many McLarens registered in the state," I said.

"My lawyer has tried to find it," Lucy Russo said. "Her investigator struck out, and now he's on another case. She hired an outside company, and they came up empty. She even hired a so-called psychic, but I told her that shit wouldn't be billable."

"I'm going to guess the spirit realm came up empty."

"Yes."

"There's one of the problems with ghosts. They have no appreciation for fast cars."

Lucy grinned. "If we can find the car, it'll get added to his assets. My settlement will be nicer, and it'll make that asshole bleed a little more. Do you think you could locate it?" She slid a piece of paper across the desk with the make, model, and registration information on the car. I searched online and saw similar specimens selling for north of two hundred grand.

"This is a very valuable car," I said.

"That's why we want to find it. I'm willing to pay you five percent of its appraised value."

I shook my head, and T.J. frowned. "We can't go by appraised value. If he thinks someone is closing in, he might take a hammer to the car out of spite. Is it low mileage?" Lucy nodded. "We'll go by comparable listings online, then, and I want fifteen percent."

"Fifteen!?"

"Your lawyer's already hired some cut-rate PI firm," I said, "not to mention a charlatan. I'll unearth the car."

"Fifteen is a lot," Lucy said.

"When you go on *Shark Tank*, you don't try to nickel and dime Mark Cuban."

"Maybe not, but you can always make a deal with someone else."

I held my hand toward the door. "Feel free to seek out a better offer, then. If your husband can afford to buy an exotic sports car and hide it, you're going to come out of the divorce with a pretty good payday."

Lucy pursed her lips and frowned. T.J. shot me a glance much like the one I gave her when our new potential client arrived. Lucy pulled out her phone, her brows knitted as she tapped away at the screen. "I can't give you fifteen percent," she said after a contemplative moment, "but I can go to ten."

Considering the expected value of the car, this constituted a nice payday. It would make up for the double murder case, allow me to give T.J. the generous Christmas bonus she deserved, and keep the business closed through the holidays. I still felt she was being a little cheap, but raking in fifteen to twenty grand for an easy job made for a sweet gig. "We'll take ten." Lucy and I shook on it.

"I'll draw up the contract," T.J. said, and the pair adjourned to her desk. I still didn't relish the idea of working two cases at once, but this one didn't seem taxing, and we weren't exactly awash in suspects on the main investigation. A short while later, Lucy put her white puffy coat back on, thanked us again, and left.

"Really?" my assistant said. "Mark Cuban?"

"You don't expect me to compare myself to Kevin O'Leary, do you?"

"He's Mister Wonderful."

"I have a lot more claim to the title than he does," I said.

CHAPTER 22

EVEN WITH A NEW client in tow, I focused on our main case.

"You're bad at multitasking," T.J. told me at some point.

"It's one of the reasons I hired you," I said.

"Any luck?"

I shook my head. "Every time I think coming back to this with fresh eyes will make a difference, I end up disappointed."

"Maybe it's time to focus on our new client," my assistant suggested.

She was right, but I still didn't want to admit it. This double murder left me flummoxed, and it was a new experience. I'd been stumped during cases before but always found something to turn the tide—often in advance of others on the job. This investigation resisted all our attempts to put anything together. I checked the BPD case files. Each saw only perfunctory updates. Officers and detectives did the legwork but had nothing of consequence to show for their efforts. The lack of concrete evidence, witnesses, or even good surveillance video from around the locations haunted everyone involved. I couldn't remember feeling so frustrated on a case, and I couldn't fathom the idea of this being part of the job. "Fine," I said after a fruitless few minutes.

"I shared her documents with you. It's all the assets they've found for the husband so far, plus a rundown of the car."

"All right. We should be able to wrap this up quickly."

"You're confident," T.J. said.

"Maybe I'm just hopeful this won't turn into another shitshow."

"Can I watch the magician at work?"

"Pull up a chair," I said. "Fetch my cape and top hat on the way."

"Should I go outside and catch a rabbit first?" she asked as she wheeled her way beside me.

I reviewed what T.J. provided. Frank Russo, aged 51, enjoyed a successful career in private equity. The divorce would bring his wife a few million simply in the fifty-fifty division most cases saw. Even if she got the short shrift on the percentage, Lucy Russo would be set for retirement and the rest of her life. The McLaren was icing on the cake, though I understood her reasons for wanting it included. Vitriol rarely needed an explanation.

After going over everything, I used my scraping script to go after Frank's social media accounts. He only used Facebook and LinkedIn but posted on both regularly. He used the latter mostly to talk about investments and dispense what he called "free nuggets of wisdom," presumably in the hope of converting someone reading his posts into a paying client. I didn't follow the markets closely, and even I knew some of his propositions ended up being total whiffs. Someone like Frank Russo would have a canned speech about the risks inherent in any investment.

Frank's Facebook was more for general use. The output

of the script allowed me to search and sort, so I hunted for car posts and ones about the McLaren in question specifically. I found no lack of braggadocios updates about the sports car. Frank looked like a typical middle-aged guy—receding hairline, getting paunchy, trying to make up for what he saw as a boring life until this point. I doubted he had any idea how to drive a vehicle like a McLaren properly, and he probably would've been better off with a new Mustang.

It's hard to rub your wealth in other people's faces with a Ford, however.

I found several posts and photos about showing off his car —and even driving it a little—at the Southern Maryland Car Club. As residents of Catsonville, the Russos did not live in or anywhere near southern Maryland, but geography seemed to be a minor consideration when it came to membership. Pictures showed classic muscle cars, modern versions like the Corvette and Mustang, and even a few 911s. As far as I could tell, Russo owned the only McLaren, and maybe the club courted him for this reason.

The owner of the Southern Maryland Car Club was a jowly man named Ray Benedict. His profile showed him posing next to and inside members' vehicles—a perk of the job—and also at his very large garage where he kept two cars and had room for several more. "Look at this," I said, and T.J. leaned in.

"I don't see the McLaren," she said.

"Me, neither. But if you were going to hide your expensive car somewhere, a garage not registered to you would be a good place."

"Makes sense."

"Let's see what we can find."

As far as we could tell, Frank Russo paid for his car club membership with an account registered to his business. I didn't know if this would be part of the pending divorce settlement, but a competent attorney could certainly get it included. "How do we prove the car is in the garage?" T.J. wanted to know.

"We'll have to gain access."

"It won't hold up in court."

"I know," I said. "Lucy's lawyer can ask for it. We can find a way to make it legitimate, and she'll handle the rest."

"You're guessing the garage has a camera system." It was a statement, not a question.

"Yes. I think this Benedict would want to protect his own vehicles. Stashing one for his rich friend is mere extra incentive. Russo probably made what he wanted clear."

"Let's find it, then."

I checked the club's website information and sent a few pings. Most people outsource their web hosting, picking a provider who does a lot of the background work. Ray Benedict liked to get his hands dirty. He operated a Windows machine using Internet Information Services to handle the web management onsite. A quick probe of the network revealed his lone machine also operated the building's security system.

A search using a different tool gave me the make and model of the cameras Benedict installed. Many people set up these components and left the default login credentials in place. I found the factory-set user name and password online, opened a remote shell connection, and tried them. The user ID worked, but Benedict must have set his own password. "He's got a leg up on most people," I said.

"Now we need to guess it?" T.J. asked.

"I don't know whether this login will fail if we guess

wrong a certain number of times," I said. "Let's try and figure it out."

"Something like 'SouthernMarylandCarClub' is too obvious, right?"

"Yes and no. It is, but most people pick passwords they can remember easily. You can't dismiss the low-hanging fruit." I tried it, and we received the *INVALID LOGIN* message again. "Let's review his posts." According to his socials, Benedict was single and had no children, which took a few obvious options off the table. He'd occasionally mentioned a cat but not in the last six months. Many of his posts dealt with being the owner of what he billed as a growing and successful car club.

His personal vehicle was a black 1969 Camaro SS, and it featured in his profile picture along with plenty of other photos. "I'm going to try the car," I said, and I entered *1969-CamaroSS* into the password field. It featured upper and lowercase letters as well as numbers, so it wasn't a bad choice except for the possibility of people like me discovering it in a social media review. *ACCESS GRANTED* flashed on the screen, and a live shot of Benedict's garage replaced it.

In pictures, it looked to be of above average height and depth and long enough to park at least a half-dozen cars. In a past life, I imagined it held construction or industrial equipment. Benedict's Camaro sat in easy view of the lens. We had a rather zoomed-in shot of the hood and grill, and the owner's was the only car on the screen. The online controls for the camera were easy enough to figure out but slow to respond. After several periods of delay between the inputs and results, we saw what we were after.

Frank Russo's shiny blue McLaren sat parked near the far wall.

"Now we need to figure out how to make it legit," T.J. said.

"Let's start with some detailed searches of the club itself." We probably should have conducted these to start, but I took a few shortcuts along the way. Ray Benedict registered the organization as an LLC with himself as the sole owner. The address corresponded to a property in southern Maryland with a figure-eight racing track and the long garage which ended up housing the McLaren. "We could send this."

"Is it enough?"

"I have no idea," I said. "I'm not a lawyer. It's a good place to start, however. Once we add the surreptitious banking information, it'll be clear Frank is trying to hide something."

"It can't be about the money," T.J. said. "Even if Lucy gets half his assets, Frank could write a check for another fancy car."

"My guess is he likes it a lot," I said. "Lucy called it his midlife crisis purchase, and maybe she was right. Frank might want to take his mistress out for drives in it." I shrugged. "We don't really know what it means to him, and it's not our job to care. Lucy's lawyer can find it honestly and get it added to the assets. What happens afterward is out of our hands."

T.J. frowned at me. "You're very Zen about this."

"I just solved our second case in about thirty minutes." I cracked my knuckles. "We'll earn about fifteen grand for this work. Pretty nice ratio if I do say so myself."

"What about our main case?"

"Don't be a spoil sport. We'll get back to it." I looked at my screen and sighed. "My guess is our efficiency will take a pretty big hit."

"We don't even have a client anymore."

"We don't need one now," I said.

———

We handed everything to Lucy's lawyer Friday morning.

Sunday evening, Lucy called to tell me everything went through. Her attorney got a search of the car club's garage approved, and the investigator and local police identified the McLaren. The car became part of the pool of assets to be contested and divvied up. T.J. and I had done our jobs, and we could expect a payday of around fifteen thousand—depending on the comparable values the lawyer found—in the next few days.

These positive developments served as a poor salve on the wound of our continued failure in the double homicide case. T.J. and I revisited both crime scenes Friday. I figured not much would come of these returns, and I was not disappointed. Rich called to give us the most non-update update in history. I gathered he was fishing for information because the BPD also had nothing new. We couldn't share anything with him.

To her credit, Gloria managed to keep my mind off the cases most of the weekend. Once Friday evening rolled around, T.J. and I decided to take Saturday and Sunday off and come back Monday morning refreshed and renewed. I had no idea how much difference this would make, though I figured very little. We'd driven along the road for a while, plowed headlong into every pothole, and now hobbled along in a car with a ruined suspension.

Maybe I needed to stop thinking about the blue McLaren . . . and the red Mercedes rocket my wife drove.

We drove back to her Brooklandville home after attending a housewarming party farther up in the county. The temperature lingered around freezing all day, and with the sun setting, the mercury dropped, too. Still full from too many appetizers and *hors d'oeuvres* at the gathering—and wondering why the hosts took care to differentiate between the two—I made a small dinner of baked salmon and a medley of fresh vegetables. I didn't mind the smell of cooking fish, but if I did, the powerful ventilation system in Gloria's kitchen whisked it away.

After dinner, my phone vibrated in my pocket. Expecting a text bringing bad news, I was happy to see two alerts I'd set for the Carroll County *Herald* went off. The first corresponded to a new column by Adrian Brown. The second promised heavy snow starting in a few hours and continuing through the morning with eight or more inches of accumulation. I checked one of the local news sites, and their forecast called for two to five inches.

Brown's column was more of the same as before, but he'd clearly read the letter I'd sent—and the *Herald* published—before writing this one. *One wonders if the police and private investigators working these cases would be better served by reviewing the facts and sticking to long-established procedures rather than engaging in wars of words with local journalists. Of these two tactics, one is good for scoring points with peers and colleagues, and the other might actually be useful in solving a double murder.*

"Fucking prick," I muttered.

"What?" Gloria asked from beside me on the couch.

"Just commenting on what passes for journalism these days."

"You sound like you're ninety."

"I have an old soul when it comes to things like this," I said. I showed her my screen with the *Herald's* weather alert. "You see this? The Carroll County paper is calling for another big snowstorm tonight."

"I thought it was supposed to be kinda minor," my wife said.

"Me, too, but they have a pretty good record of getting these right."

Gloria frowned. "I hope this doesn't mean another dead woman."

"Me, too," I said.

———

I woke up for no apparent reason at six AM.

Gloria remained asleep. I padded to the nearest window in her bedroom and looked out at the street. Snow covered it, and more was falling. From here, it was hard to tell, but I figured at least six inches already coated the ground and roads. It was Monday morning, so someone would be plowing here soon. Brooklandville streets cannot remain besmirched by the elements for long. I crawled back into bed. Gloria stirred briefly before her breathing indicated she'd fallen right back asleep.

I never got the chance.

A few minutes later, my vibrating phone created a loud buzz which made me sit up and woke Gloria. Rich called, and a feeling of dread clawed at my insides. There were several reasons he could be calling me at six-fifteen on a Monday, and precisely zero of them were good. "Hello?"

"We got another body," he said.

"Same as before?" I wondered.

"Redheaded woman found stabbed to death in a local park, yeah. ME is arriving now, so I don't know if it lines up exactly like the others, but initially, I'll go with yes."

"Let me guess . . . no obvious tracks of our killer fleeing the scene?"

"You catch on quick," Rich said. "Sharpe said we're still all hands on deck, so you're welcome to come here. I'll text you the location."

"Great." I ended the call.

"That doesn't sound good," Gloria said, stretching and propping herself up on her pillows.

"It's very much not."

"Oh, no. Don't tell me."

"Sounds like I don't need to," I said. "What you were wondering about last night happened. We now have a third victim." I got out of bed and hunted around in the dresser for some clothes. Even with us staying at Gloria's house roughly half the time now, she still enjoyed a monopoly on closet and drawer space. This was not the morning to discuss changes to the status quo.

"Are you headed to the scene?"

"I'm going to pick up T.J. on the way."

"Hasn't it been snowing all night?"

"I have all-wheel drive."

"You're not worried?"

"A third woman is dead," I said. "I don't have time to be worried about traction." I texted T.J. to give her the bad news, told her I'd be by to pick her up, and threw some clothes on.

CHAPTER 23

EVEN WITH ALL-WHEEL DRIVE, getting out of Brooklandville proved a little adventurous.

Snow still fell, and whoever was in charge of Baltimore County's emergency operations must have believed the lower precipitation estimate. Roads were still covered in snow and slush. Plow trucks pushed as much aside as they could, but a smart manager would have deployed them at least two hours ago. Once I got to I-83, conditions improved, but some white stuff still clung to the concrete, and it made everyone drive a little slower.

T.J.'s apartment was close to the highway exit, and the streets were a little better in the city. It remained early, but the roads were less crowded than normal. Schools would be closed, some folks would work from home, and I mostly shared the road with trucks and SUVs. I pulled up in front, and the building's main door opened a second later. T.J.'s blonde hair peeked out of a wool cap as she dashed to the car, performing the practiced mix of speed and caution familiar to anyone who grew up with real winters. "This sucks," she said after getting in and closing the door.

"In every way imaginable," I agreed. The victim lay in

Eager Park, a couple blocks north of the Johns Hopkins Hospital. On a normal morning at this time, I could get there in ten minutes or so. Today, it took nearly twenty. As its name suggested, the park bordered Eager Street to the south, Wolfe to its east, Chase to its north, and the narrow Dunbar Street to the west. The park was much longer than it was wide, and grass covered most of it, with trees dominating the Dunbar side. A short trail ran through it at an angle. Snow covered all of this, of course, and flurries still fell as I parked the S4 near the collection of police cars and SUVs.

So far, no news vehicles had arrived. I wondered how long this would remain true. The activity would cause some jackass to tip them off sooner or later. Thankfully, a lot of other parks and undeveloped land surrounded us with the closest homes being a bunch of townhouses on the other side of Durham Street. Yellow tape framed the perimeter as T.J. and I exited the car and approached. Two uniforms talked to a pudgy man with a very calm Labrador at the end of a leash. I presumed the canine sniffed out the most recent victim.

"Dog found her," Rich confirmed almost right away. "Owner saw a hump in the snow and wondered what it might be. The Lab cleared enough for him to see it was a body."

Two men in white Tyvek suits with *MEDICAL EXAM-INER* across their shoulders crouched over the corpse. "Any ID this time?" I asked.

"No," Rich said, shaking his head. "Same as before. "No ID or phone. We won't know who she is for a while yet. She's a redhead like the others and looks to be in the same age range."

"If the serial killer talk started after two victims, it's going to be at a fever pitch now."

"I know," Leon Sharpe said from somewhere behind me,

and the sudden sound of his deep voice made me jump. "We won't be able to stop them from speculating. All we can do is try to solve the case."

I surveyed the scene. A few sets of footprints—and one made by paws—clustered near the deceased. "The dog, its owner, and the two guys from the ME's office," I said. None of the other prints jumped out as being different. "No fifth set."

"No," Sharpe said. "Same as the first two. No tracks leading away. The little snow under the body makes us think she died early in the event. The current guess is about nine or ten last night."

"Not many houses nearby," T.J. said, pointing to the group to our west. "In the dark and with snow falling, no one over there would see anything."

"Unfortunately, you're right." Sharpe frowned and adjusted his hat. "We've sent uniforms to talk to those people and request any camera footage. The backs of the houses face this side, so we're not expecting much."

"I'm going to point something out," I said. "One of the papers covering this whole mess has gotten the forecasts right three times in a row. None of the other local papers or stations had us getting eight-plus inches this time. I don't know how useful this is."

"I doubt the meteorologist is a serial killer," Rich said.

"No, but it might be an interesting data point."

"The Carroll County fish-wrap?" Sharpe asked.

"Yeah."

The captain shrugged. "It's small compared to *The Sun*, but plenty of people still read it. I don't know what we could get there."

A black Escalade rolled up to the scene, and Mayor Vincent Davenport stepped out along with police commissioner David Ngo. "The circus is officially in town," I said. "The ringmaster and his prized pet have arrived."

Because this day was meant to be shitty, Davenport and Ngo beelined for us. "What the hell's he doing here?" the commissioner demanded, jutting his chin toward me.

"Trying to save the city again," I said. "I'm more than just the ransomware guy."

"Hell of a job you've been doing."

"I really don't think you want to go there."

"I'm sure Mister Ferguson is here in the spirit of all hands on deck," Davenport said. "Something I've encouraged. We're up to three homicides now. We need all the help we can get."

I nodded but kept my gaze on Ngo. "At least one of you realizes it."

———

We drove away just before the media vehicles slid to a halt.

"Good timing," T.J. said as another couple passed us headed to the scene.

"So far, it's the only good thing about today." I interpreted her silence as agreement. "You eat yet?"

"No, and despite everything that's happened already, I'm hungry."

"Me, too." I drove a block out of the way to find a McDonald's. I stuck to sandwiches and hash browns because their coffee has never been strong enough. The flurries stopped, and the roads were a little better than when we set out over an hour before. Even with a detour for food, we made it to the office in about twenty minutes. T.J. put coffee on while I placed our bag of breakfast into the microwave to heat everything back up.

Several minutes later, with bellies full and caffeine flowing, we got down to business. "We have to be looking at the same killer for all three," my assistant said.

"I think you're right."

"The same kind of crime scene, so it's the same challenges. The cops aren't going to find anything."

"Let's not jump to conclusions," I said, "but I fear this one will go as the others did."

"So now we have three dead women and no leads."

"I know." I crossed my arms and sighed. "We missed something. We must have. I know the conditions have been right for our killer to make things hard on us, but we must have missed a detail somewhere. I need to be smarter than this."

"Don't beat yourself up, boss." I grunted. "If you wait a few days, three goons might come and try to do it for you."

I appreciated her attempt at levity, so I smiled. "I'd like to crack this as soon as we can. No second cases right now. I don't care if it's as easy as finding a car in some rich asshole friend's garage. This needs to be our focus." T.J. nodded her agreement. "All right. The cops are probably wrapping up the scene. We're not going to have anything new to look at until they update all the files."

"The obvious link is to the weather," T.J. said.

"True, but what's the actual link? We agree thousands of people might read the *Herald*'s forecasts, and we don't really have a good way to know who they are."

"What if it's a smaller circle?"

"You mean the employees themselves?" I said.

"Or their friends and family. Anyone who might get a tip that the light dusting is really going to drop eight inches."

I sipped my coffee, thought about it, and bobbed my head. "All right. It's a start. The *Herald* has suffered the fates of a lot of newspapers. Declining subscribers and readership mean they're running with a smaller staff. The employee count can't be very high."

T.J. tapped away at her keyboard. "Let me see if I can find out." A minute later, she added, "Eleven full-time staff, four part-timers, and two interns. Doesn't count anyone like the custodians, but they could be in on it."

"They probably contract those jobs out. Especially in an era where people can work remotely."

As we developed our theory, I got an alert on my phone. The paper in question published another piece about the murders. It was another column by Adrian Brown. *The Baltimore police remain flummoxed, confused, clueless, stymied, and plenty of other uncharitable adjectives. No one on site would confirm the obvious: a serial killer stalked women in Baltimore, and the cops were powerless to protect anyone. Despite bringing in outside investigators, no one has made any significant progress. One wonders if the women of the city would be better off staying inside, locking their doors, and carrying kitchen knives around their houses. At least then, they would have a chance.*

"Fuck this guy," I said.

"He's always negative."

"I get it to a point. The first victim was from his county, and he's trying to make sure someone speaks for her."

"He doesn't need to speak like such a prick," T.J. said.

I grinned. "He certainly doesn't." I clicked on Brown's byline and saw he'd published at least one piece a day regarding the murders beginning the morning after Kirsten Valle died. His initial column trumpeted his arrival in Baltimore as if he were some crusader whose mere presence would lead to the truth. Instead, he levied accusations of buffoonery and railed against investigations he didn't know how to conduct.

"We'll still solve this," T.J. said.

"I hope you're right."

"I am. You need to believe it, too. I know you're frustrated. So am I . . . but do you really think the snow can outsmart us?"

"No way," I said. She smiled and nodded. "I thought inspirational speeches were supposed to be my job."

"What kind of executive assistant would I be if I couldn't pick up the slack?" T.J. said.

———

In the afternoon, the BPD updated the case files online.

I wondered if they did this for my benefit along with any other outside investigators they'd asked to consult. While T.J. set a PM pot of coffee to brew, I started taking in the results. "Our third victim is April Mooney," I told her. "Social media manager, twenty-eight. Like we saw, she was a pretty redhead."

"I feel like we need a big whiteboard," T.J. said.

"We may need two or three if this damn case keeps going."

"Any other information about April?"

"She lives in the county," I continued, reading the report. "Works and socializes in the city. Two brothers local. Parents' status currently unknown."

"Any idea why she was in the park?" my assistant wanted to know.

"No mention of it."

"Even if she went there to meet someone, the first two murders had happened. Someone who's frequently on social media would have seen coverage and posts about them. Why meet a man in a park while it's snowing when you know it's already turned out deadly for two other women?"

I shrugged. "People often don't believe bad things will happen to them. They overestimate their own abilities and expertise, or they think they won't be targeted for whatever reason. Cemeteries are full of people who were convinced nothing bad would happen to them."

"I guess." T.J. grabbed her chair, wheeled it near mine, and sat. "Social media manager?"

"Yeah. Private. She had a few clients. The cops don't yet know who they were."

"She's probably popular herself."

"By follower counts, she is," I said.

"We should take a look."

We started with her Instagram. "People her age aren't big on Facebook anymore," I explained to T.J. as our script scraped her account for photos and posts.

"You really have your finger on the pulse of the youth," she said.

Even though she meant it sarcastically, I inclined my head and offered my thanks. "It's true, though. I can't keep track of what generation everyone is supposed to be, but there are definitely divides when it comes to social media platforms of choice."

"Okay, boomer."

"You're fired."

"Don't you want your afternoon coffee?"

"I do," I said. "Fine . . . you're rehired."

By the time she carried two mugs of coffee back to the desk, the script finished, and we had a virtual mountain of photos to comb through. "I can't imagine living my life so online," I said as I took in the sheer number.

"Is this a spot where I can say, 'Okay, boomer' again?" T.J. wondered.

I grinned. "I'll allow it."

My first major improvement to my script—and something I should have included from the beginning—was the ability to sort and filter based on hashtags. I got rid of all the food-based posts and accompanying photos immediately. Apparently, April subsisted on sushi, paninis, and lattes. I could think of worse diets.

"We don't know when she met the killer," I said, "so it's hard to eliminate a bunch of dates. Let's confine our initial search to a week before the first murder." T.J. bobbed her head, and a few mouse clicks later, I narrowed the results further. Quite a few snapshots—and April's commentary about them—still remained, but we now faced a more reasonable number. T.J. jotted down the names of any men identified. It was a good move even though I figured it would be unlikely to pay off. Sometimes, low percentage plays hit.

After a while, we got to the day in question. The last day of April Mooney's life. At eight fifty-five, she posted a picture of herself sitting on one of the benches just past the park's snowy grass. She wore the coat we would later see ruined by slash marks and blood along with a wool cap. Her smile was bright and hopeful, and in this moment, I felt terrible for her. The caption read, *Braving the elements to meet someone new. Sometimes, you have to take a chance!*

"There are a few more," T.J. said, "but she's the only person in them."

"Let's look anyway."

We did. April snapped a new photo every few minutes. Once the hour crossed nine, her date officially became late, though a post a few minutes later mentioned he'd texted and said the weather delayed him slightly. T.J. grabbed the mouse and clicked on the arrow in the right side of the window to advance. A vehicle drove by behind April. It looked like a minivan. T.J. advanced the picture again. I closed my eyes and remembered seeing a similar vehicle in the recent past.

But where? "Boss?" she asked. I ignored her and focused on remembering. Manny called up to the office and said someone waited for me downstairs. Adrian Brown arrived, and a gray minivan with dark red lettering—a taxi specifically engineered to transport people in wheelchairs—idled outside. The identical vehicle or another from the same company came the second time, too.

"Go back one," I said.

She did. I leaned in to look closer at the vehicle. Dark gray. Red lettering. We couldn't read it, but this time, the motion of the van and pixellation of the photo were the culprits. I pointed at the screen. "I've seen this van before."

"Where?"

"Here. Twice."

T.J. spread her hands. "You want to clue me in?"

"Soon," I said. "We need to figure a few more things out first . . . but we might have a suspect."

CHAPTER 24

A FEW MINUTES after my discovery, two sets of footsteps came up the stairs. I wondered if another pair of goons would be paying us a visit. Opening the top left drawer of my desk, I pulled my 9MM out just as the door opened. Paul King and Rich walked in. I put the pistol down and closed the drawer. "Expecting someone else?" my cousin asked.

"I haven't donated to the policeman's ball yet this year," I said. "You never know how aggressive some collectors can be."

The two rolled their eyes in unison and then followed their noses to the coffee pot. While both cops were busy at the java station, T.J. leaned in and whispered, "Are we telling them about whatever it is you discovered?"

"Not yet."

"Are you going to tell me?"

"Soon," I promised. Her expression—which suggested she'd recently taken up a radical all-lemon diet—did not convey a positive reaction to my news.

"What are you two whispering about?" King asked as he approached the desk.

"T.J. wants to start a fashion blog," I said. "I'm encouraging her to wait for a couple better specimens to write about."

"My closet is an open book."

"Christ, what a thought."

"We came here," Rich said, focusing the conversation back to business, "because we made a discovery."

T.J. rammed the side of her fist into my leg under the table. I ignored it. "The kind to give you a suspect?" I asked.

"Not directly. It might lead to one."

"What is it?"

"All three of the dead women used the same local dating service," King said. "It's one of the older-school matchmaker types, but they say they've embraced algorithms in the digital age or whatever. They all sound the same to me. There's an app, but it's supposed to only be for singles in Maryland."

"Did our dead women all swipe on the same guy?"

"We don't know. The owner of the company lawyered up and said we needed a warrant."

"So get one," I said.

Rich shook his head. "Judge won't sign it."

"Why not? It's an obvious connection. Even if the service did nothing but pair people together, it's still something."

"He's a stickler for privacy. This company has thousands of user records from across the state. If we want access, we need to submit a data management plan covering how we'll filter our searches along with our means of secure disposal." He added scare quotes to the final four words.

"By themselves, those are reasonable concerns," I said, "but I don't get how they apply to three dead women."

"Neither do we." Rich chuckled. "I thought Sharpe was going to pick up the judge and snap him in two over a knee."

"I wish he would have," King muttered, sandy blond hair waving as he shook his head.

My cousin was about to say something, but his vibrating phone stopped him. He checked the screen. "The owner played ball a little. A tiny bit. Each woman eventually matched with and arranged to meet a different man. If we want the rest, we still need a warrant."

"If only you knew a smart and handsome hacker," I suggested. "Such a person, if given a few nuggets of information, could probably get the records from the company directly."

"How long would this theoretical individual need?" Rich said.

"Brilliant though he likely is, there's a fair bit of art mixed in with the science. Thirty minutes . . . maybe forty-five."

"Doesn't sound so smart to me," King said.

"Too bad you don't know him." I shrugged. "You might even glean some fashion tips."

"King, let's go get some dinner for everyone," Rich said.

"You buying?"

"Sure."

"I'm in." The sergeant stood even before my cousin did.

"We'll walk," Rich told him. "Plenty of places nearby are open. By the time we get there, order, wait, and come back, I guess we'll be at least a half hour. Maybe even forty-five minutes."

"A lot could happen," I said.

"It fucking well better," King said as the two headed for the door. "It's cold out."

"Thirty to forty-five minutes isn't a ton of time," T.J. said once Rich and King's footsteps clanged down the metal stairs.

"I guess we'd better get going, then." I made a show of

cracking my knuckles and reviewing the sparse information the cops had assembled on the firm in question. Old Line Love—drawing on Maryland's state nickname allegedly traced back to the time of George Washington—promised to pair singles using a "proprietary mix of algorithms and good old-fashioned matchmaking." I figured the word "proprietary" was being asked to expand its duties, but the agency's methodology was not why we were interested.

To see how we might be able to get in, I brought up the general interest form. It asked the usual questions about basic personal details. A key way to prevent many attacks is to sanitize inputs. This prevents someone from entering a string of code into the phone number field, for instance, because the system will reject the alphabetic characters. Most systems had a little more going on under the hood to turn what the users entered into regular expressions and strip out any attempts to add code.

Old Line Love needed to get with the new times.

Their form accepted a string of numbers in the place of my last name as well as a mixed alphanumeric set for a phone number. "I can't believe no one's wrecked them already," I said.

"Maybe their app is more secure," T.J. said. "I imagine that's how most people sign up these days. Only old people use computers."

"I use computers."

She smiled sweetly. "Yes, you do."

"I'm going to mix a pink slip in with your Christmas bonus," I said, "which is dwindling by the day."

She pointed to the screen. "I'm going to guess you'll go with an injection attack?"

"Yes."

"You think we'll be able to gain access?"

"Yes." I used a different browser to bring the intake form up again and then double-checked my anonymizer and proxy connections. All good.

"This won't be attributable to us, will it?"

"There's no need to be insulting," I said.

"I've already called you old," my assistant said. "Might as well make sure you remember how to do things."

"I got it." The injection attack would use SQL database code to gain access to the back-end system. From there, I could find any number of data points, including ways to gain full admin access to the system. I prepped my code, submitted the form, and got the window I expected. "We're in."

"What are you going to do now?"

"Export their tables," I said. "We don't know if they have some kind of intrusion detection system. If they do, it might close the connection. Let's at least get some data first." I used SQL commands to explore the database, found what I wanted, and exported it to an anonymous cloud storage account. Nothing kicked us off, so I hunted around some more. Another table mapped names of users to their submitted photos. I dumped this one, as well. So far, I'd gotten the customer base, match details, and pictures. This was probably enough, and I didn't want to expose us—and the investigation—to unnecessary risk. I covered my tracks and closed the connection.

"Now what?" T.J. wanted to know, leaning closer to my monitor.

"Now, we go through everything and see what they had."

She checked her watch. "Twenty-five minutes. Not bad for an old-timer."

"The things I could put in your letter of recommendation . . ."

"There's another boomer term. No one writes letters anymore."

"This is why no one likes your generation," I said as I poked around what we'd taken from Old Line Love. Data fields were searchable, so I queried for our three victims and got results almost right away.

"Here we go," T.J. said.

"This is our first real connection between these women," I said. "It took a long time, but we finally have one." Each matched with over a dozen men. I didn't know if this consisted of both sides expressing interest or only one. We didn't get a dump of any messages exchanged on the site or in the app, but there was a *Yes/No* column which indicated whether the internal communications happened. This allowed me to select only the men each woman used the app to talk to. I met Gloria before I needed to explore online dating, but my understanding was the conversation would eventually move off the platform via texts or something like WhatsApp.

We looked at each of the men. None matched with all three women, so there went one easy potential marker for our killer. We checked out all the potential suitors in turn. The first was a handsome chap of about thirty. He wore a popular branded sweater, smiled, and ran a hand through his brown hair. I felt certain I'd seen the same image in an ad somewhere. A reverse image search yielded a close match: the photo had been swapped left to right but otherwise unaltered. I made a note of this.

"Who knew my Tommy Hilfiger catalog collection would pay off?" I said. T.J. rolled her eyes.

A few others struck me as being used elsewhere. As before, each got tweaked or modified in some way. The tie went from blue to green in one, an arm position changed in another, and so on. I pointed at one which took the model's arm from straight to bent and also added a sixth finger to his hand in the process. "Still an AI tell," I explained to T.J. "The tools aren't good at rendering hands properly."

"Maybe he really has six fingers," she said.

"Like Inigo Montoya, we now search for the six-fingered man." She blinked at me. "*The Princess Bride?*" She shook her head. "Really?"

"Never seen it."

"It's your homework over the holidays, then."

I compiled everything into a Word file and made it easy for the police to follow along. All the men listed redheads in their preferences, and the age ranges they chose included our three victims. "How many of these profiles do you think are legit?" T.J. wondered.

"I'd be surprised if any were," I said. "My guess is the killer created them all. Casting as wide a net as he can. Look at the photos. Different hair colors. He's varied the fashion choices. Some are listed as taller than others. I think he wanted to make sure one identity in his arsenal would work."

"Sounds like he did."

Footsteps pounded up the steps, and Rich and King walked in a moment later. Each carried a bag of food. I could smell the burgers from where I sat. "We went to The Abbey," my cousin said.

"Welcome, then," I said. "Let's eat. We've got something."

———

I saved and printed my document as Rich laid out the food. He knew my preferences from The Abbey—we'd eaten together at both the Federal Hill and Fells Point locations enough times—to bring back a Santa Fe burger. The pair got T.J. a basic model which she happily accepted. They also brought plenty of fries and onion rings to go around. T.J. grabbed bottles of water from the fridge.

"What do you have?" Rich asked after his first bite.

"Hunger pangs and the means to sate them," I said.

He sighed around his food and didn't bother to finish chewing before answering. "I meant about the case."

"Check the printer."

Rich jerked his head toward it. "King, get the papers."

King spread his hands, finished his fries, and then must have realized no one else would be getting up. He stood, fetched the papers, and slapped them down in front of Rich. "I'm not reprinting for grease stains," I said. "Some of us are watching our carbon footprints."

"What do we have here?" Rich barked, ignoring my comment.

I took it from the top while T.J. chowed down. "Basically, those are the men our three victims matched with and used the app's messaging feature. You'll notice none of them are common to all the women. The photos are all modified or AI-enhanced in some way. Probably just enough to fool any system looking at popular stock photo repositories to cut down on fake profiles."

"You think these are all fake?"

"Hundred percent. I'll go even further and say the same person made them all to cover as many bases as possible and try to meet several different women."

"So he could kill them," King added. "Sick bastard."

"You know who it is?" Rich asked.

"No," I said.

"Don't bullshit me on this."

"I'm not. There's no way to attribute those names to a real person."

"What about their email addresses?"

"Temporary. Plenty of places to get throwaways."

"You have someone in mind," he said and not in the form of a question.

"I'm considering a person, yes," I admitted.

"Who?"

"I'll let you know when I have more."

"He hasn't even told me," T.J. said.

"You're putting more women in danger," King said.

I snorted. "The hell I am. When does this guy commit murder?"

"When there's a heavy snow."

I shook my head. "When one specific newspaper predicts a heavy snow . . . and is usually the only one to get it right."

"And?"

"Nothing in their forecast the next few nights."

"We're not endangering anyone," T.J. said. I wondered when she threw her weight behind my obfuscation efforts, but it was nice to have her on board.

Rich grunted. "I want updates. If your suspicion turns into something, you'd better damn well let me know."

"I will. Your medallion display needs to stay full, after all."

He snorted but didn't take the bait. We all finished devouring burgers and sides. No one wanted to leave any fried food uneaten. In the end, we only threw away crumbs and greasy paper towels. Rich washed his hands in the bathroom sink and collected the printouts. "Remember . . . you're letting us know when you have a suspect."

"I love the implication you won't come up with him yourselves," I said. "I might need to use it on my business cards. 'Endorsed by the police to be smarter than they are.'"

The two cops offered uncharitable replies and left. Once their footsteps fell silent and an engine fired to life outside, T.J. asked, "So . . . who is it?"

"Adrian Brown."

"The editor?"

"Yes."

"The guy in the wheelchair?"

"The same," I said.

"*He's* your suspect?"

"You think he can't murder people because he's disabled? I thought your generation was all about inclusion . . . even more than mine."

She snickered. "I guess I have a hard time seeing it."

"I get it, but I'm right. He's the guy."

"Now we get to prove it?" she asked.

I nodded. "Now, we get to prove it."

CHAPTER 25

WHILE C.T. CALLED Gloria to tell her he'd be working late, T.J. tried to make sense of Adrian Brown as a killer.

Few people would suspect a man in a wheelchair. Society conditioned everyone to believe the disabled truly were incapable of much. In reality, many could do a wide range of things. She thought about the crime scenes. The women were all found near walking trails which would allow Brown's wheelchair access to the area. Snow would fill in its tracks exactly like any footprints.

The challenge would be getting around.

Brown couldn't take his own car. T.J. searched the state database and found he had an official Maryland ID but not a driver's license. He always arrived in minivan taxis specifically designed for wheelchair accessibility. It was what C.T. saw when the Brown idea popped into his head. Would anyone who happened to be out and about early in a blizzard be more likely to remember a minivan taxi?

"Penny for your thoughts," her boss said.

"My bonus had better be significantly higher," T.J. said.

"I think I can manage."

"I'm trying to wrap my head around Brown being the

killer. I'm sure he's relying on this to coast under the radar. People won't take him seriously as a suspect because they see him as handicapped."

"Exactly. Are you working on anything in particular?"

"A couple ideas," T.J. said.

"All right," C.T. said as he returned to his own desk. "Let me know if you come up with something. I'll be doing the same."

"You got it, boss." T.J. dove into Brown's column archive with the *Carroll County Herald.* Prior to the Kirsten Valle case, his byline appeared infrequently. This made sense—he'd said he was an editor, and editors tended to work behind the scenes. An acquisition and cutbacks allegedly pushed him out of the newsroom and back to the laptop for the murder investigation. It was certainly a ballsy move to cover a series of homicides he'd committed himself.

Brown's initial piece following the murder of Kirsten Valle hinted at this. *From the paper's perspective, we want to cover this until it's no longer in the news. We'll demand accountability from the police if the investigation lags. If there's an arrest, and the case goes to court, the Herald will be there, too. I'll be heading out of the newsroom to lead the coverage myself. It's been a while since I've been in the field—and even longer since I visited Baltimore—but the death of one of our own makes certain demands of us.*

Brown managed to make his assignment—which he could have lobbied for—sound like a mix of obligation and woe-is-me. T.J. wondered if he'd really been in Baltimore beforehand. If he was the killer, he obviously needed to be in the city . . . and a stone's throw from her apartment. The recollection of Kirsten Valle getting stabbed to death across the street from The 501 made T.J. shudder.

Taking a taxi all the way from Carroll County was infeasible. Brown needed to be in the city already. Arranging transport to and from his hotel would be much easier. T.J. frowned. If Brown asked a driver to drop him off and pick him up at what turned out to be a murder scene, whoever was behind the wheel would remember and probably turn him in. He must have set things up to be a couple blocks away. In the area but not at the scene itself. Even this played on people's impressions of the disabled. Maybe the drivers dismissed any thoughts of their incidental involvement because they couldn't envision Brown wheeling himself a few hundred yards in each direction.

"I have a couple ideas," T.J. said.

"Go ahead," C.T. told her.

"You mentioned the taxi company being the same. I wonder if Brown got the same driver each time, too. Either by accident or request. Either way, whoever drove him might remember something."

"I've thought of the same thing."

"Did you also consider," T.J. said, "the driver would remember dropping him off and picking him up at murder scenes?"

C.T. smiled. "I did. I figure he arranged his dropoff and pickup points to be a few blocks away."

"We should follow up with the company."

"It's late. Let's do it tomorrow. Better odds of reaching someone competent."

"All right. I'm also looking into Brown himself. It's certainly an interesting choice to cover a series of murders you committed."

"It is," C.T. said.

"In his first column, Brown establishes that he hasn't been to Baltimore in years."

"Obviously a lie. He needed to kill Kirsten Valle if nothing else."

"Right," T.J. said.

"So let's catch him in his lie," C.T. said.

T.J. grinned and looked at her screen again. "Yeah. Let's."

———

T.J. started by focusing on Adrian Brown's social media accounts.

He maintained some in his own name but didn't use them often. More commonly, the *Herald*'s posts talked about his articles and columns, and one could assume Brown wrote the short snippets himself. Still, she excluded anything they couldn't tie explicitly to Brown himself. T.J. frowned at the results. "Does the script do anything more than just pull posts?" she asked.

"Like what?"

"What if he got tagged in something?"

"You can select it," C.T. said. "Just add a slash-T to the end of the string."

She appended the characters her boss mentioned and ran the script again. This time, many more results filled the screen. Brown may have only posted infrequently himself, but his friends and coworkers tagged him pretty often. For what seemed like a small paper, the staffers of the *Herald* enjoyed regular nights on the town, and Brown came along on many of the excursions.

T.J. noticed he rarely looked happy in the photos. He smiled in some, but the expression rarely reached his eyes. Maybe he was just an unhappy person. She didn't want to speculate that living in a wheelchair caused him to feel isolated—even though his peers had no trouble including him in many things—but it was an easy conclusion to reach. T.J. kept scrolling through the tagged posts until she found one which caught her eye.

"I might have something," she said, and C.T. walked close to stand beside her chair.

"Show me."

"Here's a collection of photos." She added each to a slideshow. Brown appeared with several different people, many of whom were not in the pictures of his coworkers. "The script doesn't tell us, but my guess is Brown removed the tags. Everyone else is identified." She closed the chosen snapshots and opened one more. "Here's the only one he overlooked. It must have been added recently."

T.J. and C.T. both looked at the caption, location, and embedded date. *Catching up with old friends at the Rural Journalists Convention!* The event took place at the convention center in downtown Baltimore, and the date on the photo put it two nights before Kirsten Valle died. "He said he hadn't been to Baltimore in quite some time," T.J. pointed out.

"It seems Mister Brown is a liar."

"There are more photos from the next day, too. He stuck around."

C.T. returned to his own desk. A moment later, he said, "The *Herald* pegged the heavy snowfall the day before it happened. No one else called for more than a couple inches."

"You're right." T.J. looked at the picture on her screen of a dour Brown surrounded by happier colleagues. "He's the killer."

"We'll need more than a script and some social media tagging," C.T. said. "This is a good start."

"How are we going to convince the cops?"

"We can present what we have, but my guess is Rich will want more."

"What's our alternative?" T.J. wanted to know.

"We can set a trap for Brown."

"When's it supposed to snow again?"

"I don't know," C.T. said. "But we have the app he uses to meet the women he kills. It wouldn't be hard to plant a few fake profiles of our own."

"I'm in."

"Let's not get ahead of ourselves. I appreciate your willingness to go in the line of fire, but it shouldn't be our first option."

"I want to get this son of a bitch," T.J. said.

"We'll get him."

———

Shortly after their discovery, C.T. and T.J. called it a night. It was almost nine o'clock, and both of them were tired. It felt like three days before, but it had only been in the morning when C.T. swung by to pick up T.J. and take her to the latest murder scene. She sat silently and watched the city roll by on the drive back to The 501. Road crews got the snow off the streets as best they could. It sat piled up near the curbs, blocking a few cars in completely and often eliminating at least one lane of traffic. Driving would be more interesting until temperatures warmed and the snow melted.

C.T. stopped in front of the building. "See you tomorrow," T.J. said as she hopped out. Her boss wished her a good night. As usual, he didn't drive away until she was safely inside the main door. T.J. unlocked her apartment, closed the door, and flopped on the couch. She felt more tired than if she'd run five miles. At least they'd finally made some progress on Adrian Brown.

The cops would definitely want more, and T.J. felt confident she and C.T. could deliver. Tomorrow, they could talk to the cab company and get the driver to confirm some details. The police needed to present a case to the state's attorney's office, so if a lawyer didn't sign off on it, there wouldn't be a path forward. It proved frustrating when they'd done good work. C.T. sometimes colored outside the lines when it came to legality and techniques, but everyone took care to make sure they could also get evidence via legitimate means.

When T.J. first met C.T., she tried to help him solve the case of another young prostitute who'd gone missing. Libby would eventually turn up dead, but it wasn't for a lack of trying on anyone's part. T.J., recently eighteen then, wanted out of her hazardous occupation, and Melinda offered her a lifeline. When someone needed to sniff out one of the men behind the disappearance and murder of Libby, T.J. never hesitated. She went in knowing she'd be bait and might be on her own if things went wrong.

She wondered if this case would require something similar.

If the police didn't want to take what they had to the state's attorney, then tactics would shift to trapping Brown the next time his paper called for a heavy snowfall. This had been the worst winter in more than a decade, and it wasn't even Christmas yet. The solstice hadn't even happened, so all this precipitation technically fell in late fall. What if no other major snowfall came? The idea of letting Brown off the hook because the weather changed made T.J. feel nauseated.

"We'll get you, you bastard," she said to her empty apartment.

She wondered what Melinda would think of her willingness to go into danger again. The first time, Melinda tried to forbid it, but T.J. wanted to help her friend, and she was eighteen. Now, she wanted to help the three victims, and she was over twenty-one. Melinda would object again because she would always feel protective of the young women who moved through the Nightlight Foundation.

If the opportunity arose to go undercover and try to prove Adrian Brown's guilt, T.J. would take it.

If it hadn't been late—and if she weren't already so tired—she might have capitalized on her aggressive thoughts with a heavy bag session. Instead, she changed into pajamas and got ready for bed. She would need to be awake and alert to catch Brown whatever the method used, and T.J. was determined to see him go down for what he'd done.

CHAPTER 26

THANKS to the lingering snow and cold, I eschewed a morning run.

After dropping T.J. at her apartment, I'd driven back to Gloria's house. The weather provided a convenient excuse, but I didn't like staying multiple nights in a row in Brooklandville. Gloria tabled the idea of me selling my house a while ago, but I didn't want the subject to come up again. Once conditions improved, we would need to get back on our alternating schedule.

This morning, I used Gloria's exercise bike. It didn't provide the satisfaction of a good run—or a nice ride on a bike which actually moved—but it got the heart pumping and blood flowing. As I was getting dressed, T.J. texted and said she'd be ok to drive herself in. I whipped up a quick breakfast. Gloria kissed me goodbye and took her plate to the upstairs office. I smushed my toast, eggs, and bacon into a sandwich and hit the road.

"We should talk to the taxi company today," T.J. said as soon as I set my bag down. She wore an ugly reindeer-forward Christmas sweater which lived up to its designation with room to spare. I felt bad for whatever sweatshop workers toiled away stitching the monstrosity together.

"Good morning to you, too."

"Good morning. We should talk to the taxi company today."

"All in good time," I said as I prepared a cup of coffee. "The police don't know our theory. I want to see if they've come up with anything on their own."

"You think they have?"

I shrugged and sat back down. "It depends if the dating company decided to play ball yet."

"Do we still have our in?"

"We should. I thought about sending them some snarky email about vulnerabilities. The timing would have been weird, though, and I didn't want anything to blow black on the investigation."

"Probably best you showed a rare level of self-restraint," T.J. said.

"It's all the extra maturity I get for being thirty-three," I said. "I'm going to start eating prunes at this rate."

My contemplations on aging and mortality got interrupted by my buzzing cell phone. Rich called. "The dating company is going to play ball." Road noise intruded on the call.

"Good."

"We're going to work with them later today," he said. "I'm on my way in now."

"You're late, then. What happened? Your Tuesday suit didn't come back from the cleaners in time?"

"Some days, even I get to sleep in a little." Rich ended the call.

"The cops are going to start getting some info from the matchmakers," I told T.J.

"What do you think they'll learn?"

"I don't know. It probably depends what questions they ask. Even cooperating companies tend to punt things to their lawyers, and those bastards always define compliance narrowly."

"Sounds like we still have a chance to shine," she said.

"Might as well take it. Let's get back to our data." While my assistant wheeled her chair closer, I brought up our data dump of Old Line Love's client information and matchmaking efforts.

"How much more do you think we'll find?" T.J. asked.

"I'm not sure." I glanced at the trove of information. We could probably glean a lot from it by using the right queries. "I'm going to be cynical for a minute here. Most companies today are in the data business. It doesn't matter what else they claim to be doing. Their most valuable asset is the information they collect and store about their users and customers. It's why they try to protect it . . . and why breaches can be so damaging."

"What does this get us?"

I gestured to my screen. "We don't know what Old Line Love is doing with all this. My guess is they're monetizing it in some way already. Tracking cookies, targeted ads . . . the usual. If I were to guess further, I'd say they're positioning themselves to get acquired by one of the larger players in the space."

"This bigger company would be interested in the data?"

"Right. And all the potential extra revenue streams each person brings."

"I guess I get your cynicism here," she said, "but what does it mean for us looking through everything?"

"It means they'll want to keep as much on the platform as possible. It's why they have messaging built in even in an era where everyone texts and uses something like Signal or WhatsApp. All those messages are more information to mine and harvest. It got me wondering what else they're tracking." I checked the profiles of the men we believed to be Adrian Brown. We scanned the messages he sent to each of his matches.

"Looks like he had a few irons in the fire," T.J. said.

I noticed a field marked *Scheduled Meet*. On the evening of Kirsten Valle's murder, each of Adrian Brown's three aliases scheduled initial meetups with three different women. "Look at this." I pointed at the screen. "Brown was covering all the bases."

"You think he booked three in case two bailed because of the snow?"

"Seems likely." I went back to the communications module and found one such message from a woman named Leigh David. *It's snowing to beat hell as my parents used to say. Rain check?* No response came from Brown's alias. Leigh David remained alive thanks to her unwillingness to meet a stranger in the snow. I wondered if she thought about it.

"Those other women really dodged a bullet," T.J. said. "Shit like that would keep me up at night."

"Let's keep going, then," I said. "No one else needs to have nightmares because of Adrian Brown."

———

T.J. interrupted our deep dive of Old Line Love to remind me about the cab company.

"We want to get to him while he's not busy," she said. "Right now, it's between morning rush hour and lunch."

It was ten-twenty-five to be precise, and my assistant had a point. The challenge was knowing which company to call.

None of the images of the cab produced a still where we could read the lettering. None except Manny's. A while ago, I helped him install a security system at the property and offered to manage it. He was happy to offload the work to someone who knew what he was doing, and in turn, I wanted the footage when goons rolled up. And occasionally for identifying things like a cab in question.

A couple minutes later, I got an answer. We called the very Baltimore named Crabcake Cab Company. A man answered quickly and encouraged us to use the online reservation system. "I don't want to get a taxi," I said.

Before I could explain why I called, he launched into a brief tirade. "What are you doing, then? We're a cab company. We don't sell crab cakes. You want those—"

"We can discuss the name you chose another time. I'm investigating a murder, and I need to talk to one of your drivers."

"You police?"

"Private investigator."

"I don't need to talk to you, then, do I?"

"I don't have time for your shit," I said. "If you don't want to talk to me, I'll harass every city and state agency I can think of. Anyone who might have the smallest shred of oversight for your operation. You'll have audits and compliance requests coming out of your ears . . . and on top of it all, I'll bring the actual police with me."

"All right, all right." The combative tone left his voice. "A murder certainly sounds serious."

I summoned my professionalism to avoid a tirade of my own. "It's multiple murders, actually. Before there's more, we need to talk to one of your drivers."

"You know who it was?"

"No, but I'll give you the vehicle number, dates, and

times. It would be one of your minivan models equipped for wheelchair access." I provided the information relevant regarding all three rides associated with the murders.

"Gimme a minute." Loud tapping on a mechanical keyboard filled the line. "Same guy every time. We like to put him on the handicapped taxis when we can. Hafiz."

"Last night, from the cypress branch, the nightingale sang," I said.

"What?"

"Hafiz. The Persian poet."

"Different guy," the cab company man said.

"I should hope so. The poet died over six hundred years ago."

"Could you arrange for us to talk to Hafiz?" T.J. broke in.

"I'll have him call you. Is this a good number?"

I confirmed it was, and he hung up. "Really?" my secretary said. "A long-dead Iranian poet?"

"Persian," I said. "Iran didn't exist back then."

"Sometimes, I'm amazed you get people to cooperate."

"It helps if I'm speaking to a fellow lover of the arts. This guy was not."

The phone rang a moment later, and I answered it on speaker. "This is Hafiz," the caller said in a light Middle Eastern accent. "Lou told me you needed some information."

"Don't you dare mention poetry," T.J. whispered.

"Thanks for calling us," I said. "We're investigating the recent murders in Baltimore."

"You cops?"

"Private."

"All right."

I guessed we passed some sort of test, but I didn't push it. "The guy we spoke to told us you were the driver for all three of these." I gave him the first date. "The actual murder happened in Saint Mary's Park, but the man you drove may have asked you to drop him off somewhere else."

"He did," Hafiz confirmed. "A coffee shop a couple blocks away."

"What happened after he got out?" T.J. asked.

"He waited by the door. It was already snowing, and I didn't want to sit alongside the road. He'd already scheduled a flexible return ride . . . meaning the time isn't set. I drove away to somewhere I wouldn't be sitting along the side of a snow route."

"And you then went back and picked Mister Brown up?" I wanted to know.

"Yeah. It was maybe forty-five minutes later. He was outside the same place."

"How did he seem?"

"Fine, I guess," Hafiz said.

"Did he say anything?"

"He never really talked much. I asked him how it went. He said he met a woman, and they talked but probably wouldn't see each other again."

"Yes," I said, "because he stabbed her to death."

Hafiz sighed. "I can't believe he would do those things. Mister Brown was always quiet. I don't think I would call him nice, but he was nice enough."

"It's all part of his act," T.J. said. She provided the date of Bernadette Holmes' slaying. "This one happened on the east side of Patterson Park."

"Same thing," the driver said. "I dropped him off and picked him up a couple blocks away. It was why I never thought much about what happened. Lots of people could have been in the area around the time someone died, you know?"

"Sure," I said to be agreeable. Hafiz probably felt terrible about the inadvertent role he'd played in what happened, and I didn't begrudge him his attempts to cope with it. "Let's talk about the last one. This one was a little more challenging because of the location." I provided him the date and time. "Eager Park."

"This one was a little different. There are some houses a block or two past the park. Mister Brown told me he was interviewing someone in there, and I should come back in about forty-five minutes. When I let him out, he was wheeling himself toward someone's home."

"Once you left, he went to the park. Did you pick him back up at the same spot?"

"More or less. I think he'd gone to the end of the street when I pulled up. I didn't think anything of it at the time."

"He never gave any kind of a hint what he'd been doing?"

"No," Hafiz said. "I got the idea Mister Brown was trying to meet women. He pretty much told me the first time. There was the interview story for the third one." I noticed he called it the third and not the last. T.J. and I—along with the BPD—would do our collective best to make the two synonymous.

"Does he carry anything with him?" I said.

"A messenger bag. Nothing unusual." Hafiz was right, but it could certainly hold things like a Taser and knife while appearing to be an easy way to transport mundane things like a laptop.

"How often do you drive this guy around?" my assistant asked.

"Probably a few times a week. It's been many more than just the three you told me about. I guess there's another reason I never really put it together." Hafiz paused. "What do I do if Mister Brown books another ride?"

"Take him like you normally would," I said. "His killing

spree needs specific conditions. You've probably noticed they were all times of heavy snow."

"Yes."

"If we have another one, and he wants you to take him somewhere, do it."

"Won't I be putting someone in danger?"

"Not this time. We're on it, and the police are figuring it out, too. The important thing is for Brown not to think something is wrong. Can you treat his future rides like they're perfectly normal, Hafiz?"

"I think so," he said.

"Good. You'll be an important part in resolving this if you can."

"I'll do my best." More strength filled his voice now. "You have my word."

"Thanks," I said, and we rang off. "Poor guy."

"Now, we know," T.J. said. "I hope he can keep it together the next time Brown wants to go to a grocery store."

"I think he'll be all right. Let's keep digging. Maybe we can nudge the BPD into taking action soon."

Further digging showed a pattern to the male profiles.

"They've all been established for a few months," I said. T.J. leaned closer and looked at the data on my screen. "Inactive for the most part. Once the bad weather hit, Brown started using them."

"Why would he leave them dormant?"

"I've never used a dating app. My guess is he didn't want the accounts to look like they'd just been created."

"Can the other person see stuff like that?" T.J. asked.

I shrugged. "No idea. Maybe assholes create profiles and spam women with them."

"It wouldn't surprise me. You have no idea what it's like to be female online."

"I definitely don't," I agreed.

"I guess it makes sense if his matches could see how long his accounts had been around." She paused and frowned. "Do we know how many people he tried to match with?"

"I think I can retrieve it." It took a little massaging of the database, but I got it to show us the number of people Adrian Brown in his various guises expressed interest in. "The majority didn't get reciprocated. It makes sense. Men outnumber women on the platform, even adjusting for someone like Brown and his many accounts." For each successful pairing, three more went unanswered by the ladies. I clicked on a few. All were redheads. All were pretty.

"He clearly has a type," T.J. said.

"But why?"

"A woman with red hair left him at the altar?"

"I suppose people have murdered for less," I said. "Seems like a small thing to become a serial killer over."

"Did his profiles specify a hair color?"

"No." I pulled one up. The chap in the photos was handsome, didn't look much like Adrian Brown, and was standing in a couple of the photos. "I wonder if him showing up in a wheelchair was a deal-breaker. When the women didn't want to go out with him again, he killed them."

"Maybe," my assistant said. I heard a tone in her voice. The question of why was a good one. These weren't random slayings—Brown absolutely had a type, and there must have been a reason for it. In my days as a lone wolf private eye, I would have done the research myself, and I was tempted to even today. Instead, I knew T.J. would do it. Her curiosity would force her to. All I needed to do was give her the space to get it done.

"You can see in the profile it doesn't offer a spot for things like hair color preference. Age, gender, religion, and location look like the big factors. I guess you can tell most of the physical details by looking at someone's photos."

"If they're accurate."

"True," I said.

Rich called while T.J. and I went through Brown's accounts. "We have the data from Old Line Love," he told me. "Our tech team and King are going through it all now."

"Glad you're finally catching up."

"We need to be able to do this legitimately. It's got to hold up for warrants and judges."

"I know," I said. "T.J. and I will be snickering at how far behind you are for a while, though." My assistant smiled and pulled out her phone. I got the feeling she'd be doing research into the life of Adrian Brown.

"Save the chuckles. We're going to take a deep dive through all of this. Let's sync up later today. Maybe we'll have enough to take to a prosecutor."

"Maybe." We arranged to go to police headquarters in the afternoon. Once Rich hung up, I went back to the list of accounts. "I wonder if he used any kind of anonymization. Like a VPN or some other way to mask the real source of his traffic."

"You think Brown is that savvy?" T.J. wanted to know.

"Maybe. He also might not need to be. If he has a friend who is, it's good enough. Hell, his paper could have a smart tech reporter."

"Seems unlikely."

"They have the best weather forecasts in the state somehow," I said. "It's possible." I ran a few more queries. "Look.

Each account shows a different IP address at the time of registration. We're pretty sure they're all Brown, so unless he has nine different internet providers, he's doing some shenanigans behind the scenes."

"Shenanigans?" T.J. asked with a grin.

"It's a very technical term. They only teach it to graduate-level computer science students."

"I'm sure the police can use it."

"I'm not sure they could spell it," I said. "We need to find as much as we can. Can't count on them to discover everything we do."

T.J. and I got back to work. I noted the knowing smirk on her face and realized she'd have whatever else we needed.

———

At the end of the workday, T.J. and I drove to police headquarters.

She paused and sighed as we approached the building. "I'm not sure I'll ever get used to coming here," she said, "but it's so much better to do it on my own terms."

"I'm basically in the same boat." We headed up the elevator and stepped off into the homicide bullpen. Paul King jerked his head, and we all walked toward Leon Sharpe's office. The captain sat behind his large desk. Tall cherry bookshelves held the expected cargo plus an array of awards. Rich already occupied one of the guest chairs, and King snagged the second one. Despite being in a desirable corner location, Sharpe's office didn't boast much square footage. It was about the size of a third bedroom in a townhouse. T.J. and I standing made the room feel very full.

"Close the door," Sharpe said. I did, and it added to the claustrophobia. "We had people go over this shit all day. A bunch of men . . . or at least several different profiles . . . tried matching with all of them. They all exchanged messages and set initial meetings up in the app. The developer told us they encourage this for safety, especially for the women. Didn't seem like it helped much here." I stayed quiet. If this was all the information they'd gleaned from most of a day with Old Line's Love's records, we were in trouble.

"None of the male profiles are the same," King added after a few seconds of silence fell over the office. "I asked one of the techs to run all the pictures through a reverse image search. They're close enough to stock photos for us to think they've been downloaded and lightly edited."

"You came to these conclusions already," Rich said.

I nodded. "Yes."

"I could tell. You looked bored."

"I usually am when you talk."

He rolled his eyes. "Anyway, none of this gets us a concrete suspect. So, genius, any bright ideas there?"

"We have one, actually," T.J. said.

"Who?" Sharpe demanded.

"Adrian Brown," I told them.

"Who?"

"The Carroll County editor who's covering the case."

Sharpe snorted. "The cripple?"

"Just because he's a killer doesn't mean we should be politically incorrect," I said.

"Fuck him," the captain said, and I couldn't argue. "You really think he's the guy?"

"We do."

He leaned back and crossed his arms. "All right. Convince me. How does a guy who doesn't look very big or strong in a wheelchair murder three able-bodied women?"

"The Taser helps," I said. "We first thought it might be

the sign of a sadist, so we went down the rabbit hole of guys cited for abusing women."

"Long list, unfortunately," King observed.

"It is . . . and it also didn't give us a credible suspect. What we eventually realized was our killer could also use the Taser to overpower someone easily."

Rich nodded. "Even if Brown's stronger than the women, being in a wheelchair really limits him."

"Right," T.J. said. "If they fend him off for a second, they can run away a lot faster than he can chase them."

"And like Doctor Hunt observed," I added, "firing a Taser in windy, snowy conditions is a crapshoot. So he made sure to be at personal range with the women, used it like a stun gun, and once they were shocked, killing them was easy. They couldn't fight back anymore."

"The snow would hide his wheel marks," King noted, assembling pieces of the puzzle. "Just like footprints. Maybe easier because they're so narrow."

"Why go after these three women?" Sharpe wanted to know. "This guy . . . and let's say you're right, and we're talking about Adrian Brown . . . has targeted a specific type of woman."

"I looked into this," T.J. said. I knew she would. Once we identified Brown as our suspect, the missing piece was his motive. Sharpe was right—Brown selected pretty redheads within a certain age range. If T.J. hadn't looked it up, I would have, but I wanted to give her the space to take initiative on some things. "It goes back a while." She took out her phone and pulled up an article from sixteen years ago. "I'll send this to all of you, but the gist is Brown is going after women who look like the one who paralyzed him."

"Explain," Sharpe said.

"After he graduated college, Brown was in an accident.

The other driver was at fault. She ran a stop sign and plowed into him. While she was mostly okay, he suffered a spinal injury that left him paralyzed."

The captain nodded his large shaved head. "Sure, it's bad."

"Worse. Brown's passenger died. We don't have very much info on her, but she was a woman around his age. Probably a girlfriend."

"So why now?" Rich asked. "This all happened years ago."

T.J. had the answer ready. "At the trial, it came out she'd been drinking, her car inspection was overdue . . . just a mess all around. She got twenty-five years, and her record in jail wasn't going to see her get time lopped off for good behavior. Four months ago, though, she got out on compassionate release."

"Why?"

"Metastatic breast cancer. She died a month after going home."

"So this sick bastard couldn't get even with the actual woman who paralyzed him," King said, cutting to the chase as usual. "Instead, he sought women who looked like her and acted out some revenge fantasy."

"Basically," I said. The cops exchanged glances. "You think we have enough to throw him in jail? I volunteer to toss him in the cell, by the way. Especially if it's at the bottom of a long flight of stairs."

"Get in line." Sharpe's momentary amusement faded into a sigh. "I'll take it to the state's attorney, but I think they're going to tell us it's circumstantial." He put up a massive hand to stem any objections. "I know what you're going to say, and I agree. His history gives him motive. What we haven't done is conclusively tie him to any of the dating profiles. C.T., you can probably tell me the kind of tech he used, but let's be quick and dirty. Can we conclusively attribute any of those accounts to him?"

"No."

Sharpe spread his hands. "We're coming up on an election year. Let's not forget. People like the SA are going to be a little gun-shy. They don't want to get laughed out of court on a serial killer case. Pretty quick way to lose the public's trust."

"I hope no more women have to die in the name of someone's political ambitions," I said.

"If you want to try and set a trap for this asshole, I'm all for it," Sharpe said. "Based on what he's done so far, we'll need to wait for another snowstorm."

"One predicted by his newspaper," I added. "I have alerts set for it. If they come up with a big figure, I'll know about it, and we can set something up."

"Captain, you still need to plead our case," Rich said.

"I will," Sharpe said. "I'll do it tonight, in fact. Let's see where we stand in the morning."

I wasn't optimistic, which was par for the course when it came to this case.

CHAPTER 27

THE NEXT MORNING, T.J. and I drank coffee at our desks and waited for news from the cops.

"What do you think we're going to hear?" she asked.

I leaned back in my chair and kicked my feet up onto the desk. "If you set your expectations low, you'll rarely be disappointed."

"Sounds like you're pessimistic about it."

"I am," I said. "I think Sharpe is right on a lot of the points. We have no way to prove any of those accounts belong to Adrian Brown . . . certainly not to anything approaching a standard of reasonable doubt. He's not a registered Taser owner. The cops haven't recovered a murder weapon. There's also the fact people will tend to see him as less capable of murder because he's disabled. It's a lot to overcome. I can see the state's attorney's office passing on it until we have a lot more conclusive proof."

"You'd think this is the kind of case they'd want to take up." T.J. shook her head, and her blonde ponytail wagged. "Three women murdered. How do you pass on that?"

"By playing politics. If the current state's attorney wins re-election, maybe he'd be willing to take up the case then."

"How many more women will have died by that time?"

"If we have anything to do with it," I said, "zero."

"You still want to set a trap for Brown," T.J. said.

"Damn right I do. I think Sharpe and Rich will be on board with it to a point. We might get a little help from the BPD. If we don't, though, we'll figure out a way to make it work."

"Rich would probably help off the books."

"He'd grumble and moralize a little, but I think you're right." My phone buzzed, and I glanced at the screen. "Speak of the devil, and he shall call you." I picked it up. "What's the good word?"

"There's word," my cousin said, "but I don't know if I'd categorize it as good."

"The prosecution has cold feet?"

"Basically. Hard to blame him, really. As much as we might buy into it, we haven't exactly presented an airtight case."

"You met with the SA this morning?" I asked.

"Sharpe and I, yeah. I don't think I've ever heard one man say 'circumstantial' and 'how do I prove it to a jury?' so much in a single day." He snorted. "Sharpe predicted it. I hoped it wouldn't happen, but it did."

"The mills of justice will continue to grind while our prosecutors fret and plan for their next terms," I said.

"What do you have in mind?"

"We're going to catch Brown. If you want in, fine. We're going to trap him."

"You'll need someone as bait."

"I'll need three someones, actually. Remember, Brown hedged his bets in case anyone canceled."

"If you manage to put something together, let me know. I might want in when I'm off the clock."

"You know, you could use actual police to do this, too," I pointed out. "If only there were a convenient name for an operation where you tried to sting someone."

"We'll see," Rich said. "Sharpe might need to run it past the commissioner. He's been drubbed enough for one day."

"All right. I'll keep you in the loop." I ended the call and set my phone down with an exasperated sigh.

"Sounds like it went well," T.J. said with a smirk.

"They're accepting defeat too quickly. The cops could run a sting themselves."

"If they won't, we will."

"And we'll catch the bastard, too."

———

"This sucks," my assistant said, perfectly and succinctly recapping the morning.

"This coffee is the only good thing we have going." I'd just started my second cup here and third overall.

"We need a plan to take down Brown."

"I agree."

"Which means we need a few women lined up. I heard you tell Rich you needed three."

"At least," I said. "Brown seemed to narrow his choices to three each time."

She frowned and drummed her fingers on the desk. "He was working from a decent pool of candidates."

"And still would be. We know all about the ones his various accounts ended up matching with, however. We can also recognize his sock puppets. I think we could craft three profiles he might not be able to resist."

"We have to wait for the weather." T.J. frowned. "I hope

it snows again soon. Before Christmas at least. I don't want this case to drag into next year."

"It's supposed to be a harsh winter," I said, "and it's technically still fall for another eleven days or so." I checked the *Herald*'s website, and it promised a forecast update "based on the latest global models and our own proprietary projections" later tonight. The local news I watched last evening promised mild weather for the next five days. "Let's get people lined up just in case we need to act in a few days."

"You know I'm in," T.J. said. "I want to get that bastard. I want to toss him out of the chair and kick his ass."

"You could have been more receptive when I told you I wanted to push him down the stairs," I said.

"In my defense, we didn't think he was a murderer then."

"If I had, we'd be on to another case by now."

"Speaking of—"

"No. I indulged you once. If there's a long time until we can set our trap for Brown, I'll think about it. Otherwise, no. We're sticking with this one. Ride or die."

"Maybe we should talk to Jessie Valle," T.J. suggested.

I shrugged. "We could. She fired us, so I guess we'll see how important it is to get justice for her sister."

T.J. called our erstwhile client and handled the introductions. "You don't need to give me updates anymore," Jessie said. "A few more might have been nice while I was paying you, Mister Ferguson, but now that we've moved—"

"We identified a suspect," I broke in, having no desire to hear her screed.

She fell silent for a few seconds, and then in a small voice asked, "Really?"

"Yes."

"What happened? What changed?"

"More information," I said. "I wish we'd had it a couple weeks ago."

"Me, too," Jessie said.

"Do you want to know who it is?" T.J. said, her tone suggesting she didn't care to put up with a shitty attitude, either.

"Yes."

"You'll need to keep it under your hat," I told her. "We're still building a case, and loose lips might compel someone to hop a flight to Mexico."

"I won't say anything."

"It's Adrian Brown."

Another couple seconds of silence made me tap the screen to make sure we remained connected. "The newspaper guy?"

"Yes," T.J. said, "and we know he's in a wheelchair. It's a long story, but he's the man who killed your sister." I didn't like telling her. Though I supposed I wouldn't lose any sleep if Jessie Valle took this information, grabbed a rifle, and blew Adrian Brown's head off. The right lawyer could probably even get her out of jail time.

"It's hard to believe," she said, "but I'll take your word for it." Her voice cracked. "Wow. He sat in our home with us and promised to tell our story, and the son of a bitch killed her."

"We're working with the police to take him down," I said.

"Would you talk me out of killing him?"

"No." T.J. frowned, but I meant it—and the next part. "I think your family might."

Jessie let out a light, dry chuckle. "I think you're right. I'll try not to do anything rash."

"We would appreciate it."

"And I appreciate the update." We ended the call. One

major question remained, and my assistant got right to it as soon as I put my phone on the desk.

"Who else are we bringing in? We have me. Still need two more."

"Rich will probably want to use a cop," I said.

"You don't?"

"No."

"Why not?" T.J. asked.

"Because they always look like cops. We don't know who Brown's going to pick if we manage to make this work. The last thing we need is him thinking something is off and just leaving." I shook my head. "No. Rich might hate it, but we need civilians for this one."

"You got two more in mind?"

"As a matter of fact, I do," I said.

I asked T.J. to try Amy first.

The two worked on the streets together, and I met them both on the Parsons case over three years ago. Amy went by her *nom de rue*, Velvet, which she used until earlier this year. She wound up involved with the wrong people, and Melinda took care of the rest. Now, Amy was close to landing a real job, marking another success for Melinda's Nightlight Foundation. "We need your help," my secretary said.

"What's going on?"

"You've heard about the three women killed."

"Kinda hard not to," Amy said. "It's all over the news. Some reporter seems to have it in for you guys, too." She paused. "How's your boss, by the way?"

"He's good." Even though the call was on speaker, I

stayed quiet and let T.J. handle it. "We both need to ask you a favor."

"You've both helped me, so name it."

"It's taken a while, but we think we've identified the killer."

"That's great!" Amy said.

"It is," T.J. said, "but the police can't get the prosecutors to take up the case right now. So . . . we want to set a trap for the prick."

"I'd be bait."

"I would, too. We need three people total. You and I would be the first two."

"I'm not sure I want to be alone with a serial killer."

"You won't be," T.J. said. "We're also lining up some folks to stay nearby. C.T. would be one. We'll have a line open between whoever's waiting for the killer and the guy watching them. You'll be safe."

"What's life without a little risk, right?" Amy asked with a chuckle. "Sure. I'll do it."

"Thank you! We really appreciate the help."

"I guess I need to look like a redhead. That's who this bastard is going after, right?"

"Yes," T.J. said. "A wig is fine."

"Maybe it's time for a new hair color. If I'd thought of this sooner, I could have called myself Red Velvet." The two young women shared a laugh.

"We'll be in touch," T.J. said. "This guy only seems to strike when there's going to be a heavy snowfall, so we have to wait until then."

"I'll be ready," Amy said. "Just give me the word."

"We're one for one," T.J. said after hanging up. "Who's next?"

"I want to ask Melinda," I said.

"Do you want me to?"

"No. I honestly expect her to say no, and I don't think it matters who poses the question. She's become pretty risk averse the last couple years."

A knowing look passed over T.J.'s face, and she nodded. I wondered how many times Melinda tried to steer her into another job after placing her with me. Any time I had a dangerous case, probably. "It's worth a try," T.J. said.

I called Melinda and posed the question. "Is T.J. doing it?" she wanted to know.

"Do you really need to ask?"

"I guess not."

"We'll make sure there's a line open between the woman and whoever's with her. One will be me, one will probably be my cousin the homicide lieutenant, and we're working on the third."

"I'm sure you'll make it as safe as possible under the circumstances," she said.

"None of this sounds like a yes."

Melinda said. "I can't. I'm sorry. I know it would help your case, and you're my friend, and I want to pitch in, but . . ."

"It's all right," I said.

"I'm worried he'd recognize me. I've had to be more public than I wanted to for the foundation several times, and my dad's getting me to appear in some of his re-election commercials. They'll be hitting the air before Christmas."

"He might be running unopposed."

"Coke still does commercials in Atlanta," she said. "I know I'm a natural redhead, and I'd be a good choice for this . . . but what if the killer recognizes me from TV? Then, he probably realizes something is up. There's no way the mayor's daughter is meeting a serial killer on a local dating app."

"We could touch up the pictures so they don't look like you," T.J. suggested.

"You said you're lining up three people, right?"

"Yeah."

"So there's a one in three chance he picks me if this works," Melinda said. "Once he sees me in the park, he might still recognize me. Look, I'm not saying no to be a chicken. I don't want to mess up your operation. I hope you catch the bastard, and I'd feel awful if I somehow made that not happen."

"I understand," I said. "We understand. Thanks anyway, Melinda."

"Good luck," she said and ended the call.

"Any ideas for the third?" T.J. asked.

"Not at the moment." I glanced at my watch. It was nearly five PM. "Let's call it a day. Maybe I'll get a bolt of inspiration tonight."

"I'll try and come up with someone, too."

I was out of ideas, but I didn't need T.J. to know this.

———

I arrived at my wife's house to a sight I normally dreaded.

Gloria was cooking in the kitchen.

Traumatic flashbacks came to mind. The first time she used my blender, she neglected to apply the lid, so my cabinets and walls got the first taste of her breakfast smoothie. She tried to cook burgers indoors on a rainy day, managed to avoid triggering the smoke alarm, but made them several shades beyond well done. I could have used them as briquettes in my charcoal grill. These all happened at my house. So far, she'd been far less risky in her own kitchen. She must have read the horror on my face, because she smiled. "Don't worry. I'm trying a meal kit."

My level of worry would be abated with the knowledge I'd refreshed all the fire extinguishers in both houses over the summer. As I approached, I spotted the menu card on the counter. Gloria worked over a green pepper which lay splayed on a cutting board. Thankfully, the poor vegetable couldn't see her irregular chopping. "What are we having?"

"Chicken cacciatore," my wife said before shooing me out of the kitchen. "I got this. Go be a detective for another half hour."

I declined to tell her I foresaw a visit from the fire department and plopped onto the comfy leather couch. I turned on the TV to see continuing coverage of the multiple murders in Baltimore. Despite no real news coming out recently, the talking heads on the local broadcast found plenty to complain about. They didn't reference Adrian Brown's columns, so their ire remained focused on the BPD. One of them possessed the good sense to mention the prosecutors played a hand in this, too. Even if the police had a suspect, the loud man said at unnecessary volume, the state's attorney's office needed to bring charges. I wondered how many people watching the 6 PM news needed a civics lesson, figured it was probably an alarming number, and stopped trying to think too much as I watched.

About forty-five minutes later, Gloria summoned me to the table. National news had started, and I'd been tuning it in and out as I scrolled through my contacts looking for someone who might want to play our third potential victim. The food smelled good. I'd made the dish a couple times before, and it took over an hour. The meal kit must have come with some shortcuts built in. A large chunk of chicken surrounded by a vibrant red sauce filled a bowl. Brown rice peeked out from under it. Gloria smiled as I sat. "It looks great," I said.

"I hope it tastes the same."

I tried a forkful. The sauce, while fragrant, turned out a little bland. It needed more basil and oregano. Still, this dish was supposed to be more stew than pasta, and considering Gloria's past culinary misadventures, today's dinner represented a huge leap forward. "Very good," I said. She'd even paired with a glass of red wine for each of us. "Chianti?"

She nodded. "How'd you know?"

"I didn't." I shrugged. "Sounds Italian."

We ate in silence. Gloria's bowl contained maybe two-thirds the portion mine did, and she took her usual small bites. Even after getting up to refill our glasses and moderating my eating pace, I threatened to lap her. "How's the investigation coming along?" she asked when we were both almost finished.

"All right, I guess."

"You guess?"

"We have a good suspect. Even got the cops to buy in, though the state's attorney won't bring charges. The plan is to set a trap."

"Sounds like things are moving along," Gloria said.

"Sort of. Laying the trap means we need three potential victims. I only have two."

"What are the requirements?"

"Be pretty is the first," I said. "Then, have red hair even if it's fake or temporary, go on a local dating app and try to draw out our guy, and then meet him in a park when it snows. Accompanied by someone like me or Rich, of course."

"Still sounds like it might be dangerous."

"I think it's minimal. T.J. and her friend Amy are in. Our

suspect always had three prospects lined up, so we want to present him a trio of options."

Gloria set her fork down. "I'll do it."

"What?"

"Me. I'll be the third."

"No." I shook my head.

"Why not?" Before I could answer, she did it for me, "Because I'm your wife?"

"Well . . . yeah," I said.

"You'll let T.J. risk it."

"I'm not married to T.J."

Gloria waved a hand. "You see her five days a week and sometimes more. Your parents invite her over for holidays. She's the little sister you never had. Tell me you wouldn't be torn up if something happened to her."

"Of course I would."

"She's still doing it," Gloria said. "It's her choice . . . just like it's mine. You're big on people making their own choices."

"I am," I admitted even knowing where this would land me.

"I'll be your third, then. You'll be with me to make sure nothing happens. I'm not worried."

"Makes one of us," I grumbled.

"You think I'll make a convincing redhead?" Gloria ran a hand through her chestnut locks.

"I think you can pull any look off." I didn't like this. Not one bit. Gloria was right, though. I always preferred to let people make their own choices, for good or for ill. I'd be with her the whole time. Odds of Brown picking her were only one in three, and this presumed our plan worked, and he liked all the options we gave him.

Now, I had another reason to wish this damn case would wrap up quickly. I didn't want anyone else to die, but I would do everything in my power to keep Gloria safe.

CHAPTER 28

"WHY THE HELL do you have a red wig?"

Gloria made a trip to the attic, and I was today years old when I learned she knew how to access it and use it. A door and pull-down ladder provided access from the bedroom Gloria used as an office. An exquisite pair of tennis-toned legs backed down from the loft, followed by a box in Gloria's arms which originally held a case of paper and now bore markings reading *Theatre Supplies*. I noted the British spelling and approved.

"I did some acting in college," she said. "Nothing major. The big-time theater nerds did those productions. The smaller things were more my speed. I kept a few of the props in case I wanted them for costumes." This made sense. My wife did like dressing up for Halloween. She took the wig out of the bag and shook it. It was a dark fiery color, and I knew it would look good on her. She tried the red hair on and spent a few seconds adjusting. The perfect fit confirmed my suspicion. "What do you think?"

"I think I wish you'd kept a bed in here," I said.

She blushed and swatted my shoulder. "Have you started setting everything up yet?"

"No. You'd be the first."

Gloria grinned. "Might as well be the best, then. Let me set things up. We'll use my phone. It has the better camera." She left the room to get ready. I made sure the overhead and ring lights were on and pointing where she'd be sitting. A few minutes later, Gloria returned. She'd set the wig so well it looked like her real hair. In addition, she wore a low-cut sweater which would catch the eyes of anyone who saw her eventual profile. A pair of costume glasses looked real and changed her face just enough. We didn't need reverse image searches turning up Gloria Reading Ferguson, rising fundraiser. The thought of Adrian Brown ogling my wife made me want to push him down the metal stairs again.

"I set the lights up," I said.

"Not bad." She sat behind the desk and adjusted the standing ring light. "Good to go." Gloria handed me her phone. I chose portrait mode because it would focus the shots on her and also blur any details in the background. Over the course of ten minutes, she struck a variety of poses, and I snapped over a hundred pictures. We would find the best handful and use those. Once our impromptu photo shoot ended, I offered a suggestion. "Do you have any shots of just you? They can be a few years old. We can use software to change your hair color."

"Good call," she said. "This shouldn't look too staged. We want him to see some casuals and candids, too."

While Gloria took off her wig and—unfortunately— donned more modest clothes, I scrolled through my amateur photography work. Of the many snapshots, I identified about twenty as favorites. Gloria would need to look through them, and I could see her opinion differing. She came back, checked our work, and picked five she really liked. Four were among the ones I'd starred. She looked terrific in all of them.

An easy confidence, obvious sex appeal, but also an inviting warmth. "I think I'd break my screen swiping on these," I said.

"Let's hope the killer feels the same," she said. Gloria brought up some pictures on her laptop. They ranged from a few months ago to the bleak and dark times before she met me. She found three she wanted to use and handed the computer to me. "I'm not very good at retouching."

"Let's hope I am." I took the laptop, brought up a different photo, and used it as practice. It took a few attempts to change her hair color and match the shade to the wig. Once I had the settings dialed in, I made the edits on the three she chose. "There you go." I passed the computer back to her, and she set it on the desk. "You're a redhead as far as Old Line Love goes."

"You think he'll dig into these pictures? Try to find out who I am?"

"Maybe." I shrugged and wheeled my chair a little closer to hers. "As far as Brown knows, the cops don't have anything, and he can continue to write his hit pieces. I'm sure he's not going to take foolish risks, but we don't have any reason to think he's especially on his guard."

"Good," she said. Gloria created an account on the site using a temporary email I'd made for her. The profile setup filled the screen. "I need a name."

"Katniss Everdeen," I suggested.

She chuckled. "I'm pretty sure he'd recognize that one." She opted for Susan Smith. "My mother's first name," she said. "I've been hearing it my whole life, so I guess I can respond to it if I need to."

"Smith?"

"When in doubt, keep it simple."

I found no fault in her logic. Susan Smith was 29—a year

and a half younger than my wife, who would turn 31 in the coming summer—and split her time between working as an office manager and going to grad school. "You'd better hope he doesn't ask you your favorite filing system," I said.

"Dewey Decimal."

"I thought you looked a bit like a hot librarian earlier." I leaned over and kissed her neck. Gloria gasped but gently pushed my head. "Easy, tiger. Let's set our trap first." She filled out the rest of the profile with boilerplate information. Susan enjoyed the beach, hiking, reading, and pickleball. So did Gloria. She was interested in men from thirty to forty-five years old, did not want hookups, and expressed no preference when it came to religion.

"I think I'm done," she said, giving it a final once-over.

"Looks perfect to me," I agreed. "Prepare to have your inbox start blowing up."

Gloria grinned. "We'll have to go over the matches together. You know the kinds of things Brown uses."

"Sounds good."

"You think it'll work?"

"I don't see how he could resist the considerable charms of Susan Smith."

"And you'll be there to protect me if I'm the one he picks."

"You know it."

"I do," she said, "and I'm not worried."

"I'll worry enough for both of us."

Gloria stood, slid over to my chair, and eased herself onto my lap. "Let me take your mind off of things, then."

———

The following morning, I experienced another shock.

T.J. sat at her desk, her normal blonde hair now a deep red. It didn't look like a wig, either. "I dyed it," she confirmed a moment later. "You can stop staring. Ten dollars at CVS."

"You're dedicated," I said.

She shrugged. "I didn't have a wig, and it was cheaper and easier to get a bottle of hair color."

"You look like a different person."

"I'm still getting used to it." Her frown indicated the transition might take a while. "Do we have a third?"

"We do."

"Who?"

"I'll show you in a minute." I fixed myself a cup of coffee, woke my laptop, and logged in. Gloria shared her credentials for Old Line Love with me. She would use the app, and I would keep an eye on things via their website. I waved T.J. to my desk. She walked next to me, leaned in, and did a double take.

"Is that Gloria?"

"In the flesh . . . and a red wig she apparently kept from her college theater days."

"You asked your wife?" T.J. wanted to know.

"She volunteered. I couldn't talk her out of it."

"Looks like you also couldn't talk her out of letting you play photographer."

"We picked a few of her older pics, too," I said. "Just recolored the hair to match her wig."

"I know she got a writeup in the *Sun* a few months ago. You worried Brown will recognize her?"

"It's a concern. We hope the red hair and glasses will be enough to throw him off."

T.J. grabbed my mouse and scrolled through the photos we'd chosen. "Looks like the old ones show her in sunglasses or with something covering part of her face. Not bad."

"Between the two of us, we're pretty smart."

"I guess you do all right," she said, returning to her own desk. "If we're pairing people up with protection, I guess you're going with Gloria?"

"I am," I said. "We'll find some people to go with you and Amy." While my computer remained on, I checked the Carroll County *Herald's* weather page. Below a banner trumpeting the accuracy of their forecast, they posted an update: snow expected Tuesday evening. Today was Thursday morning. "Our favorite paper is calling for snow in five days. Might as well line things up now."

"What about Joey?" T.J. suggested.

"If nothing else, he could sit on Brown."

"Why don't you call him?"

I did, and my longtime friend said he would stop by after twelve and bring lunch. "A refreshing change," I said. "Usually, my debit card feels the effects of your appetite for a week afterward."

"I'll add it to your tab," he said.

In the interim, we worked on T.J.'s profile. She'd never been publicly associated with me or the agency, so even if Brown ran reverse image searches on her, he wouldn't find anything. She chose a few pictures from the last few months, and I took a couple new ones with the inside of the office door serving as a nondescript backdrop. Once I retouched her blonde locks in the older set, she presented a consistent hair color across all her photos.

As with Gloria, T.J. used the app, and I kept an eye on things via the Old Line Love website. The hardest part was coming up with a name. Eventually, she sighed, grunted, and entered *Tami Jean White*. "I hate that fucking name," she said. "Weasel Boy and Jacko used to call me that."

"Pick something else."

"No." She shook her head. "I hate Adrian Brown, too. If all goes well, we won't need to use this for more than a handful of days. I'll live with it."

"All right." She finished setting up the profile, and it went live. I wondered how many random guys would try to match with her, and if one of them would be an Adrian Brown sock puppet account. "We'll have to look over some of the guys who swipe on you."

"I think I can dismiss basic dudebros outright," she said. "Brown didn't use any accounts like that."

"Yeah," I agreed. "Flexing gym selfies are a red flag in so many ways."

A short while later, heavy footsteps rang on the metal stairs. I grabbed a pistol just in case, but Joey Trovato came through the door. He was a black Sicilian of good humor and boundless appetite. While we were about the same height, Joey outweighed me by a good hundred pounds and basically always had. His girth belied some real athleticism, however, and I knew several people who regretted underestimating him. He closed the door and eyed my gun. "Expecting someone else?"

"I want to hear your delivery fees before I put it away," I said.

Joey carried a bag—the common combo of paper inside plastic—and I could smell bread and tomato sauce even from a few feet away. "No fee this time." I put the gun away, and he carried the bag to the table, where he dumped out the paper one and tore it open. Three chicken parmesan subs and as many orders of fries were inside along with an order of mozzarella sticks. "Those are mine," he said, marking his culinary territory.

"I had no doubt. Where'd you go?"

"A hole in the wall Italian place," he said. "I like it when I can speak the language with whoever's at the counter."

I figured this described many Italian restaurants in the area, but I could only fake the language with my knowledge of Spanish, so I stayed quiet. Joey started eating before T.J. and I even sat down, devouring a mozzarella stick in two dunks and a pair of large bites. "I heard you got caught up in the serial killer case." As usual, Joey didn't wait to finish chewing. His manners were better when he ate with my parents, but when it was just us, he reverted to a pig.

"How?"

"The guy from Carroll County seems to think you suck."

"Yeah, well . . . he's a fucking murderer, so I guess he sucks worse."

Joey blinked. "The guy writing the columns? He's the killer?"

"Yes."

"Ain't he a cripple?"

"He uses a Taser," I said. "The police have kept some details out of the press. Wheelchair or not, it's easy to overpower someone when they can't move."

"Jesus Christ," Joey said. "Pretty brazen son of a bitch to keep writing about the shit he's done."

"We expect we'll have a chance at catching him Tuesday night," T.J. said as I ate some of my sub. Among the chicken parm sandwiches I've eaten, this would rank near the top. The sauce carried a terrific tang. "He strikes when there's a big snowfall. It covers his wheel tracks."

"Makes sense. How are you gonna catch him?"

"It's a long story, but he uses a local dating app. We'll have three people on there as potential matches . . . including me."

"You want me to stay close in case he picks you," Joey said.

"Yes," my assistant confirmed. "I'm not sure where we'll be. Hell, I don't even know if he'll try and match with me. If he does, we need someone there to help collar him."

"I can't run many people down, but I'm pretty sure I could nab this prick."

"Then you could sit on him until the cops arrive," I said.

"It's right in my wheelhouse," Joey agreed.

"Good," T.J. said. "I hope he does pick me. I want to catch this bastard."

"You ain't worried?"

Her head wagged. "Not if I have someone to keep an eye on me."

"No running out for dinner," I said.

Joey chuckled. "Now you're cramping my style."

CHAPTER 29

IT TOOK A FEW DAYS, but T.J, finally got used to the red hair.

By Saturday, she stopped frowning at herself in the mirror. She would go back to being a blonde when this whole mess was done, but the red look wasn't so bad. Melinda even complimented her on it. "And I'm an OG redhead," she said.

It was Tuesday, and tonight should see the Adrian Brown case conclude. Baltimore news outlets called for three to four inches of snow. One had the good sense to cite the *Herald*, which expected rapid accumulation and a total north of eight inches. "Maybe plan for the bigger number," the beleaguered meteorologist said with a shrug.

T.J. knew Adrian Brown would be.

As expected, a bunch of men came out of the woodwork once her profile went live. She'd kinda hoped the cute guy she occasionally saw in the apartment's gym would find her, but no such luck. Most of them were the kinds of just-out-of-college bros who were way too impressed with themselves, their degrees, and their cars to care what a woman really thought. She eliminated them right away. If she thought an account might have been Brown undercover, she consulted with C.T.

He told her he'd seen a few from Gloria's profile. "She has the same problem. I can't imagine what it's like to be a woman on one of these apps."

"You really can't."

"Someone sent her a dick pic," he said, his face darkening.

"What happened?" T.J. wanted to know.

"I found a lot of his accounts and posts. It was as cringey as you might expect. His boss received an interesting email including the photo he sent Gloria. He got fired pretty quickly."

"Seems excessive for a dick pic."

"It was a pattern of behavior . . . and his boss is a woman."

Before T.J. could say anything else, her phone vibrated. It was a notification from Old Line Love. "One of my matches is sending me a message," she said. C.T. came to her desk, and they checked it out.

Hey gorgeous. I know there are flurries in the forecast, but I really want to meet you tonight. I love sitting outside in the snow, and I hope you do, too. How about 8:00? I'll bring an umbrella, hot cocoa, and great conversation. You just bring yourself. :)

The message came from an account with the name Brian Cooley. Based on the pictures—stock photos manipulated just enough to throw off reverse image searches—T.J. and C.T. flagged it as one of Brown's likely aliases. "No proposed location," her boss said.

"Let's find out where he has in mind, then." T.J. tapped out her answer, which began a messaging chain.

> I like the snow, too. :) Where do you want to meet?

> You're in downtown Baltimore, right?

> Yes.

> How about Saint Mary's Park? Pretty small, nice walking trail, and they have benches.

She looked up. "Going back to the scene of the first murder."

"At least you won't have to walk far to get stabbed," C.T. said.

"Very funny," T.J. said. "Should I tell him yes?"

"Might as well. I'd make sure to take a roundabout way to get there, too. Make sure he doesn't see you coming from your apartment."

T.J. nodded as she answered the message. *See you there.*

C.T.'s phone went off next. "Gloria got a hit, too," he said. He returned to his own desk and brought up the match-making site, logging in with Gloria's account. T.J. wheeled herself there and read the incoming message from an account named Steven Gullett.

Hey gorgeous. I know there are flurries in the forecast, but I really want to meet you tonight. I love sitting outside in the snow, and I hope you do, too. How about 8:00? I'll bring an umbrella, hot cocoa, and great conversation. You just bring yourself. :)

"Same exact message," she noted.

"Nothing says romance quite like copy and paste," C.T. said. His phone vibrated again. This time, Gloria called, and C.T. answered it on speaker.

"T.J. got an identical message."

"Did she reply?"

"Yes. They have a potential meetup at eight."

"I guess I should say yes?" Gloria asked.

"Might as well. Brown had a few irons in the fire each time. We want the pattern to hold as much as possible. There's no way to know which one he'll pick, so we need to give him options."

"Are you in my account now?"

"Yes."

"Go ahead and say yes, then."

C.T. typed a reply. *I'm a fan of the snow, too. Let's do it.* After a short back and forth, he set something up with the Brown burner account. "Looks like we'll be waiting at City Springs Park."

"That's not far from here," T.J. said. She'd walked there before on nicer days. Depending on how long it took to wait and cross some of the busier roads, it was ten to fifteen minutes by foot from the office.

"True. Not too close to Saint Mary's if anyone needed to drive between them, but it's doable. Orleans Street will get you most of the way there."

"Sounds like we have a date tonight, stud," Gloria said.

"Catching a serial killer is my love language," C.T. said.

T.J. winced. "Jesus, get a room."

"We might once this is over." Thankfully, husband and wife ended their call with a minimum of further mushiness.

"Let's see if Amy got the same thing," T.J. suggested, texting her friend. "Looks like she did. Copy and paste strikes again."

"Have her set something up, then."

After a moment, T.J. said, "She's a go. Madison Square Park."

"Much farther north."

"Who's going with her?"

"I have Rollins covering her." T.J. had only met the mysterious Rollins once before. She knew he was an ex-army guy who now worked private security and protective details. She didn't know how he and C.T. were acquainted, but her boss vouched for him, so she trusted the man, too.

"We got pretty lucky here," T.J. observed. "Three for three on matching and getting a potential date tonight."

"My guess is the pickings are a little more slim with all the coverage of the murders," C.T. said. "Even though the public doesn't know about the Old Line Love connection, Brown probably can't be as choosy as he was originally. Anyone who says yes at this point is a potential victim."

"We're going to get this son of a bitch tonight," she said.

"Yes, we are."

"I'll be ready."

Snow fell Tuesday evening.

T.J. arrived at Saint Mary's Park early. She exited her building from the rear, walked around the block, came up Eutaw Street, and approached the area from Franklin. A dusting covered the sidewalks and grassy areas. So far, the streets were wet but not covered. As the temperature dropped into the overnight hours, the forecast called for this to change. The *Herald* ended up calling for a range of eight to ten inches for the city. Even local outlets upped their own predictions into the six to eight band.

A small Bluetooth earpiece about the size of a tiny hearing aid sat in her right ear. Her wool cap—which went well with her boots and coat—would hide it even if Brown got close to her. T.J. shuddered and pushed that thought out of her head. As she walked, she dialed Joey Trovato. "I'm headed to the park," she said. "Crossing Paca from Franklin now."

"I'm in a coffee shop just past George Street," he said. "It's across from the old seminary."

"You'll need to move when Brown comes, then."

"I will. Let me know when he's here. I want to stay out of sight as long as I can."

"All right," she said. "I'll keep the line open. He's used minivan taxis before, so give a shout if you see one drive by."

"Will do," Joey said.

T.J. walked north up Paca Street. She wore boots in case the snow grew heavier while she waited for Brown. Having her foot slip could be disastrous. She trusted Joey to be available, but she also needed to be able to rely on herself. She adjusted her coat and disliked how it felt stiff over her torso. She passed the old seminary, then a loop and parking lot before turning left at the red walking trail. No benches were setup at the lower portion, so she headed under the trees and found them around the center of the park. T.J. sat with her right side against the bench. Joey would approach from her left, and she wanted him to be invisible to Brown for as long as possible.

She waited. C.T. told her this was the toughest part of the job, and right now, she agreed. This case had dragged on for weeks, and one victim turned into three. It would stop tonight. Here if Brown chose her. She wondered if everyone else was in place by now. Gloria and Amy would be in similar spots at two different parks, their protectors nearby, everyone waiting for something to happen. T.J. took a few deep breaths to calm herself.

No one else entered the park. It made a useful cut-through for anyone walking between Paca and St. Mary Streets, but foot traffic was at a minimum thanks to the current snow and impending forecast. Cars still rolled by at what looked like a normal pace for almost eight PM on a Tuesday. As T.J. waited, the snow came down heavier. This would combine with the latening hour to limit vehicular traffic soon. She glanced at her watch—7:59. "Anything?" she said.

"Not yet," Joey replied.

T.J. wanted this to be over, but she also wanted to be the one to end it. She pushed for C.T. to take this case initially, and when Jessie Valle came to see them, it was serendipity. The whole thing spiraled and turned into a mess from there, and she wanted to be the one to clean it up. Adrian Brown would find he couldn't do to her all the terrible things he'd done to his three victims.

"I see a minivan," Joey said. "Looks like it has taxi markings on the side. It's got a raised suspension."

"That's probably it." T.J. felt her pulse quicken. She adjusted her coat again. It was big and puffy and looked like any other jacket with similar attributes. She glanced at her watch again—8:03.

"It went up Paca. I don't see it anymore."

"Hold your position for now."

T.J. waited. She didn't see the van appear on any other road. If Brown came here, he would be wheeling down Paca. A moment later, Joey's voice filled her ear again. "I see a guy in a chair headed toward the entrance."

T.J. kept her eye on the area. Sure enough, a man in a wheelchair came into view moving toward her. "Let's go. Tell the others he's here."

"I will," Joey said. "I'll be in position shortly."

T.J. tried to look happy—or at least not nervous—as the man in the wheelchair drew closer.

———

The snow seemed to increase in intensity as the man neared T.J.

Over his shoulder, she saw Joey slip into the trees. The guy—she presumed it to be Brown—proceeded as if he didn't notice. In her ear, Joey spoke in a quiet voice. "I've let everyone know. They're going to converge on this position. We just need to keep Brown here long enough."

"Understood," she whispered while moving her mouth as little as possible. She doubted Brown could make out her lips through the white flakes falling, but why take the chance? As the wheelchair approached, Joey stayed low and emerged from the first group of trees to another set closer to the bench. He didn't have any cover past there. The line remained open, so if things went south, T.J. knew he would react.

"Hello," she said as Brown wheeled up to the bench.

"Hi. You must be Tami Jean."

T.J. suppressed a wince at the name and tried to maintain a happy expression. "I am. Brian?"

"In the flesh." He patted an armrest. "And metal and plastic. I didn't mention the chair because I didn't want to bias you against me from the start."

It's not the fucking wheelchair, she thought. "I don't care about that. Did you bring cocoa?"

"Sorry, no," Brown said. "The place closed for the weather. I didn't even think it had gotten too bad." Like her, he wore a wool cap over his head. In the lights of the park, Brown looked to be in his late thirties. What she could see of his hair looked brown with some sort of product in it. He had a hookish nose, and if he kept his head canted downward, the effect lent him a sinister appearance.

"At least we have the snow," T.J. said. Brown checked out

her face and hair. She'd made sure to skip the usual ponytail and let her dyed red locks flow freely. He needed to see the color. His eyes traveled below her neck, but between the coat, jeans, and boots, she was basically ogle-proof.

"We do." He put on a grin. "You look young for your age, Tami Jean." Brown paused. "Do you go by both names?"

"My friends call me T.J."

"I hope you'll count me as one of them . . . T.J."

"You're doing all right so far," she said. "I was hoping for the hot chocolate, though. It's gotten colder just since I've been here."

"I was annoyed, too," he said. Brown pushed his chair to the rear about a foot, leaned his head back, and stuck out his tongue. Falling flakes soon dotted his entire face. "Wow." He wiped them away with the back of a leather-gloved hand. "I guess it's hard to catch one when hundreds are falling."

T.J. wondered if he did this same routine with his three victims. "Brian, it's cold and snowy. *I'm* cold and snowy. It was nice to meet you, but I want to go somewhere warm."

"By yourself, I take it?" Any mirth previously on Brown's face was gone.

"I think it's for the best." T.J. knew he might attack her at any moment, so she stood. "Have a good night."

"You bitches are all the same," Brown growled.

"Excuse me?"

"You say you don't care about the chair, but you do. You do. I can tell. You're dismissing me. Not even giving me a chance."

"Maybe you should have taken the chance to bring us some goddamn hot chocolate."

"There was no cocoa!" Brown's hand went into his jacket pocket, and it came out holding a Taser. The metal barbs gleamed even in the inconsistent light.

T.J. made sure to stand up straight. With her height and the short distance between them, Brown couldn't reach her neck. "Why don't you put that away?" She made sure to say it loud enough for Joey to have no doubt what went on. He appeared from behind a tree.

Brown wheeled himself forward suddenly. T.J. registered the motion with just enough time to take a step back. She was in his arm's reach, however, and the Taser surged toward her, a bright bolt of electricity arcing between its two metal endpoints as it slammed into her coat.

The thud rang out in the park.

Brown grimaced. He drew his arm back to try again. T.J. delivered a side kick with her rubber-soled boot, whacking the stun gun from his grasp. She knocked on her torso, and the wooden thunk filled the air again. "I came prepared, asshole."

"So did I." Brown pulled a long knife from his coat.

"Put it down." Joey walked toward them, a pistol in his hand. "Drop the knife. Now."

"I'd listen if I were you," C.T. added, jogging up from the opposite side. He also held a gun. "We got you, Brown."

"Mister Ferguson," Brown muttered. "It seems you took your grievance with the free press a little far."

"Let's not talk about running the Olympic mile with something."

"I can't run. It's kind of the point." Brown jutted his chin toward T.J. "What's under your coat? Bulletproof vest?"

T.J. unzipped her jacket. The rounded wooden front of Manny's old cabinet radio was strapped around her torso. "A little bulky and uncomfortable," she said. "Good thing I can wear a heavy coat."

"Smart thinking," her boss said with an appreciative nod.

"What now?" Brown asked. He still held the knife, but

T.J. had stepped out of reach, and two men with guns kept their eyes on him.

A siren drew near. "I called my cousin the homicide lieutenant," C.T. said. "You can ask him yourself if he thinks the police have been buffoons."

"I imagine his answer would be uncharitable."

A couple minutes later, two BPD cruisers pulled close, along with an unmarked sedan and a van. Red and blue lights filled the area. Rich, Paul King, and a bunch of uniformed officers climbed out of their vehicles and descended on the scene.

CHAPTER 30

I WATCHED as the police took control of the scene.

Once Rich, King, and crew arrived, Joey and I put our guns away. Brown still held the knife a few seconds after the cops ordered him to drop it. He didn't have a play other than stabbing himself or slashing his own throat, and in the end, he tossed the weapon into the snowy grass. I harbored no objection to Brown killing himself. The families of the victims would get closure either way, and the murderer cutting himself open would save everyone the emotional headache of a trial.

An obvious police SUV rolled up, and Captain Leon Sharpe unfolded himself from the rear seat. Snow continued falling. Everyone shook it out of their hair or off their clothes and hats periodically. "We arresting this asshole?" the captain asked as he walked toward the BPD contingent.

King read Brown his Miranda rights. A uniform held an evidence bag with the knife safely inside. I wondered if Brown used the same one the first three times. "Thanks for your help," I said to Joey.

"Happy to do it," he said. "You got here fast."

"The cab driver tipped me off. Sorry you didn't get to sit on Brown."

"I'm willing to try. You just need to create a distraction first."

I chuckled, and we bumped fists. "Let's do lunch again soon."

"Sure," Joey agreed. "You're buying, though."

"I'll be sure to have plenty of money in my account."

Joey exchanged a few words with T.J., they shared a quick hug, and he headed away from the park. "I want to know who the hell she is," Brown said, jabbing a finger at my secretary.

"I work for C.T.," she said. "I'm his executive assistant."

Considering the success of her foray into the field tonight, I doubted I could deny her the promotion. "You let him use you as bait?" Brown sneered. "I thought you young women were supposed to be about independence."

"It was my choice, you miserable asshole. I wanted to catch you for what you did to those poor women."

"They had it coming."

She turned to me. "You're right. I should have agreed with pushing him down the stairs."

"It's all good," I said. "My guess is men in wheelchairs who murdered women aren't among the most popular inmates in prison."

"You think you're scaring me?" Brown said.

"Me? No. Your cellmate, however . . . yes."

"Enough guff from you," Sharpe said, standing between me and the disgraced journalist. "Ten years ago, I would have thrown your sorry ass in the street and let someone run you over. We're a kinder, gentler police force now. So shut up, and we'll load you in the van."

"Is it still all hands on deck, Leon?" I wanted to know.

"What do you mean?"

"You still need to question this prick."

"Sure," he said. "Come on down. You're making the coffee."

I found it a fair trade-off.

———

Rich and King stood in an interrogation room with Brown.

Captain Sharpe, T.J., and I watched from the other side of the one-way mirror. Speakers mounted into the walls above the glass let us hear what went on. A standard push-button microphone enabled observers to talk to those in the main room. Sharpe stood in front of it, and I wasn't moving him without a bulldozer. Probably for the best. Brown's defense team didn't need me heckling him to try and gain some sort of advantage.

"Why the hell did you do it?" Rich asked for an opener.

Brown ran his left hand along the handcuff chain affixing his right to the desk. He sat in his own wheelchair. The normal metal one stood in the corner behind the cops. "You're presuming I'm the killer."

"Aren't you?"

"It's up to you to prove it."

"All right," King said. He opened the beefy manila folder in front of him and pulled out some papers. "Here are the accounts we believe you registered with Old Line Love. Here are the women you matched with and your communications within the app. Dates and times you met the first three victims and your attempted fourth tonight all line up. All redheads, all young and pretty. No reason for any of them to be dead."

"You're going to have to prove every item," Brown said. "Do you think I can't get a good lawyer?"

"What's an editor for a smallish county newspaper make?" Rich wondered. "If your outfit still employed enough reporters, they wouldn't have sent you here, so the place can't be swimming in cash. I'm not exactly worried about you assembling some legal dream team." Brown didn't say anything, and I wondered why he hadn't already summoned an attorney. "We'll come back to our initial question. Why'd you do it?"

When Brown remained silent, King spoke up. "Look, if you confess now, maybe you'll actually get out of prison before you die."

"I'm supposed to think the state's attorney will offer me a deal?" Brown scoffed. "You're going to say I murdered three women and tried to kill a fourth. There's no death penalty in this state anymore, so it's either life without parole, or maybe I get out when I'm already close to the grave." He waved his left hand. "Pass."

"Suit yourself," Rich said. "We're not going to coerce a confession out of you."

"Where's your cousin?"

"What the hell does he have to do with this?"

"Seems like he figured it out when you couldn't. Maybe I'll get to write a few columns from my cell."

"Write what you want," Rich said. "Landing on you as a suspect was a team effort."

"There's no I in team," I said, "but there is a me."

"And me," T.J. added.

"I didn't see any of you until the scene played out," Brown said. "Your cousin's assistant in the field? Why not send a cop? You must have some young women who graduated the academy recently."

"Why'd you do it?" King asked, not taking Brown's bait.

"Are you familiar with the name Monica Clark?"

"She the one who hit you?"

Brown flinched as if someone threatened to clobber him. "How do you know about her?"

"Like we told you," Rich said, "we've put quite a few things together."

"That's the royal 'we,'" T.J. said.

After sulking for a few seconds, Brown nodded. "Yes. Dumb bitch. Her SUV was a death trap she never really bothered to maintain. Plowing into someone was inevitable. It just happened to be my car." He paused for a deep breath. "If you know about her, then you know I wasn't alone in the car."

"We do," Rich said.

"I made sure to put the screws to her as much as possible. One of my dad's friends was the meanest, sharkiest lawyer I knew, so I hired him. He dug up all the stuff about her vehicle. Considering what happened to me plus the death of Yvonne, Monica was going away for a long time. I really wanted her to get old and die in prison." Brown let out a dry chuckle. "I used to imagine myself as an old, dying man visiting her in jail so I could spit in her face one last time."

"Her getting cancer caused all this?"

"She wasn't supposed to get out early. She was supposed to rot in a cell. Compassionate release." He made air quotes with his free hand and snorted. "Where was the compassion for me and Yvonne? Her family?"

"Terminal cancer often gets someone out," Rich said. "It had been quite a while."

"Not long enough."

"You feel you'd been denied justice," King said. I figured he was right. Even though Monica Clark spent years in jail,

Brown created a scenario where she needed to die behind bars. When she didn't, it upended his world.

"Of course I do," he confirmed.

King took a photo out of the folder and slid it across the table. "Wasn't heavy use of social media back then, but we found a picture of Miss Clark. She's pretty. Red hair. Ever since she escaped her fate, you've been trying to find and kill her."

"Can you blame me?"

"Yes," Rich said, providing the common-sense answer to a question devoid of self-awareness. "We can. A jury will, too."

"Now, you'll get to be the killer who dies in prison," King said. "In a roundabout way, you're getting your wish."

"Go to hell," Brown grumbled. "Get me a lawyer."

———

The next morning felt warmer—and not just because Adrian Brown was in custody.

The mercury was climbing. It would reach the high forties today and stay there through the weekend, which would melt the most recent snow and at least some of the mounds remaining from earlier blizzards. After several laps around Federal Hill Park, I showered, dressed, and drank coffee downstairs. "You're not making breakfast?" Gloria asked.

"I'm celebrating today. Want to get some bagels with me?"

"Thanks, but I'll pick up something else." Gloria smiled and kissed me. "You deserve to celebrate. This case was a mess."

On the way in, I made a small detour to Goldberg's and got T.J. her favorite sandwich—sausage and egg on a sesame bagel—and got a double-toasted whole wheat bagel with lox and cream cheese for myself. If you're going to celebrate, you might as well do it right. I arrived at the office a few minutes later than normal, dropped a paper bag wet with grease onto T.J. desk, and waited for her reaction. She eyed it, opened it enough to inhale the aroma, and smiled. "We're celebrating?"

"Damn right."

"Did you get your weird fish thing again?" she asked.

"We don't question other people's revelry," I said.

After breakfast, I washed my hands and checked the *Herald's* website. I wanted to see them try and clean off the entire carton of broken eggs covering their faces. To the paper's credit, they covered the story. A column written by the publisher accompanied it. "Check this out," I said, and T.J. wheeled herself to my desk.

A City Shaken: The Unmasking of a Monster

The <u>Carroll County Herald</u> finds itself confronting a truth darker than any headline we've ever printed. Adrian Brown, our esteemed News Editor, has been exposed as a predator, a cunning murderer responsible for the senseless deaths of three innocent women: Kirsten Valle, Bernadette Holmes, and April Mooney.

Readers will remember his coverage of his crimes, including his columns taking the police to task. How he could carry out the crimes and then write about them as if someone else committed them is another level of depravity.

Words cannot express the depth of our horror and betrayal. We trusted Adrian, relied on his journalistic integrity. The very man who championed truth and accountability was weaving a web of lies and brutality. We, like the rest of Carroll County, are reeling.

The Baltimore Police Department, in collaboration with private investigator C.T. Ferguson, deserves our immense grat-

itude. Their meticulous investigation, fueled by unwavering determination, brought this monster to justice. Their work has ensured that the families of these victims can finally begin to heal.

As a newspaper, we hold ourselves to the highest ethical standards. We strive to be a pillar of our community, a source of truth and justice. In this instance, we failed. We allowed a monster into our midst, and for that, we offer our sincerest apologies to the victims' families, our readers, and the entire Carroll County community.

We are committed to a thorough internal investigation to ensure such a lapse in judgment never happens again. We will review our hiring practices and implement stricter background checks.

Now, we must turn our attention to the victims—Carroll County's own Kirsten Valle, a rising star in local public relations; Bernadette Holmes, a dedicated office manager; and April Mooney, a young social media manager. Their stories deserve to be told, not eclipsed by the darkness of their killer. Remember their smiles, their laughter, their dreams so cruelly cut short.

Adrian Brown may have sought to manipulate the narrative, but the truth is undeniable. He is not a journalist, not a colleague, not a human being worthy of our empathy. He is a cold-blooded killer, and the weight of his crimes will forever stain his name.

In the coming weeks, the <u>Carroll County Herald</u> will dedicate space to the victims, offering their families a platform to share their memories. We will also provide in-depth coverage of the investigation and the trial. This is a story which demands our complete attention and demands justice.

We, the <u>Carroll County Herald</u>, stand with the victims, with the families, and with our community. We will move *forward, scarred but determined to rebuild trust, to be the beacon of truth and accountability that Carroll County deserves. Let us learn from this darkness, let us honor the lost, and let us ensure such a tragedy never befalls us again.*

"Not bad," I said once we'd both finished reading it. "Doesn't sound like the lawyers got hold of it first."

"Vindication," my assistant said.

"I'm glad the focus was on the victims and their families. Along with the paper completely fucking things up."

"You think they'll survive?"

I shrugged. "If they keep covering things honestly, they have a good chance."

"We might need to keep the celebrations going with lunch later," T.J. suggested.

"We just might."

"WHERE ARE WE GOING?" I asked as Gloria drove us toward the highway.

"A belated birthday celebration." She merged and quickly got ahead of most traffic owing to her car's rocketlike attributes. The red color alone added ten horsepower. A racing stripe—which she sensibly eschewed—would have been good for five more. The AMG didn't need it, of course. I liked cars enough to identify most models, but I didn't know all the specs and details. Still, this coupe must have been north of five hundred horsepower, and it drove with alacrity no matter what.

"With whom?"

"My parents," she said.

We hadn't seen them too often since our wedding, mostly on holidays and special occasions. This technically counted, too. They used to live in Brooklandville like Gloria but moved to a gated community near White Marsh in Baltimore County about a year ago. The Mercedes lapped up the miles, and we soon zoomed past the exits for White Marsh Mall, which somehow still managed to stay operational. About five minutes and at least as many turns later, we approached an imposing black gate.

A sign read *The Estates at White Marsh*, and it seemed accurate. The homes on the other side of the barrier were bigger than those in Gloria's neighborhood. Probably pricier, too, even being farther away from the city. Someone had to pay for the gate, guards, and so on. The sentry approached the car. Gloria rolled the window down, we provided our IDs, and drove through a moment later.

Her parents' house was large and blocky. White brick and stone made up the exterior, and a bright red door split the outside at the center. It was two stories above ground, and I figured these homes all came with finished basements because you don't want to look at bare stone and support posts for one and a half million dollars. Total square footage must have been over four thousand. It was a lot for a family of five. For two middle-aged people, it was an extravagance.

Gloria rang the bell, and I quelled my disappointment at it merely ringing versus queueing up a symphony recording. No fanfare greeted us as Gloria's mother opened the door. We walked into the stately foyer, covered in elegant tile and sharing a vaulted ceiling with the neighboring living room. As usual, I felt underdressed despite wearing a nice pair of jeans and one of my best sweaters. Gloria's father Hugh wore dress pants and a blazer. He got around well on his new hip now more than a year since replacement.

Her parents were age peers of mine, so while I didn't know their exact ages, I guessed early sixties. Gloria shared a strong resemblance with her mother, and if Susan served as the model for what my wife would look like in about thirty years, I would continue to be a lucky man. After a round of hugs and handshakes, we adjourned to the dining room. A long table dominated the space, a fancy white cloth hanging from it. Eight chairs stood around it. We took the ones at the left end. Gloria and her mother brought food out from the kitchen—they declined my offer of assistance—and set it on the table.

"Happy belated birthday," her dad said as we all served ourselves some chicken, vegetables, and dinner rolls. I couldn't identify the recipe, but everything smelled great, and I got a strong rosemary note from the bird.

"Thanks. I mostly spent it working."

"We heard you were working the serial killer case," Susan said. "It must have been frightening."

I shrugged. "In the end, we got the right guy."

"He's being humble," Gloria said. "The cops didn't have much until the first victim's family hired C.T."

"To be fair," I said, "we joined them in not having much until recently."

"You think the publicity will help your business?" Hugh asked.

"I haven't really thought about it. We do well enough for me to pay the bills, give myself a decent wage, and pay my assistant bonuses for things like Christmas. I'm not sure how much else we could do without expanding."

"What's the problem there?"

"I didn't get into this to manage people."

"A good number of managers say the same thing," he pointed out.

I wondered how many people Hugh Reading—a man who had not needed to work in years—spoke to about this but didn't say anything. I liked Gloria's parents, but they were similar to mine in being a few layers removed from most people. After dinner, Gloria and her mother returned to the kitchen and came out with a birthday cake. It was a round Bundt with stripes of white icing covering dark chocolate. They inserted two sets of three candles and lit them.

"Make a wish," Gloria said and kissed me on the cheek.

I thought about the conversation her dad and I just had. Maybe wishing for just enough business to keep the agency's current model alive would be the play. I went for it, blew out the candles, and endured an off-key rendition of "Happy Birthday" for my troubles.

There were worse fates.

———

The next morning, I arrived at the office to the unusual sound of a ringing landline.

I felt like a Boomer for even having one. At least I could console myself in the fact it used voice over IP technology rather than the traditional telephone service. At the end of the day, however, it was a relic but one most people still expected businesses to maintain. The thing normally rang once a day apart from the occasional spam caller. This morning, T.J. kept placing people on hold.

"Ferguson Investigations, one moment please," she said, pushing the button and letting out a deep breath. "What the hell is going on?"

"We got a lot of good press this morning," I said. "Once the *Herald* denounced Adrian Brown and lauded our work, the other outlets covering the story did the same. Even California papers are talking about how indispensable we were to the investigation."

"Good. Maybe they can send some extra phone coverage."

"Anything promising?"

"I've only managed to talk to, like, two people," my

assistant said. "I wouldn't categorize either as a client we wanted to take on."

I walked to her desk and pushed the button to hang up the current call twice. "Turn the ringer off."

She did. "Why? Don't we want the business?"

"Some of it, sure," I said. "People can leave messages. Our mailbox size is unlimited." I pointed to her empty coffee mug. "You have any yet?"

"No," T.J. said. "Once I set the pot to brew, the floodgates opened."

I fixed us each a mug, setting hers down on the plain cork coaster where it normally rested. "This is the first big publicity blast we've gotten in a while," I said. "Maybe since you came aboard."

"We often get a little coverage."

"True, but it's pretty minimal and always local. Brown called me out, so his paper had to go back and issue a *mea culpa* when he turned out to be a murdering asshole. By then, the story got national attention."

"What are we going to do?" T.J. wanted to know.

I sat at my desk and kicked my feet up. "It'll be Christmas soon. I vote we not work too hard until then."

"And take off the week between Christmas and New Year's?"

"Sure."

"With pay?"

I grinned. "Sure. Enjoy the bonus you're going to get, too. You earned it."

"Thanks," T.J. said with a smile. "I meant about all these calls, though. Even if most of them turn out to be shit we don't take on, we'll get a decent number of prospective clients."

"Maybe."

"Have you thought about bringing someone else in?"

"Not really." This veered into the territory Gloria's dad and I touched on last night. "I'm not sure I want any other investigators. Managing you is enough of a chore most days."

T.J. flipped me off. "It's something to think about."

"After the holidays."

"All right," she agreed with a nod. "After the holidays."

I opened my email to find a slew of inquiries, requests, and the like. "I think this is a great day for a long lunch."

THE END

AFTERWORD

Thanks for checking out this novel! I hope you enjoyed reading the book as much as I enjoyed writing it.

I write mysteries and thrillers with action, snark, and flawed heroes. If this sounds like something you like, you can check out my catalog below.

The C.T. Ferguson Crime Novels

1. The Reluctant Detective
2. The Unknown Devil
3. The Workers of Iniquity
4. Already Guilty
5. Daughters and Sons
6. A March from Innocence
7. Inside Cut
8. The Next Girl
9. In the Blood
10. Right as Rain
11. Dead Cat Bounce
12. Don't Say Her Name

13. Night Comes Down
14. Concrete Angels
15. Conduct Unbecoming
16. Bleeding into Winter
17. Unreasonable Doubt (December 2024)

The John Tyler Action Thrillers

1. The Mechanic
2. White Lines
3. Lost Highway
4. Four on the Floor
5. Forced Induction
6. The Low Road
7. Backfire
8. Redline (September 2024)

I release 3-4 new novels per year. For the most current list of books, please visit:

- https://tomfowlerbooks.com - Direct sales
- www.tomfowlerwrites.com
- https://books2read.com/tomfowler

(**Note**: C.T. Ferguson appears in *White Lines*. John Tyler appears in *Don't Say Her Name*.)

While the suggested reading sequences appear above, each novel is a standalone mystery or thriller, and the books can be enjoyed in whatever order you happen upon them.

Connect with me:

For the many ways of finding and reaching me online,

please visit https://tomfowlerwrites.com/contact. I'm always happy to talk to readers.

This is a work of fiction. Characters and places are either fictitious or used in a fictitious manner.

"Self-publishing" is something of a misnomer. This book would not have been possible without the contributions of many people.

- The great cover design team at 100 Covers.
- My editor extraordinaire, Chase Nottingham.
- My wonderful advance reader team, the Fell Street Irregulars.

www.ingramcontent.com/pod-product-compliance
Lightning Source LLC
Chambersburg PA
CBHW011134190726

48289CB00012B/3038